KILLING MIDAS

Other Books By RW Hague

Surviving Midas

Escaping Midas

find more from RW Hague

www.rwhague.com

KILLING MIDAS

RW Hague

Young Adult

Suspense

To Baby–

We do not yet know your name, but you have all our love!

RED HANDED

"What time is it?" Tucker whispered, swiping his wrist across his forehead. Each of his heavy breaths caused the leaves in front of his face to rustle, and his thin frame trembled beside Katie as they lay prone in the underbrush five yards from the road.

Katie's own tongue clung to the roof of her mouth and her heart thundered in her chest, but if they had any chance of success, one of them had to be brave. So, she squinted at the foreign sky and declared, "After midnight," as if she really knew how to decipher the constellations.

The overhead light of the warehouse illuminated Randall as if he were on display. The great boulder between them and escape.

The red cherry glow from his cigarette intensified then fell to the ground beside his canvas chair to be extinguished underfoot. He crossed one leg over the other and turned the page of his magazine. It was strange, his being on guard duty tonight. Generally, his elevated position kept him from such unpleasant drudgeries. Not that it mattered. Randall, Stanton, anyone else. The docks did not go unwatched and they'd have the same problem regardless of who was here tonight. And if tonight failed, they would just have to try again.

But their chances were good. They still had three hours before their absence would be noticed. Surely Randall would have to take a piss break by then.

But you need time to get away too. They'll come after you.

Katie bit her lip until the taste of metal filled her mouth. A tear escaped her eye, and she swatted it away before Tucker could notice it. Another cherry glow roared to life at the end of Randall's fresh cigarette. With a loud groan and a stretch, he stood, rounded the corner, and disappeared from sight.

Katie lay still, staring at the empty chair. *Go*, she ordered herself, but her legs had gone numb. *GO!*

She propelled herself forward, darting from the underbrush to the side of the warehouse, Tucker right on her heels. Upon reaching the side of the warehouse away from the light, Katie flattened herself against the wall and moved down the length of the building toward the ocean. The waves gently lapping against the shore prevented her from hearing any sound of Randall's return, but Katie reasoned that if Randall couldn't be heard, he probably couldn't hear them either.

The sand sunk underfoot as Katie neared the water's edge, and soon her sneakers were soaked by the lapping waves. Tucker followed her, silent as a phantom, until they were chest high in the water. It being high tide, the warehouse jutted out into the ocean for a few more yards. Behind the warehouse, a long dock and marina stuck out into the ocean where five boats sat rocking.

Katie grabbed Tucker's shirt and pushed him ahead of herself. He did not want the responsibility of going first, but that was tough. She had gotten them out of the house. Now it was up to him to get them off this damn rock.

Silently, Tucker swam to the boat at the end of the marina, and Katie followed. After pulling himself up onto the dock, he lay flat on his stomach upon the wooden planks and looked back down to the warehouse bay. Apparently satisfied, he climbed over the edge of the boat and vanished inside. Katie followed suit and was soon facedown in the carpet of the boat.

"Untie the stern," Tucker said.

Katie slunk to the back of the boat and released their tether. Once freed, Tucker took a paddle from the floorboard and pushed them out of their slot. Katie searched the shoreline for Randall's burly shadow, and, upon seeing it, she ducked down out of sight.

Tucker dug his paddle into the ocean in time with the waves lapping on the shore. It was slow going, but they dared not try the engine until they were away from land. Hope thrilled through Katie as the warehouse and docks grew smaller and smaller. Was this really happening? Were they really escaping?

Escaping to where? her annoying practical side chided. *You don't know where the hell you are, and you're sailing blind into the ocean. You'll be shark bait by morning.*

With a sneer, she silenced the voice and turned to Tucker. "Are we far enough out?"

"I think so." He set the paddle back onto the floorboard and pulled out a wad of wires from beneath the motor cover. As he picked through them, Katie continued to watch the shore. Still no sign that Randall had been alerted to their leaving.

After a few minutes of inactivity, however, she grew curious about the delay. Tucker sat unmoving, the wad of wire in one hand and the pliers in the other.

"What is it?" she asked.

Tucker cleared his throat. "I think it's these two."

"You *think?*"

He snipped through them. When he tried to connect the two wires together, however, nothing happened. Tucker made a noise like a wounded cat and tried connecting the other halves.

"Hurry, Tucker," she hissed.

"I'm trying!"

Again and again, he pressed the wires together. A chortling sound erupted from the engine, but it did not catch. Katie strained her eyes to make out the distant shoreline. Where was Randall? Was that tiny light his glowing cigarette?

Tucker pushed past her to the other side of the motor. He yanked open the gas cap, but nothing could be seen in the darkness.

"Is it empty?" asked Katie. "Please tell me it's not empty!"

"I…I don't know!" He moved to the driver's seat and checked the gage. "Shit!"

"Tucker, you idiot!"

"Help me, Katie! Look for a gas can!"

But Katie ignored him. For the tank to be this low, the gas had to have been siphoned. There would be no gas can on this boat. Katie searched the shore once more, but saw nothing. No shadow passed beneath the light of the warehouse, no glowing ember on the end of a cigarette roll. Tucker tore open the cabinets at the front of the boat, unrelenting in his pointless search.

"Grab an oar, Tucker," said Katie, reaching for her own.

"Are you insane? We can't make it across the ocean with—"

"We're not. We're going back."

"Back? We can't go—   "

"When a job goes sideways, it gets scrapped," she ordered. "Now come on and—"

She was interrupted by a purring sound coming from across the ocean. It mingled with the lapping of the waves against the boat but grew steadily louder. The glint of another boat bouncing across the ocean reflected in the moonlight.

"Grab an oar!" she ordered, digging her own into the waves. "Hurry!"

Tucker floundered around for it, but soon joined her in panicked strokes. In his haste, he only skimmed the water, splashing her instead of moving them forward. She barely felt the water.

In and pull. In and pull, she chanted to herself over and over.

The purring sound grew louder, and she did not have to look back to know the boat was gaining on them.

In and pull. In and pull.

Tucker started blubbering, and his strokes continued in their chaotic motion. He swerved them sideways away from the dock, and Katie corrected them with a back stroke.

In and pull. In and pull.

A powerful light flashed across the waves, and Katie ducked into the boat as the light illuminated the top of their dead vessel. A cry came up from the docks.

There was no more reason to hide, to pretend not to be seen, but Katie continued to crouch beneath the blinding light. They had been caught red-handed. There was no escaping what came next, and yet…

On the other side of the boat lay a vast ocean. If she jumped in now, would she drown before they reached her? Would she have the courage to make it happen?

The hum of the approaching boat grew louder as a new rumble came from the docks. Katie peered over the side of the boat into the black waters. Randall's light illuminated each strand of hair swirling around her head and hurt her eyes as it reflected on the surface of the water.

Tucker tried again and again to connect the wires. He blubbered and wept, but nothing happened. The boat remained as dead as Katie felt. But there was a big difference between feeling dead and being dead. For the past three years, ever since Midas had first taken her, one goal had dominated all others: survive. But even if her body remained trapped, it didn't mean that her mind had to as well. Katie felt herself slipping away, ascending. The world faded into a fog as the lights from the boats approached. She made no effort to stop the ascension either. They might have her body, but her mind she still kept for herself.

What followed was a lot of shouting and cursing. Tucker cried. Someone dragged her from the boat, and she collapsed onto rough carpet, the fibers of which tore at her scarred cheek. Then a hand raised her chin from the floor, and she met Midas's dark eyes. "Katie Belle, shouldn't you be in bed at this hour?"

Had there been anything in her stomach, she would have vomited. Suddenly, Randall's presence made sense. As Midas's little errand boy, he had been waiting on the boss's arrival that night, not just guarding the docks.

Stupid, stupid stupid!

"Dammit!" Randall shouted from the boat they had stolen. He had pulled up in another boat on the other side. "What the hell did you do, kid?"

The big man crossed to Midas's boat and struck Tucker with the back of his hand. Tucker collapsed onto the floorboard, and Randall followed the blow up with a kick to the stomach. Tucker reeled.

"Nelson, get us to shore," Midas called to the driver. "Randall, tow the other boat back, then deal with *this*." He shoved Katie backwards into a seat. There was no headrest, so her neck cranked back as she fell, but Katie barely felt it as she reached her point of ascension once more.

Once they reached the docks, Katie was told to get out and walk. She complied robotically, stopping only when she reached the vehicle bay where several SUVs and golf carts were parked. Tucker came along too, babbling. Midas and Nelson loaded up in an SUV, leaving them with Randall. Midas knew they were in good hands.

Katie stared at the floor as Randall approached, sizing them up. Thinking of a fitting punishment. He brushed Katie's hair behind her ear with a grin that penetrated her ascension and churned her stomach once more. Then he turned to Tucker. "Take off your shirt."

As Tucker was flogged, Katie continued to stare at the floor, neither here nor there. She didn't know when it started or ended. She didn't count the blows. And then Tucker was gone—sent hobbling up to the house with his back bloodied and gaping.

Then Katie was next.

BLOOD TRAIL

Balancing the giant cloth bag filled with groceries on her hip, Tonya slid the tip of her key into the lock, but then the chain slipped from her fingers and fell to the porch with a clatter. For a moment or two, she stood staring at the keys as rain continued soaking through her coat, chilling her further. As if the day hadn't been long enough already.

After setting the bags on the wet stoop, she managed to gather the keys and enter her apartment. When the door opened, her kitten exited with a "Meow." Tonya started to greet the cat, but it sped straight past her and bolted into the bushes by the front porch.

Rude.

The heavy bags strained her arms as she squeezed through the door sideways. She left them on the kitchen floor before peeling off her soaked coat. She undid the top buttons of her blouse and tossed her silly diner cap onto the counter top. The groceries looked up at her, demanding to be put away, but not until she changed clothes.

Her heels clicked on the laminate flooring as she stepped down the hall while undoing her frumpy apron. She kicked one shoe off, then the other before leaning against the wall and massaging her feet. *Three more weeks*, she reminded herself. Three more weeks until she could leave this place and head to Vegas.

Not that Vegas would be much better, but the thought of moving made everything more tolerable. Phoenix, Chicago, and Denver had been about the same. One diner was as good as the next, but she needed to keep moving. The regulars at the diner had learned her name. It wasn't her real name, but if anyone came around with a picture, they'd point her out regardless of her new hair color and style.

Tonya opened the bedroom door and tossed the apron onto the bed, which was still unmade from that morning. Who had time to make beds when you were working doubles?

The door closed behind her with a click. Breath stolen, she spun about to face the stranger in her bedroom. And his gun.

At first, the gun was all Tonya saw—that and the suppressor screwed onto the end of the barrel. It was not, however, pointed at her, but at the floor. But that could change in half a second.

The man was not tall by any stretch, but his t-shirt did little to hide his muscular physique. Curly brown hair peeked out from beneath an Atlanta Braves cap, and a neatly trimmed beard followed his jawline. Beneath thin-rimmed glasses were a pair of piercing green eyes that studied her with a silent intensity.

For a long while, they both stood there—her struggling to breath while he stood leaning against her bedroom wall as if he had no better place to be. Finally, he asked her, "Do you know me?"

Tonya swallowed hard and gathered any moisture that had not fled from her mouth. "You're one of Midas's men," she said.

He cocked his head to the side in question.

"I have a friend in the DEA. He keeps me up to date on all of the members of Midas's crew so that if one of them comes to kill me..." She clutched her throat.

He shook his head and slid the gun into the holster on his hip. Tonya guessed he could pull it in an instant if necessary. "You don't know me then," he said. "We've met before, Tonya. Nearly two years ago."

She shook her head and reached for the bed behind her. A gun was previously hidden in her nightstand, but it now lay on top of it, the magazine separated from the weapon and empty. Another weapon was in the kitchen and a third in her bathroom, but she guessed he had found those as well. "I'm…I'm sorry. I don't remember that."

"I snuck into a camp trying to save my girlfriend," he said. "And I was about to escape through a hole I had cut into a fence. Two of your co-workers were going to shoot me, but you shot them first."

Tonya's mouth parted. Of course she remembered. But she had saved a kid—a little blonde-headed teen, not this man standing before her.

"Ironically," he continued, "the only person who *wasn't* saved during that raid *was* Katie."

"Wh-why are you here?" Tonya ventured.

"I need to take the next step in infiltrating Midas's organization. In exchange for your head, I get a seat at the table. And hopefully, a chance to find Katie and bring her back home."

Tonya didn't understand. Was he here to kill her then? Or save her? When he pulled a rubber glove out of his pocket, the thundering in her chest ramped up even further.

"This world is full of irony, isn't it, Tonya? Midas sending the guy you saved to kill you for saving him? We might as well get started though. We're going to have to make this look convincing."

JUST A NICK

Katie shut the door to their room as silently as possible. The others still had an hour of sleep left. No reason to shorten it.

Stepping around the other kids sleeping on the floor, Katie knelt at Tucker's side as he lay on his belly whimpering. Katie's own back roared in pain, but she had work to do. "This is going to hurt," she whispered, "but try to be quiet."

She had awakened in the bathroom, wet washcloth in hand. She was not sure why her dissociated mind had taken her to this location—it was not an approved place and could have gotten her into further trouble. She didn't try to figure it out, however, but merely accepted the washrag as a gift and brought it with her.

Now she dabbed at the red, raw cuts on Tucker's back. His body tensed beneath her touch and he let out a whine, but she ignored it and continued. This he would survive. An infection—not as likely. She tried to be quick, which meant she lost a little gentleness, but speed was preferable anyways.

The wounds hurt. They would hurt no matter what she did. Just getting it done and over with was the best she could do. When finished, Katie collapsed onto her own mat and stared at the wall. She had run out of tears.

"I'm sorry," whispered Tucker.

Katie bit her lip. She was tempted to say, 'It's not your fault,' but it damn well was his fault. The boat was *his* job. Not checking it for gas was an egregious oversight. But instead of chiding him for his stupidity, she continued to stare at the wall until the cook opened the door, flipped on the lights, and shouted at them in a language Katie didn't understand. The intent was clear: Get up.

Sally, the only other 'older' girl, rubbed her blue eyes and stretched. When they had first arrived on the island there were twenty-five of them. Now there were ten: Sally, Katie, Tucker and seven young ones to look after. Sally was two years younger than Katie. Originally from New Zealand, she spoke with a Kiwi accent. Her fiery red hair typically hung in waves but frizzed out in a giant ball that morning from sleep. When she finished rubbing her eyes, Sally finally noticed Tucker's and Katie's state. "What the hell did you do?"

"Nothing," Katie muttered. "That's why we're still here." With great effort, she managed to rise to a sit. Her shirt clung to her wounds and she knew she had bled through it.

Mouth agape, Sally shook her head. "Idiots. Have you cleaned them yet?"

"Just Tucker's," said Katie.

Sally rolled the back of the shirt up to Katie's shoulders and cleaned the skin as much as possible with the washcloth. Having no other options, Katie's old shirt was rolled back down over the wounds.

Sally had not been invited nor informed about last night's escapade for this very reason. She was far too sensible. If a plan didn't have a higher than fifty percent probability, she was not interested.

But they had already tried those other plans.

Wincing, Tucker pulled his shirt over his head before leaning heavily against the wall to stand. He hobbled to the door and past the young ones gazing up at him as red lines oozed a pattern onto his shirt.

Katie stood and followed him. There would be no day off, no moment to heal. If she kept her mind fixed solely on the task at hand, the pain would continue, but in the back of her mind. Day one was the hardest, and sometimes Katie wished to claw her way out of her own body just for a minute or two.

Once in the hallway, the older kids divided up responsibilities for the younger ones. Today, the task fell to Sally alone since her partners were out of commission. Everyone started in the kitchen before leaving for their various jobs. Most of them were house jobs—cooking and cleaning. No fields existed on this island although there were flower beds to tend to. The food rations, however, had not changed. Stealing scraps was risky, and years of this and lack of sleep made each day feel like a day in the fields.

Katie took jobs around the house that day, kept her head down, and tried to stay out of trouble as much as possible. While she was in the barroom, she caught sight of her reflection in the mirror behind the bar and averted her eyes from the strange girl looking back at her. Her scar, a ragged cut dominating half her face, was the main feature anyway.

After Midas's attack, Katie had been left alone in her cell for the next two days without food or water. All the time, she kept reliving the moment, trying to figure out why he hadn't just killed her. By the end of the time, she was half-delirious, convinced that his attack had been motivated by her looks. Taking the rusty nail hidden behind the mattress, she had reopened her scar.

Midas had laughed when he saw it that evening when the time had come for them to leave the country. "Do you really think *that* will save you, Katie Belle?"

But it *had* worked. So far. The scar coupled with her matted hair and stench kept everyone but her fellow captives at arm's length. Flogging, she had learned to live with, but she doubted she could survive another attack like that.

Another person entered the bar, and Katie's stomach flopped. Randall placed his hands upon her shoulders. "Morning, Scarface."

Katie froze as his meaty hands lingered on her thin frame. Then he chuckled and stepped behind the bar, helping himself to a drink.

Staying rooted in place, Katie clutched the mop with white knuckles until he left.

When he was gone, she looked into the mirror again, seeing the strange, ragged girl looking back at her. Was it time to re-open it once more?

Jared leaned against the willow tree and sipped on his tea, enjoying the warmth that spread through him from the beverage. He had not yet returned to his bosses after the incident with Tonya, and his mind played over the events as he came at the situation from every angle. Was there anything he had missed? DNA—check. Dental records—check. Kill video—check. But he felt the tingling of tremors shoot through his arms, nonetheless. He took another sip of the tea.

One by one, the lights on the house across the street went out. The moon, a waxing gibbous, dangled above the hill to his back. If he waited a couple more hours, it would be hidden completely.

When the appropriate time came and Jared was sure the neighbors were asleep, he pulled up his hood, crossed the black tar pavement, and strolled down the driveway. No need to crouch or be otherwise suspicious. If by chance someone *was* looking, that would be a dead giveaway. Once he reached the downspout hanging off the porch, Jared climbed it and pulled himself onto the roof.

Being on the roof was suspicious enough, and he was thankful for the pine tree growing in the yard, hiding him from at least one direction of the street. He pressed his palms flat against the window and raised it up. As he lowered his leg inside, a shadow moved across the room, grabbed him by the back of the head, and kissed him on the lips.

Jared shuffled back, nearly tumbling out the window and onto the roof. The kisser, too, retreated, and a lamp came on seconds later. Leida stood before him, hand over her mouth, her eyes wide.

"What the hell was that?" Jared hissed as he stepped inside the house.

"I…I did not know it was you," she managed.

"Who the hell else would be coming in your window?"

"Uh…nobody. Never mind."

Jared stuck his head back out the window and scanned the street up and down. *Whoever it is, they'd better hope I don't catch them.*

Leida sat upon her bed, legs tucked beneath her. Although his sister wore blue and green plaid pajamas, her make-up, eyeliner, and braided hair implied she had not been sleeping. For a moment, Jared considered pressing the issue further, but he had no time. He had a plane to catch.

"Why are you here?" Leida asked instead.

"Nice to see you too." Jared knocked a stack of clothes out of her desk chair and took a seat. "I'm probably not going to be back for a while. I wanted to see you before I left."

"Any luck?"

"There are some rumors that Midas has some leftover Comms on an island he's been basing his operations out of, but nothing more than that."

"An island where?"

Jared scratched the beard running up his jawline. "Southeast Asia."

Leida's mouth dropped. "You're going to Southeast Asia? Jared, you've got to be kidding me!"

"I'm only going where the breadcrumbs lead."

Leida peaked her hands against her mouth as if to hold in a reply. Moisture gathered about her eyes, but she did not let any of it fall. Jared took a seat on the bed beside her and slid his hand into hers.

"I'll be careful, I swear."

"What if Katie's dead? What if you're going there for nothing-"

"Midas isn't dead," Jared said. "If all I can claim is his head, then I'm still doing this."

Leida rested her head on his shoulder. "I don't want you to go."

Jared resisted the urge to pull away from her. Why did she have to do this to him? Didn't she know how guilty he felt leaving her already?

"I know," he said softly. "But you know I have to do this."

A thump sounded on the porch roof, and Jared looked to Leida in question. She scrambled for the window and whispered into the night. "No, don't! Go—"

"Hey, Leida," a male greeted and pulled her into a kiss. Jared gripped the collar of whoever-it-was's shirt and yanked him inside, spilling him onto the floor. Bryan landed on his back, staring up at him. "Hey there, Jared—"

"You son of a bitch! What the hell are you doing here?"

"I don't know what you mean." Bryan grinned. The lamp light caught beads of sweat already gathering on his forehead. "I just came by to check on her. With you being gone and—"

The door to Leida's room burst open. Dad entered, pistol drawn. "Freeze! Don't move."

Both Jared and Bryan raised their hands.

Dad bought a gun, Jared thought. *Good for him.*

"Bryan, Leida," Dad ordered them to come with a jerk of the gun. Leida complied, but Bryan continued to lay upon the ground.

"Who the hell are you?" Dad demanded of Jared.

"Relax, Dad," Jared replied.

"Jared?" He lowered the weapon a fraction.

"Yeah, Dad, it's me." He gestured to Bryan. "Did you know about this?"

Dad tucked his pistol into his pajama pants as he eyed Bryan up and down. "Did I know my daughter's boyfriend was sneaking into my house after 1 a.m.? No, I did not."

Bryan grinned sheepishly and rubbed the back of his head. He started to stand, bracing his ribs as he did so. For a split second, Jared considered leaving him to do it on his own—as a payback of sorts, but he ended up grabbing his arm and pulling him up the rest of the way.

"Thanks," said Bryan chipperly.

"Don't mention it," grumbled Jared.

A thump sounded in the hallway followed by footsteps on the stairs. "That would be your mother going downstairs to make hot chocolate," said Dad. "I guess since the whole house is awake now, let's go and join her."

Jared motioned to the window. "I have a plane to—"

"No, you're going to go say hello to your mother first. Now, come on."

Jared glanced hesitantly to the open window but trudged out of the room with the others. Mom already had a kettle of water warming on the stove. When he stepped into the room, she wrapped her arms around him in a stifling embrace—that Jared loved every minute of.

"Your hair." Mom ran her hand through his brown waves. "You look so much older."

He smiled. "Hi, Mom."

"Marie, we've got some unhealthy snacks around here, don't we?" Dad asked as he pilfered through the cabinets.

"There's some frozen yogurt in the freezer." Mom joined him to find it.

"So, you're not *really* mad at me, right?" Bryan asked Jared as he leaned against the stove, holding Leida's hand. "I mean, you were all talk to Dakota too, but…"

Jared narrowed his eyes. "Don't count on it."

Bryan laughed and scratched the back of his head. "How is that fake ID I got you working out?"

Dad peeked out from around the freezer.

Jared saw right through the effort to change the subject, but shrugged anyway, playing along. He didn't like *anyone* dating Leida, but…well…it was Bryan. "I'm not dead yet, so—" Jared answered.

"No problems with the passport or anything—?"

"Alright." Mom set down the cartons on the counter with a thud, a sound reminiscent of a judge bringing down a gavel. The discussion of his "'side business'" as they still called it ended.

As Dad handed out bowls of dessert, he paused before giving Bryan his portion. "Don't think that you're off the hook or that this dessert is somehow a reward for sneaking in tonight. We're going to be discussing that later."

Bryan gulped. "Yes, sir."

Dad eyed him closely before relenting the bowl to him. More talk? Probably. But it seemed Dad was just as obligated to play hardass about Leida as Jared. She was, after all, still a minor.

Soon, the rest of the group had been served and started to move into the living room.

"Hang on, Bryan," said Jared before he left. "I do need to talk to you for a moment. Sorry, Mom."

"Fine," she said. "But I don't want to hear about it." She continued on into the next room, but Jared suspected she would be listening by the doorway. Dad remained in the kitchen.

"Do you recognize this guy?" Jared asked as he pulled a picture from his pocket. Every time a new face came up, he asked this question. This time, however, Bryan flinched. He then let out a guttural noise and gripped the countertop with pale fingertips. Tears brimmed his eyes and he rubbed them off onto his sleeves.

"I'm sorry," said Jared.

"It's fine," he said with a sniff. Flashback, brewing panic, Jared didn't know what exactly was going on with Bryan. It didn't matter. The results were the same.

"Let me see it again," he said after a few moments.

Jared handed it back and Bryan tromboned it as if he were near-sighted. "Yeah," he said. "It's who I thought it was. That's the guy that took Katie."

If Bryan had not been in pain, Jared would have punched the sky.

"How do you know him?" asked Bryan, handing it back.

"He's my latest contact."

"Be careful with him, okay?" said Bryan. "He's bad news." He pressed his hands to his eyes and took a shuddering breath.

When one of his people said something like that, Jared listened. If bad was worth mentioning, then it had to be very bad. "What can you tell me about him?"

"Jared," said Dad, "I don't know—"

"It's fine, Mr. Kelley," said Bryan. "I got a decent look at this guy at the gas station where Katie was hiding. He claimed to be FBI then, and he looked and spoke like a cop. After they ran us off the road though…He's the one that jabbed Katie with the needle. While his partner took her to the road, he tried to question me a bit."

"What did he want?"

"To know my name," said Bryan with a shrug. "I told him to go to hell. He put a gun to my head." The tears started again, but Bryan swiped them away without fanfare then chuckled. "I just looked between the gun and the steering wheel crushing my chest. There was blood coming out of my mouth, gurgling up with every breath, you know? So, I straight up asked him, 'Are you serious?' and the bastard laughed at me."

He continued, "I guess the guy thought it was a weird thing for me to say. Or he thought I was acting too calm for…you know…a dying person. He tugged on the back of my shirt collar. When he saw my scars, he just laughed again and left. I must have blacked out shortly thereafter because the next thing I know, three months had passed and I was waking up with rods and plates in my chest." He ran a hand over his ribs. Jared, however, gazed at the scar on his neck where they had cut open his throat to plug in a ventilator.

Jared hid the pain the memory brought him as well. For months after the accident, he had remained glued to his phone, waiting on a call from Agent Rogers. Since Jared was not allowed to contact Bryan directly, the call about whether Bryan lived or died would have come from him.

"Sounds like a typical Watcher," he said, choosing not to linger. "What makes you think I need to worry about this guy in particular?"

"Do you remember the way Clayton used to look at us?" asked Bryan. "Like the time he dislocated your shoulder…"

Jared nodded. His damned pupils had dilated, like he was getting off on it or something.

"They had the same eyes," said Bryan. "He's—he's something else, man. He's not like Bartrum or even Tweedle Dee or Tweedle Dum. There's something in him that's just wrong. Watch your back."

Bryan gathered his bowl for the living room while Jared poured himself another cup of tea instead of hot chocolate. He was about to join them without a bowl when Dad said, "Try this, son." He handed him a single-serving bowl of sorbet. "Mom always keeps these around in case you come by."

Jared took it with a faint smile. Ever since the first day home, Mom had always made sure to keep his lactose intolerance in mind, but the anxiety on Dad's face killed the gesture.

Dad lowered his voice. "Son, I don't want to know what you've been up to. I would ask you to stop if I didn't know it was pointless, but—" He pulled his gun from his waistband and set it on the counter. "I *do* want you to be safe. You can take this if you promise you'll use it only for good."

"Dad, I'm currently carrying three firearms and five knives." He slid it back to his father. "You'll be better off carrying it than I will. It is only because I know you will protect them that I can go do what needs to be done." Jared met his father's eyes, looking into them purposefully.

Dad nodded, slid the piece off the counter, and tucked it away. "Take care of yourself, son. Please."

Jared nodded, and Dad pulled him into an embrace. And while his face was pressed against his father's shoulder, a tear slid down his cheek. He would miss them. More than they knew.

DEAD FAINT

By dinner time, Katie neared exhaustion. More than once the cook caught her staring off into space rather than chopping up vegetables. . . or whatever she was supposed to be doing. Her vision swayed as her back continued to throb. She kept forgetting where she was and what she was doing, even if the task were right in front of her.

Vaguely, Katie noticed Tucker washing dishes in slow motion at the sink. His face was pale and more than once he held onto the sink to steady himself. His shirt had turned brown and clung to him.

"Katie, you're bleeding!" shouted Sally.

"Hmpf," said Katie, unsurprised that one of the flog marks had started up again. But Sally took her hand and wrapped it in a dish cloth. Without realizing it, Katie had cut her finger instead of the carrots. She stood staring at the dish cloth as redness spread across the fabric.

"I've got it, Sally," said Katie, taking the cloth. "I need to put the brownies out now—" But as Katie turned for the bake room in the back, dizziness overtook her and she fell, losing consciousness as her head hit the floor.

*   *   *

Jared shook his head again, trying to remove the cobwebs. Twice he had nodded off, but thankfully, no one had noticed. At night, his dreams persisted in ruining his sleep regardless of what he did, but he was determined not to show his tiredness. After rubbing his hands over his face, he surveyed the room full of strangers sitting in their own little groups, waiting for their rides. Stanton said he'd be back in an hour after he cleared the boat through customs.

Seeing a pile of magazines nearby, Jared moved to thumb through some boring pages. Perhaps the motion alone would help keep him awake. The selection was sparse, mainly fashion and gossip pieces, but one stood out among the others: *Science and Engineering of the Modern Age.*

Jared glanced around the room. Jack wouldn't choose this magazine, but the temptation for Jared was too great. He picked up the booklet and started reading an article about a new theory in geothermal energy.

"Excuse me?"

Jared peered over the pages to see a young blonde woman smiling at him. He frowned in return and tossed the magazine back onto the pile. "Yes?"

"Is this where we are supposed to meet for the trip to Pali Island?" she said.

Jared checked his watch. "Yes, but you're a half-an-hour early."

She shrugged and took a seat a couple of places away. "I like to be on time."

Jared picked up a magazine on men's fashion. The drowsiness returned.

"Do you work on the island?" she asked, pointing to her shirt, mirroring the position of the insignia on Jared's polo reading 'Pali Island Spa.'

Jared fluffed out the magazine. "I do now."

"Oh. So, I guess you don't really know anybody yet." She twirled a strand of hair.

Jared returned his attention to the magazine, and the girl twiddled her thumbs for a few minutes before pulling a book out of her bag. Jared narrowed his eyes as he looked at the title: *To Kill a Mockingbird*.

"Any good?" he asked.

She shrugged. "I'm supposed to write a book report on it. It's alright, I guess—"

"For college?"

"Uhm, sure."

Jared peered over his magazine once more and studied the girl. *To Kill a Mockingbird* . That was something he had read in his high school courses. Did college students read that?

He thought back to his English Lit class. It was possibly on the list. But this girl…

Her face, although painted in make-up, had acne blemishes. Her hair was tied in the back with a pink ribbon and she overall looked very young. It was possible she was older, but just looking at her, Jared guessed fifteen. Maybe even fourteen.

Jared did not need to get involved with this. Stanton could come back any minute, or any one of the people here could be watching him. Shoving away his suspicions, Jared stared at the text before him.

But his eyes refused to focus.

The girl set her bookmark, a Harry Potter Puppet Pals popsicle stick, to the side. His eyes might not be able to focus on the magazine, but he could not pull them from the bookmark. Then he saw the stamp on the back of her book stating 'Oakdale High School Library.'

"What are you doing here?" Jared asked.

She tilted her head to the side. "I'm sorry?"

"Why are you coming to the island?"

She shrugged. "I was invited to come."

"By whom?"

She smiled a wide pleasant smile, and a dimple appeared on her cheek. "I met this guy at a party. A college party that I really wasn't supposed to be at, but my friend knew him and—"

"Yeah, yeah, yeah," Jared said. "What's his name?"

Her brow knit at his rushing. "Mr. Stanton. He's a college professor at UCLA. I'm trying to get into their Engineering Program, but it's really competitive and he said he could help. He invited me to this party on Pali Island where his dean is supposed to be and—"

Jared pinched the bridge of his nose. Of all the things his new boss was, college professor was not one of them. "He invited you to come get on his boat and go to his private island in a foreign country for a college interview?"

"Well, it's not like an official interview or anything. He said it was more of a social opportunity. A lot of other people are going to be there too and—"

"How old are you?"

"I'm…eighteen."

"No, you're not. How old are you?"

The girl lowered her head and ran her finger over the cover of her book. "Sixteen," she said barely above a whisper.

Jared wasn't sure that was true either, but perhaps the kids he knew looked older than their actual age. "And your parents let you come?"

The girl didn't raise her head.

"They don't know you're here, do they?"

"They wouldn't understand! They don't realize how the world works anymore. It's not all about grades and extracurriculars. It's about meeting people, putting yourself out there."

"Well, you're definitely putting yourself out there," Jared muttered. "What's your name?"

"Connie."

Jared glanced up at the security cameras watching their every move before leaning in. Stanton was still nowhere to be seen, but he lowered his voice anyway. "Connie, I am about to give you the best advice of your life. Go home. Now. Forget about Stanton and this party and the dean. Work hard in your classes and get into the engineering program the *right* way. Do you understand me?"

Connie stared at her shoes.

"Do you understand me?" he repeated.

"Yes," she whispered. "Yes, I think—" Tears crept into her eyes, and she covered her mouth.

"Then get out of here."

With tears sliding down her face, Connie stood and ran for the exit. Jared shook his head as he watched her go.

"I'm never having kids," he muttered and picked up the magazine once more.

A few minutes later, Stanton, with his crew cut and muscle shirt, arrived with the boat keys in hand. "Ready, Warner?"

Jared stood and set the magazine back onto the stack. "Ready."

Stanton frowned as he looked around the terminal. "Did you happen to see a little blonde girl running around here somewhere? About yea-high?" He held a hand up to his chest.

Jared stepped past him toward the port. "Nope."

PHOENIX RISING

Katie woke on her mat alone and unsure of how long she had been out. Her wounds had been cleaned and left open to the air, and a new shirt sat folded beside her. She guessed she had gained a little pity from the Watchers after passing out.

Katie felt along her back, finding the rifts scabbed over, but still tender. A voice in her head urged, *Get up!* but her body declined to obey. If she lay still enough, the person watching the camera over her left shoulder wouldn't know she was awake. This was, after all, the first break she had had in recent memory.

When the door opened a few hours later, Katie closed her eyes and pretended to still be sleeping. Whoever it was knelt beside her—Katie could hear the fabric of their clothes shifting. Then, to her surprise, her own warm breath reflected back against her nose.

Confused, Katie opened her eyes. Sally knelt before her, her fingers beneath Katie's nose, checking for breath. When Sally saw Katie's eyes open, she sighed with relief and petted Katie's hair.

"Thank God, you're alive," she said.

Was that such a good thing though? Katie wasn't sure.

"You've been asleep since yesterday. It's lunch time now."

That *was* a long time to be unconscious. No wonder Sally was worried. That's how the others had died after all. They had just passed out and didn't wake up again.

"The Watchers are telling me either to get you up or to grab shovels," said Sally. "I think you're going to have to come with me."

Katie let out a sigh. She had expected no less, but a girl could dream, couldn't she? So, with the help of Sally, she sat, shrugged on her shirt, and followed her out of the room.

"Katie!" the kids cried as she entered the kitchen. They swarmed her, hugging and tugging on her until Sally shooed them away. Again, Katie stayed close to the house that day, not wishing to further rupture her wounds by doing yard maintenance. The bar room, as usual, was a mess when she arrived, and she set to cleaning it.

When two men entered the pub, Katie kept her head down and migrated to the back of the room. Safely behind the bar, she kept her back to them as she wiped down the sink, but watched them from the mirror above her head. Stanton, she knew, but the other had an unfamiliar bearded face.

"Ooh, a fully serviced bar!" the bearded one said in a deep voice.

"Just another perk of this place." Stanton pulled out a stool and sat before the shiny counter. "You can have two free drinks a day as long as you're not on duty."

"You, girl, I'll take a shot of your finest brandy," he said.

Katie kept her head lowered as she scrubbed on an invisible stain.

"The girl only cleans," Stanton called in Burmese to the back of the shop, and the bartender entered and bowed to them. The bartender's name started with a Lu-sound, so Katie called him Louie.

"Brandy, two,   " Stanton said and Louie pulled out a pair of glasses from beneath the bar. Other than drink orders, Katie doubted he knew any English. Whenever he needed to communicate something, it was always done in gestures like the rest of the staff. Not that it mattered. She was forbidden to speak to them anyway.

Katie continued down the bar away from the sink as Louie selected a glass bottle from the shelves above the mirror. When she glanced back, however, she noted the bearded one watching her.

Why was he watching her? She moved even further away.

As Stanton and the newcomer sat at the bar and chatted for some time, Katie ventured out from behind the counter to continue wiping down the tables. She made a point to stay quiet as she worked, invisible, but the damn man continued with his gaze. Katie studied his face in her occasional glances to determine his intentions. She hoped for revulsion, but didn't find it. Sympathy perhaps? Doubtful. Attraction? Oh gosh, surely not.

Please, no.

Suddenly, she wanted to bolt, but she couldn't leave until she was done. Three more tables to go then the floor to attend to.

The newcomer accepted another drink from the barkeep, and Stanton patted him on the back as he dismissed himself to the bathroom. Louie returned to the back to continue…doing whatever it was he did…and Katie and this man were alone in the front.

The man slid down from the barstool and moved to sit at a table. Katie stopped mid-swipe. Why that table? Didn't he see the crumbs on it? Ten other tables, and he picked that one? Sweat broke on her brow as Katie moved to the table next to him and wiped it down.

"Hello there," he said.

Katie kept her head down and ignored him. She was required to speak to members of Midas's crew, but this guy was new. Maybe he didn't know the rules yet.

Dammit. Why is he looking at me? She tried to slip past him to the bar, but he grabbed her arm. Not painfully, but firmly. Katie froze.

"Look at me," he said, and a lump filled her throat. "Look. At. Me."

Katie's eyes flitted to meet his, but she could not sustain a longer gaze. He frowned, and her heart pounded. She knew she had displeased him. She tried, she tried so hard to look at him, but could not.

"Find something you like there, Jack?" Stanton returned. "Oh phew! You must not be able to smell."

"Deviated septum," he said.

"Well, trust *me* then."

Jack released Katie's wrist, and she moved behind the bar. He leaned back in his seat, but his gaze continued to linger on her. "I need some help bringing my stuff to my room. Would you mind if I borrowed her?"

Katie wrung the rag in her hands. *Come on, Stanton. Say no. Say she needs to finish her job—*

But Stanton shrugged. "Sure. Once you get unpacked though, meet me at my office. It's on the second floor. I have a placard on the door."

"Sure thing, boss."

Stanton left once more and blood drained from Katie's head. Again, she was alone with this man. This vulture.

Jack gestured with his head to the door. "Come with me."

With trembling hands, Katie set the rag on the counter and walked ahead of him out of the bar.

Midas had built a leisure palace on the island. It was staffed primarily by people from the mainland, but Katie wasn't sure what that was. Most employees lived on the island, but traveled back home once a month.

Jack had come by boat that morning, and his belongings had been loaded into an SUV and driven up from the docks. Two giant suitcases and a small overnight bag sat in the back of the hatch. Katie grabbed the strap of one of the navy blue monstrosities and pulled. Jack grabbed the strap on the side before it slid out of the vehicle and eased it to the ground with her. It *was* heavy, and Katie was glad of the assistance, but confused by it.

It was because he was new. It had to be.

Jack opened his mouth as if to speak, but Randall approached from behind and slapped a hand on his shoulder. "Hey there, Jack! Glad you could make it!"

Katie flinched at the other Watcher's greeting and kept her eyes locked on the ground.

"Good to see you again." Jack smiled and shook his hand.

"Well, I gotta run, but I'll catch you later." Randall walked backwards a couple of steps before jogging into the house.

Katie pulled the extendable handle of the suitcase and gently set the overnight case over her shoulder. The sores howled and she lowered it to her bicep. She was about to grab the other suitcase to have them both trail behind her, but Jack already had it in hand. He grabbed the strap of the overnight bag and pulled it from her arm, swinging it onto his own.

Katie frowned but did not question this. He gestured for her to go ahead into the mansion.

Staff quarters were down the corridor to the right of the entrance, across from the bar. The entire building was reminiscent of a hotel with most halls having rooms on either side of the corridors. Jack stopped at a room midway down on the right, shoved the key into the lock, and pressed his thumb onto the scanner. The door unlocked.

Katie hesitated, hoping he would enter before her and leave her near the door, but he gestured for her to enter ahead. The knot in her throat tightened. With her head hung low, she obeyed, rolling the bag into the small apartment. The walls were a generic beige, but the sheets and comforter were better quality than most hotels Katie had stayed in. A small kitchenette stood on the far wall with a mini-fridge and a microwave. Beside the microwave was a sliding glass door leading to a staff courtyard. A round table sat between this and the bed. Across from the bed was a TV cabinet and a closet beside that. As Katie rolled the suitcase to stand in front of the TV cabinet, Jack shut the door and locked the dead bolt.

Katie stood still as stone, staring at the tan carpet, her hand on the suitcase. Jack stepped further into the room, stopped beside the bathroom door, and leaned against the wall. "Look at me," he said.

But Katie did not move. Nor did she hear him above her own pulse pounding in her ears.

Why her?

Her stomach churned, and she feared she would vomit. She closed her eyes, and a tear fell down her cheek. Jack took her hand, but she pulled it away.

"I'm not going to hurt you," he said and took her hand again. Was it hers who trembled so or his? The room walls expanded and contracted. She felt herself slipping outside her body. Ascending it—

"Katie…" He brushed a hair behind her ear.

At the sound of her name, she was brought back. But no! No, she needed to leave!

"Look at me, please," he said.

What cruel game was he playing with her? Her eyes darted to his face, but then away again.

Leave, dammit, leave. Get out. This isn't real. This isn't happening to you…

"Katie, it's me," he said, placing a hand on her cheek. "It's Jared."

Jared? But Jared…

"Jared is dead," Katie whispered neither here nor there.

"Not yet he's not," he said. "Look at me, Katie. I'm right here in front of you. Can you see me?"

For the first time, she managed to raise her eyes to his face. There was nothing familiar about him. Not at all. Except…

Except those eyes. She knew those green eyes. "Jared?" she whispered.

He smiled softly. "Hi, Katie."

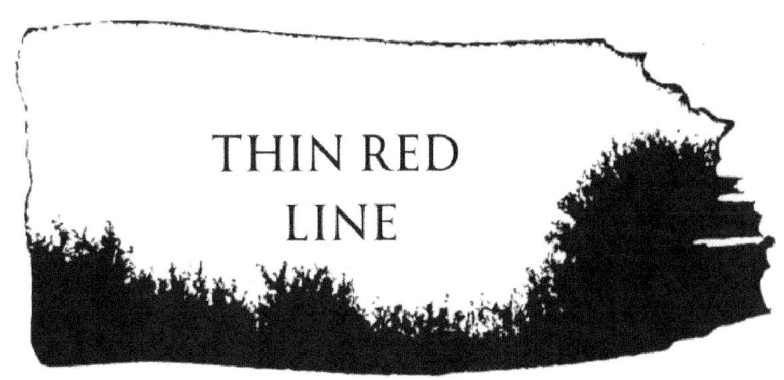

Katie wrapped her arms around Jared's neck, and Jared held her tight to himself as his body trembled.

"You're alive?" she finally managed, taking a step back.

Jared caressed her cheek with his thumb.

"But…I watched Clayton shoot you. Midas…Midas said—"

"Midas lies."

Katie pressed against his chest again. It was broader than she remembered. Thicker. Then, with sudden realization, she pulled away once more. "You're working for Midas now?"

"No, I'm undercover. I've been looking for you."

"But…but it's been two years—"

Jared smiled sadly and ran his thumb against her cheek again. "I'm sorry it took so long."

She shook her head. "That's not what I meant."

"We found all the camps, and you weren't there. I had to find you, Katie." Jared moved to the sliding doors and pulled the curtain across an uncovered gap. "I'm working on a plan to get you out. They've got me working maintenance on the docks, so that's promising."

Her wounds throbbed. "They watch the docks closely."

"Yeah, I know, but I'm one of the Watchers now. I might be able to find an out…"

Katie sank into a chair and buried her head in her hands.

"What is it?" Jared knelt next to her chair and rested a hand on her knee. Katie tensed, and he removed it.

"I'm just…I'm just so tired," she said.

He took her hand. "I know." He smiled at her again, and Katie wrapped her arms around him once more.

"Thank you," she said. "Thank you for coming for me."

"Always. But I think it's time I sent you back to the bar. You looked pretty busy when I pulled you away."

Katie held on to him, not wishing to let go.

"This is the beginning of the end, alright?" he said. "I'm going to get you home."

Katie sat next to him, this boy whom she thought until this moment was dead, and she desperately wanted to believe him, but her heart was too tired.

Was this real? Or had she transcended reality for good? She recalled the note she had received from JAK while in Camp 3. A note from a ghost.

But did it really matter? So what if she had broken from reality? This was a good fantasy and she would live it for now.

Katie returned to the bar in short order to finish the job. Like usual, Louie was nowhere to be found. She finished her work in silence and processed Jared's arrival. Now that she was not in the same room with him, she truly doubted his presence. It had been a hallucination, nothing more. Finally, she was losing her mind.

About damned time.

But then Jared walked past the bar. She froze as she watched him standing in the doorway. He looked so different, but his eyes were unforgettable, even hidden behind the thin wire glasses. Katie could also not ignore how much of a man he had turned into—had he grown taller? Even his voice was deeper than she remembered. But more than anything, he looked not only healthy, but athletic.

He did not linger long in the doorway, just long enough to wink at her before moving to the staircase further down the hall. She was glad to see him, truly, but puzzled too. What did this mean? Were the FBI far behind? Could there actually be hope in her future?

*   *   *

As Jared passed by the barroom on his way to the stairs, he glanced in on Katie. She looked worse off than he had feared. Her lively eyes were dull and sunken and her spirit was nonexistent. And what had happened to her face? Her scar had been healing so well, but it looked like someone had reopened it.

Whoever it was would be feeling his blade against their throat soon enough.

Jared had witnessed this wasting among his peers repeatedly, but Katie—she had been so vibrant. She had been a spark and reminder of what life was like on the outside. Sometimes her naïveté annoyed him and downright scared him, but her resolve to damn the consequences for the sake of others had been what attracted him to her. Everything about her now screamed terror. If something didn't change, she was on the cusp of being lost.

Jared longed to take her hand right then, lead her to the boats, and flee for their lives. But that was not an option. Midas's men would be on them before they stepped out the door. If by some miracle they made it to the boats, they would be followed. And there were other kids that needed their help too. People he wouldn't just abandon. No, they needed a better exit strategy. He just hoped she could hold on long enough.

Jared stopped before Stanton's office door and hesitated. Should he knock? Should he just enter? What did the Watchers at camp do?

Jared knocked twice and peeked inside. That was a good middle-ground, no?

Stanton waved Jared in as he sat with his long legs on the oak desk studying a stack of papers. The office was dark with only a lamp on the desk and the computer screen lighting the area. The window behind Stanton, if Jared had his sense of direction correct, opened up to a beautiful view of the ocean, but it was covered in light-shielding curtains.

Jared's instincts told him to hang at the back of the room and wait to be invited to sit, but that's not what Jack would do. So, instead, he yanked back on one of the upholstered chairs, dropped into it, crossed his legs, and leaned back.

"I was just reviewing your hit," Stanton said and turned the screen to Jared. He clicked play, and the video showed an empty living room with a shabby couch across from a TV. Then a door opened, blocking the view of the camera momentarily, and a woman with dark hair entered, closing the door behind her. Two pops sounded, and two red holes appeared in the back of the woman's shirt before she collapsed on the floor.

The video shuffled and turned to the wall momentarily, then rotated back to the woman. A foot rolled her over showing her pale face and open eyes. The videographer knelt and slipped a rectangular device on the woman's index finger. A heart rate slowed then tapered to a stop. Then the video quit.

"Efficient," noted Stanton. "Was this your first kill?"

Jared shrugged. "Would it matter if it wasn't?"

A thin smile crept over his lips. "At this level in the organization, we like to know everything about you."

"Yeah, well, tough." Jared crossed his arms. "I don't kill and tell. And I clean up my messes."

The smile grew. "Fair enough. I won't press you anymore about it." Stanton slid a spiral-bound book across the table. "The Handbook. Since no one actually reads it, I'll fill you in on the bigger issues. No drinking while on duty. No fighting with your co-workers. The native staff are not part of the crew, so don't divulge information to them."

Jared leaned forward in his seat. "Tell me more about the girl in the barroom. A…Comm…I think they were called?"

"Yeah." Stanton dropped his feet to the floor. "Midas's trophies. There's not much to know, really. They're captives. Don't let them leave the island, use the phones, or get your gun. They are required to do what you tell them to, instantly and without question."

Stanton eyed Jared up and down. "If you're looking for—romance—Midas brings in whores every Friday. If one of the Comms strikes your fancy, which I have no idea why one would, there used to be a rule against that, but no one enforces it anymore. Just don't get attached. These Comms don't last long."

Jared slid the book from the table and flipped through it. "My childhood therapist informed me repeatedly that attachment is not something I have to worry about." He closed the book and met Stanton's eye with a sly smile.

Stanton laughed. "Mine too." With a grin, he extended his hand across the table. "Good to have you on board, Warner." Jared stood and took the hand. "Come with me and I'll show you the docks."

As they exited the office, Jared asked, "How often does Midas come through here?"

"Who knows? Whenever he feels like it."

Stanton led Jared back down the stairs and out the front door. Along the path to the docks, a boy was raking fresh mulch along a hedge row, and Jared guessed his age to be sixteen. Of this age guess, Jared was rather sure.

It was one of his people after all.

Like the others, he was gaunt, although a touch of hair dotted his chin. His shirt was covered in what appeared to be copious amounts of dirt along the back—as if he had been rolling in the flower bed. Stanton grabbed the boy's shirt collar without slowing his pace, dragging the kid out of the bed. The kid fumbled the rake, leaving it in the mulch. Stanton shoved him in front of himself as they continued down the path.

The kid clutched his arm and kept his head down as he went with them down the path. Jared wasn't sure why they were bringing the kid, but his presence made his stomach do flips. He reminded him of someone—a friend from long ago.

They stopped before a large warehouse on the edge of the shore. Stanton unlocked the padlock on the garage door and lifted the hatch. "Here's where you'll be working, Warner. We've got five sedans, two trucks, three SUVs, and twelve golf carts. This, of course, does not include the water vehicles. You will be in charge of those as well."

Each of the vehicles in the garage bay were no older than a year and shined with fresh wax. At the end of the warehouse, a long dock extended into the ocean where several other boats were tethered. "Nice rides," Jared said.

"Keep them that way," Stanton said. "Each vehicle receives an oil change every six months as well as a tire rotation. Any time the vehicle returns to the bay, it needs to be cleaned. Golf carts included."

"Sounds like I'll keep busy."

"Which is where the kid comes in." Stanton shoved the boy forward. "This one's not too bright, but he'll do as you tell him. Or else." The boy kept his eyes fixed to the shiny slab floor, and Stanton continued, "If you have any questions, let me know." He slapped Jared on the back and headed back up the path.

"Yes, sir," Jared muttered before turning his attention to the kid. The boy's shoulders came to his ears. His sun-bleached hair was matted and greasy, and his eyes were gray.

Jared walked to the vehicles, and the kid followed a couple of paces behind. Jared kicked the waxed tires and popped open the door of an SUV. The car smelled of stale leather and Armor All. "What's your name?" Jared asked.

"Tucker," the boy whispered.

"Have you ever changed oil in one of these monsters before, Tucker?"

"No, sir."

"Neither have I," Jared said. "But I understand the general concept. Come on. Let's get to work."

Tucker followed Jared to a work table in the corner where Jared opened and closed multiple drawers until he had found his needed supplies. Unable to carry everything, he had Tucker carry the rest and set all this beside the first SUV. The boy winced as he lifted the load.

Jared climbed inside the driver's seat and used the key ring he had found on the workbench to start the vehicle. "Put the wedge ramps against the tires."

Tucker looked to the ramps leaning against the wall and bit his lip. He dragged one ramp over with sluggish movements, but Jared didn't rush him. Once the ramps were in place, Jared drove up onto them.

After exiting the vehicle, Jared lay on his back and slid underneath the vehicle. Tucker lingered above, still holding his arm.

"Whatcha still doing up there?" Jared said. "Plug's under here."

Tucker hesitated momentarily, then lay on the concrete floor beside Jared. Slowly, he shimmied his way backwards until he was shoulder-to-shoulder with Jared beneath the car. Sweat dripped down from his hair and tears glinted in his eyes.

Still not putting the pieces together, Jared turned his attention back to the plug. "Damn, this is tight," he muttered as he tugged on it with his wrench. Tucker opened his mouth, then shut it. "What?" Jared asked.

He swiped his hand across his forehead. "You know what you're doing."

Jared paused. "I think we established earlier that I don't know what I'm doing. So out with it."

"You may be turning it the wrong way."

Jared frowned. "Hmm." But as he tried the opposite direction, it still refused to budge. "Hang on a second." Jared slid further under the vehicle and set his foot onto the wrench. With considerable force, he kicked the wrench, and the bolt turned. Tucker flinched at the kick.

As Tucker moved the oil basin under the plug, Jared scooted out from beneath the vehicle. "We've got three pans, so let's get three draining at a time."

Tucker crept out from beneath the vehicle and clutched the car grill to stand. His breath came heavy, but he said nothing. After getting the next car up on blocks, Jared was about to send Tucker under when he spotted a red spiderweb pattern creeping out the top of Tucker's shirt.

Jared tugged on the collar of the shirt, revealing the fresh wounds beneath. Tucker pulled away, turning to face him. Jared held up his hands. "Didn't mean to startle you."

Tucker stared at the floor, but Jared's stomach continued to do flips. *Dammit, how could I have missed that?* He couldn't send that kid back under the vehicle with open flogging wounds again, but what else was he supposed to do with him?

Jared palmed the car keys and took a deep breath as he made a decision. They were on an island. Where was the kid going to drive off too? Surely, if he allowed him to switch jobs no one would care. But would that tip the kid off?

Jared didn't know, but he tossed Tucker a set of the keys anyway. "Get the next one up on blocks," he said before sliding under the second vehicle and setting it to drain. This was going to be harder than he thought.

After crawling out from under the third vehicle, he frowned to see Tucker standing against the wall with his head down. The boy rubbed his arm incessantly, a classic self-soothing motion.

Jared longed to put the kid at ease, but knew this to be unwise. "Let's check out these golf carts."

The boy trudged behind. What had the kid done to receive the latest flogging? And just how recent had it been? These were questions he couldn't just up and ask, so they rolled around his mind on a loop.

Jared shook his head as he entered the golf cart. He didn't know that Mercedes made a golf cart, and here were twelve of them. An electric control panel sat in the center of the dash, and after fiddling around a bit, he managed to turn the damn thing on.

"Heated seats?" Jared muttered. A map of the entire island appeared on the screen. "Midas, you've got more money than sense. Tucker, how do you charge this thing?"

"I think it has an automatic charger."

"Of course, it does," Jared said, peering at the boy sideways. Surely the kid thought he was an idiot. In all fairness, he had no idea what he was doing, and he was too distracted by his new slave to really focus anyway.

Tucker sat beside him in the golf cart with his back erect as if afraid to touch anything. He kept rubbing that damn arm, causing Jared's stomach to sink into his colon. Knowing he shouldn't, but desperate to calm him at least a little bit, Jared pulled a granola bar out of his pocket and kicked his feet up on the dash.

Tucker licked his lips and peeled his gaze from the morsel.

"Did you miss breakfast?" Jared said.

"No, sir."

"Then why are you eyeing my food?"

Tucker rubbed his arm again and kept his eyes glued to the floor. Without looking at him, Jared pulled another bar from his pocket and handed it to him. The boy's mouth parted as he accepted the wrapped gift, but Jared pretended not to notice his surprise and inspected the oats on his own bar.

The other granola bar disappeared in seconds.

Jared took both wrappers and stepped down from the cart. "Let's check on that oil."

Every morning at exactly four-thirty, while the rest of the house slept, the cook would fetch Katie, Tucker, and Sally to boil a giant pot of gruel. Then, once the task was securely underway, the cook would set her head on the prep table and snore, her cup of coffee chilling beside her. Of all their chores, Katie minded this one the least. Breakfast time in the hall behind the kitchen guaranteed food. Not so much the other meals when poaching became frequent. Only rarely did they see any adults at this hour, especially since the average wake time neared ten.

Once revived with a few calories, they would talk before being fetched for staff meal prep. If not for the gaunt faces of her friends and the cold tiles beneath them, Katie could imagine she were having breakfast at some sort of boarding school, not hell island.

"How's your new boss?" Katie asked Tucker once her bowl was empty. She had not seen him for most of the day. Jared had dropped him off on time for lunch, but Katie had been late. Then, in the evening, she had been delayed for bed thanks to a dishwasher malfunction.

"Fine, I guess. He's an idiot though."

Katie stifled a laugh. Idiot was not what *she'd* call Jared, but of course, she couldn't say that.

"I don't know how he got the job," Tucker continued. "The guy knows nothing about cars. We changed the oil in all the vehicles yesterday, and he did it all with hand tools. Didn't use the lift or the power wrench."

Katie doubted Jared had much experience working with vehicles while he was at the camps. Their camp definitely didn't have a garage as well stocked as the one here.

"But he did half of the work," Tucker said. "That's the nice thing about the newbies. They haven't figured out that they don't have to lift a finger yet."

"Is he treating you well though?"

He ran his spoon around the edge of his empty bowl. "I guess. He hasn't hit me."

And he'd better not if I have anything to do about it.

"He's no good guy though." Tucker set his bowl on the tiles. "I heard some of the Watchers talking. In order to get the job, he murdered some woman. Two in the back as soon as she walked through the door. He's cold as ice."

"Perhaps they deserved it," she breathed, and Tucker quirked a brow.

Stanton stepped into their little hall from the kitchen, and silence fell as everyone lowered their heads. "We have some guests coming in today around noon. Anyone not in their room by eleven will be flogged." Then he turned and left.

"Does everyone know how to find eleven on the clock?" Katie asked, and the little heads around her bobbed. "Sally, if you'll watch the kitchen today, I'll try to round up the stragglers before time."

"And the rest of you, don't dilly-dally for Katie," Sally said in her Kiwi accent. "Do as you're told."

It was Katie's turn to list off assignments—something that should have been easy if she could get past the brain fog. Sally and Katie traded off days supervising, and on her days outside the kitchen, Katie never assigned herself a starting position. This allowed her the ability to roam around and check on kids. She would fill in as needed or get poached for various jobs.

On this day, she started her rounds outside to shoot for a job near the docks. As she ambled down the paved path, she spotted Tucker plucking blades of grass next to the warehouse as he waited on Jared. He waved to her when she passed. Katie replied with a thumbs-up, asking if he were okay. Tucker raised his thumb but then paused. His expression shifted to concern as he looked to something behind Katie.

Katie jumped to find Jared behind her. "What the hell?"

"I'm a Watcher," he muttered, looking past her to Tucker.

Katie nodded and lowered her eyes to the pavement. "Why are you all sweaty?" Moisture stains collected beneath his arms and around his neck.

"I went on a run."

"Midas sent you out last night?"

"No, a run around the island. Listen, we probably can't talk right now, but I'm working on a way for us to get together, alright?"

"Did you kill someone?" Katie blurted, and his brows shot up.

"I…uh…" He scratched the back of his head. "No. Not how you think. Later, I promise." Jared stepped past Katie, collected Tucker, and entered the warehouse. But what did he mean, not how she thought? That wasn't a no.

*　　*　　*

Jared shut off the water hose and frowned as the ringing continued. Was that a phone?

He called to Tucker, "Where's that coming from?"

Tucker made wide circles with the sponge leaving behind lines of suds on the SUV. "Probably your office."

Jared set down the hose. "I have an office?" he muttered and trudged through the puddles into the vehicle bay. At the back of the garage was a door he had not noticed before, and the ringing came from inside. He entered to find a desk, a few chairs, a couch and a file cabinet. On the desk, a phone rang, and he answered, "Hello?"

"Damn, Warner," Stanton replied. "Didn't think you were going to answer. You have a boat arriving in about fifteen minutes. Unload the contents into one of the vehicles and drive it around to the kitchen door."

"Can do," Jared said, and the line went dead. He stared at the receiver for a moment as a shiver of fear crept up his spine. That had been abrupt. He hoped Stanton wasn't pissed at him for not answering sooner.

Upon returning to the vehicles, he found Tucker had finished sudsing and was hosing off both vehicles. "Here—" He tossed Tucker the keys. "We've got a boat incoming. Dry the vehicles off and park them." Tucker nodded, and Jared re-entered the warehouse, walked to the edge of the dock, and cupped his hands over his eyes. Just visible on the horizon was a new dot growing ever larger.

Jared moved one of the SUVs to the edge of the dock for ease of loading. As the boat pulled in, he received the rope from the driver and pulled it to shore. Tucker caught the second rope and pulled in the stern.

The people bringing in the delivery didn't speak English, but they chatted quietly to themselves as if fearing Jared could understand them. Everything came out of the boat in a hurry. Jared got the distinct feeling these guys knew what this island was and were intent on getting off it as fast as possible.

You and me both.

As Jared was taking a load to the trunk, he noticed Katie standing at the edge of the garage biting her nail. Clearly, she wanted to say something, but then she left.

Jared turned back to his work, but Tucker glanced at the clock. It read ten forty-five. Was there something significant about the time?

When Jared returned from loading another box into the SUV, he found Tucker looking at the clock again, but the boy returned to work when he saw Jared watching him. Five minutes later, Katie showed up biting her nail again. Her gaze darted from Jared to Tucker.

Tucker set a box inside the SUV and turned back to get another, but Jared grabbed his arm. "That's the second time that girl has shown up, and you keep looking at the clock. Is there something going on I should be aware of?"

Tucker swallowed hard. "I'm…I'm supposed to be in our room by eleven. Otherwise, I get flogged."

The clock read five 'til eleven. He shoved Tucker to the exit. "Then go. And next time, if there's something I should know, tell me. Don't leave my ass hanging out there again, do you hear me?"

"Y-yes, sir," Tucker said.

This lack of communication bullshit was going to get someone killed.

After packing up the mountain of supplies by himself, Jared drove up to the big house and parked outside the kitchen door. Upon entering the kitchen, he frowned to see Tucker peeling potatoes at a work table. Tucker glanced back at him then lowered his gaze back to his work. Had the kid just conned him for a better job?

"Hey, Warner." Stanton stood from his stool at the work table. "Hope you don't mind me poaching your help. We've got some guests coming in for the evening and we keep the Comms close to the house during these events. I'll be sending Randall down to work with you though."

Jared inclined his head. "Good to know. Thought for a second the kid had played me or something."

Stanton laughed. "Kid's not clever enough for that."

A red hue crept up Tucker's cheeks.

"Boy—" Stanton grabbed the back of Tucker's shirt and the color fled from Tucker's face. "Unload the truck. You too, Miss Scarface."

Katie startled as she had just stepped out of the walk-in cooler with a bowl of lettuce. Jared rubbed the back of his head and looked away, determined to appear indifferent about her arrival. From the corner of his eye, however, he caught a faint smile float over Katie's face. It vanished as if it were a ghost, but if Stanton happened to see it…

Tucker stepped past Jared to the door. As he did so, he scrunched his shoulders together as if fearing to even touch Jared. Katie, however, stepped right past him, even looking him in the eye. Jared's breath caught, and not from infatuation. A vanishing grin was one thing, but this wouldn't do. Whether she realized it or not, she was acting far too familiar with him. It was only a matter of time before someone started asking questions.

Stanton pulled a radio from his belt and handed it to Jared. "I forgot to give this to you yesterday. Call if you need me."

"Right, boss." Jared nodded, and Stanton left.

As Katie and Tucker entered the house with their wares, Jared leaned against the wall and watched. He needed a solution to Katie's inappropriate body language, but more than anything, they needed to talk. He had an idea, but she was going to hate it.

Katie brought in a box labeled "Lemons," and Jared followed her into the walk-in cooler, closing the door behind him.

"What?" she asked. She glanced at his eyes but seemed to have trouble holding her gaze there. In fact, she seemed to struggle focusing on much of anything. A red flaky rash covered the backs of her hands and crept out of her shirt collar.

Pellagra. No doubt about it. Which meant she probably was not thinking clearly. He needed to tap into something deeper than surface knowledge. To a raw nerve just below the surface. Her survival instincts.

"Do you trust me?" Jared asked.

"I…think so."

She was going to hate this. If her rational mind were in charge, he wouldn't need to do this, but something else was at play.

"Roll with this," he said, "but know in your head that I'm still your friend."

"What?"

The door behind them opened, and Tucker entered with another box.

"Do you want me to keep unloading the truck?" Katie asked.

Had she noticed him entering? Did she realize that Tucker was a threat to them too?

"What do you think?" Jared sneered.

Katie frowned in question, confused by the sudden change. She tried to take a step past him, but he stepped in her way. She tried to go the other way, brushing her chest against his, but he blocked this too.

"Can I help with something?" Tucker's voice came as a whisper.

"Did I tell you to stop unloading?" Jared asked. Tucker bit his lip, set the box down, and left.

"What are you doing?" Katie hissed.

"You're forgetting I'm a Watcher."

"Do you want a medal or something?" She tried to shove past him.

Grabbing her arm, he pushed her back. He raised his hand to her, and she flinched. Jared lowered it back down. "This will only work if we sell it. You have to do your part."

Katie hugged herself. Fear and confusion were written across her face. Jared's heart tore, but he forced away the sentiment, turned to the door, and entered the kitchen once more. She had to learn, or they were both going to die.

GUNPOWDER SPARK

"Warner!"

Jared winced as his alias was called down the hall of the staff quarters. His hands had not stopped shaking since he had last spoken with Katie, and he had hoped to steal away a cup of tea before anyone noticed them.

Holding his shoulders high while taking a shuddering breath, Jared turned to find Stanton at the end of the hall with a man in a navy silk suit, shaved head, and a golden earring. Jared caught the distinct smell of cleaning products but wasn't sure if that was real or imagined.

"Warner, I'd like you to meet someone," Stanton said as he waved him forward.

As Jared walked stiffly to them, sweat broke on his palms.

"This is Alexander Chase," Stanton said with a grin. "Our Gatsby."

"Gatsby?" Jared shoved his hands into his pockets, seizing the moment to remove the moisture. Too bad the tremor wouldn't go away so easily.

"Like the movie?" Stanton smacked his hand against the man's chest, and Chase's lip curled. "He's the 'billionaire playboy' who owns the island." Stanton put air quotes around the "billionaire playboy."

Jared had not seen the movie, but he had read the book. Still, Stanton's meaning remained elusive. "I'm sorry, I don't understand."

"Midas is a well-known name. We can't go around slapping his name on everything. So, most of his properties are under the name Alexander Chase. Carl here is the face of that name."

"Why do you have to go and tell him my real name?" Chase complained. "He doesn't need to know that."

Stanton raised his hands. "Relax. Warner is one of my guys. He knows how to keep his mouth shut."

"Well, he'd better," Chase muttered as he brushed past them. "I'm going up to my room. See you tonight."

Stanton checked his watch. "Our first guests will be arriving in an hour. Go get on your tux."

*　　　*　　　*

Katie did not know what guests came and went from Midas's island, nor did she care. They came, ate, and left. While their presence generally required more work from the Comms, she had stopped caring about that as well. One day blurred into another. One pile of linens or room to clean was as good or bad as the next.

Through burning moisture, she chopped onions for the cook and started on the next set. Beyond the thin kitchen walls she could hear the chatter of their fancy guests, but did not perceive any meaning. The young ones remained in their room behind the kitchen leaving Katie, Sally, and Tucker to feed the lot. Katie might not be thinking the best, but she had enough awareness to not wander into the crowd. That was not as likely among the young ones, and talking to one of the guests would be the equivalent of contacting someone on the outside—a capital offense.

Katie had just sliced into another onion when a shadow passed over her shoulder. Instinctually, she froze, knife trapped between the layers.

"Whatcha making?" Jared whispered in her ear. The warm moisture of his breath skittered goosebumps across her arms and neck.

"Why are you doing that?" she whispered back.

Jared spun her hair with his finger. "Roll with it."

Katie leaned away from him. Sweat beaded on her brow. He had said that earlier, and, in part, she recognized what he was doing. Oh, but she hated it!

Jared wrapped his arm around her to claim a carrot from the counter. He chomped loudly into her ear before leaving the kitchen for the main hall. A knot formed in her gut as he disappeared through the door.

"Dick." Tucker joined her at the table. "If you'd like, I'll ram him with an SUV. I could make it look like an accident…"

"Like that'd matter," she replied. "They'd kill you anyways."

When time came to clean up, Katie peeked through a crack in the door to see Jared standing midway down the wall watching the fancy people eat. He was dressed just like them in a suit and tie, but the bulge on his side and the cord protruding from his ear gave him away as security. His job was to watch the guests, ensure that no one tried to enter unauthorized areas, and provide polite assistance if needed.

These men were nothing like the thugs from Katie's past lives. Tweedle Dee and Tweedle Dum might have done well at Camp 1, but they couldn't have made it here. There was a difference between those uncouth brutes and these suited men with silencers. A big difference. *Professionalism*, Katie thought.

And Jared fit in with them perfectly. Or rather, Jack did.

The dinner went off without a hitch. Paid servers took plates from the kitchen to the guests and brought back the trays. They were not allowed to speak to these people either, and the servers didn't attempt conversation. Even if they didn't know exactly who the western kids behind the counter were, they knew better than to ask. Finally, the dinner ended and the guests migrated to other parts of the mansion, leaving a wreck in their wake.

Once the guests left the dining hall, the doors were locked and the other kids brought in to clean. Together, they managed to get the place back to its original state, but it was past one a.m. when they were allowed to rest. As soon as Katie's head hit her mat, she was asleep. Only rarely was this ever not the case.

*　　*　　*

"How's it going, Warner?" Randall leaned against the wall beside Jared, placing one foot against the bricks.

"That depends," Jared said. "Can Armani suits get wet? Or are they dry clean only?" He raised his arm to show the wetness on his gray sleeve from where an overweight and overzealous guest did a bellyflop into the pool, showering Jared with chlorinated spray.

He had been assigned to the pool for an hour now. His primary task had been pointing them to the towel desk or advising them to take the plastic wine glasses into the pool rather than the glass ones. Besides this, there were not many rules, but the sheer volume of the obnoxious partygoers jolted his nerves. He longed for a cigarette.

At the center of the action stood Alexander Chase. The guy had done so many Jello shots, Jared marveled at his ability to stand. Perhaps that was the qualification that got him the job. Jared didn't see Midas as the party type. How long had Chase been their Gatsby?

Randall laughed at Jared's soaked sleeve. "You worry too much, kid. Listen, Stanton is going to need you down by the docks tomorrow morning to help load the guests onto their boats for home, so you're officially relieved for the night. Go get some rest."

Jared needed no further prompting to leave his post, and soon he stepped into the hall, closing out the noise. As he walked the corridors, he bumped into a few guests weaving their way to their rooms. He doubted any of them would recall the party they had had the night before. As he stepped into the hall behind the kitchen, however, a man he had never met stood near the door to the

Comm's room. He was East Asian and wore a waiter's outfit. Perhaps he was lost?

"Excuse me," Jared called. "You're not supposed to be down here."

The man said something in Burmese as he pointed to the exit at the end of the hall.

"Yeah, I don't know what you just said, but this is an authorized area. You can't be back here."

The man continued to talk as he approached Jared with exaggerated gestures.

"Warner!" Stanton called behind Jared. "Detain that man!"

The man charged at Jared, but Jared stepped to the side and extended his arm. The man ran full tilt into Jared's arm, hitting it with his neck. As he lay on the ground, choking, Jared pulled his pistol. "Don't move."

"Nice work, Warner." Stanton grinned as he approached with his pistol drawn as well. "We caught him on the security camera trying to pick the locks."

"The lock on the Comm door?"

"Secure his hands and take him out back."

Jared rolled the man over and tied his wrists with a pair of zip-ties. He hauled him to his feet and led him out the door at the end of the hall. All the while the man complained in Burmese, a little hoarser than before, but he only resisted minimally.

Once outside, Stanton shoved the man against the brick wall beneath the floodlight and pressed his pistol against his head. "Who do you work for?"

"No English." The man's lip curled as he spoke.

Stanton pulled a knife from his pocket and handed it to Jared. "Cut his shirt open."

Jared sliced through the buttons on the man's shirt revealing an intricate tattoo of a serpent twisting and coiling across his chest, wrapping around gray skulls with black eyes. At the center of his chest was a white lotus.

"You're one of Arhrit's men, aren't you?" Stanton asked.

The man sneered. "Go to hell."

"I thought you didn't speak English," Jared muttered. "What do we do with him, boss? If he was looking for the Comms—"

"He was looking for drugs. Two million in heroin to be precise." Stanton gripped the man's throat. "I told your boss we didn't rip him off. It was some other crew."

The man's lip raised, exposing a row of crooked teeth. "He doesn't believe you."

Stanton pulled the radio from his belt. "Randall, come to the kitchen side door, please."

"I'm with the guests," Randall replied.

"Do as I ask. Now, please."

Randall did not reply back, but soon exited through the side door. "What the hell is this?"

"A spy," Stanton said. "You and Warner get him down to the docks. Take him for a ride. When you're far enough away that the guests won't hear, shoot him and dump his body on the Myanmar coast."

Jared's mouth fell open, but he quickly closed it and swallowed hard.

"Arhrit will kill you! He will kill all of you!" the man shouted. "He can try." Stanton jerked the man off the wall and offered him to Randall. The man yanked free and tried to bolt for the woods. Before Stanton or Jared could react, Randall drew and fired at the man, hitting him twice in the back.

THE SCARLET LETTER

The suppressor muffled the blast partially, but it still set Jared's ears ringing. The man collapsed onto the pavement in a pool of blood, sputtered briefly, then fell still.

"What the hell!" Stanton shouted. "What part of 'we have guests' did you not understand?"

"Yeah? Did you want him running around free on the island while we had guests, Stanton?" Randall rolled his eyes as he approached the body and nudged it with his foot.

Stanton glowered at Randall. "Warner," he said with measured tone, "go to the garage and get an SUV and a tarp."

"Right, boss," Jared said and took off for the garage.

Holy shit, holy shit, holy shit, kept running through his mind as he jogged down the path for the vehicle. The guy was no one Jared knew and probably a bad dude, but still. Soon he returned with the tarp and Stanton ordered him and Randall to wrap the body while he returned to the guests.

So much for a break.

Jared rolled the man up on his side and tucked the tarp beneath his back, then rolled him onto the other side to spread it flat beneath him. Then he folded the tarp over the body and tucked it beneath the man's side. "Do you have any rope?"

"Is this your first time doing this?" Randall asked.

He shrugged in reply, wishing he could say yes, and Randall grinned. Together, they loaded the big man into the SUV, being careful to keep the edges together.

"Put this SUV off to the side and be sure no one uses it tomorrow," said Stanton. "Once the guests are gone, we'll sneak him off the island."

"Right," Jared said and climbed into the driver's seat. The clock on the dash read three. It was going to be an early morning.

*   *   *

Around three a.m., the door ripped open and slammed shut, jolting Katie awake. Above her, a shadow moved. She scooted away until her back hit the wall, but the shadow grabbed her arm and pulled her to her feet.

"No!" Katie cried. The man hoisted her up by her collar and pushed her against the wall.

"And I say yes," he said levelly. The smell of cigarettes and bleach wafted around him.

Katie startled as her eyes adjusted to the poor lighting. *Jared?*

"Are you going to disobey?" he asked.

Tears filled her eyes, but she was more confused than frightened. Beside her, Tucker watched with fear, but he would be no help. "I will come," she said.

"Good." Jared released her and shoved her toward the door. Once in the hall, he shoved her again, causing her to stumble. When Katie looked back to him, he shook his head, and she swallowed hard. Was she wrong about him?

He led her to the staff wing of the mansion, and Katie hesitated at the head of the hall. Her fingers went numb, and she glanced back at Jared. If she didn't go, would he shove her again? But Jared's hardened expression had softened. He waited.

Katie forced herself onward. It was Jared. He was her friend. In her head, she knew all this, but she couldn't feel it. Not really.

Once at his door, he ushered her inside and closed the door behind him. "Katie—" he said, and she smacked him across the face. Then trembling, she brought a hand to her mouth and backed away. Had she actually done that? Why? Now what would he do to her?

But Jared stared at the floor and bit his lip. "I guess I deserved that." With nothing more said, he stepped past her into the room.

Katie watched him close as he kicked off his shiny, polished shoes into the corner on his way to the mini fridge where he pulled out a Styrofoam box. Her mouth watered at the sight of the box. Was she anything anymore besides raw instincts?

Jared opened the lid and took a sniff. "I asked your brother what your favorite meal was. For some reason, I was thinking of sushi or a panini or something. I was surprised when he told me what it actually was." He turned the box to her, revealing a sirloin steak inside. Her stomach gurgled in response.

"It's not fresh," he continued, holding it out to her. "But—"

She snatched it from him. Using her hands, she lifted up the steak and took a giant bite. She closed her eyes and smiled as the juicy flavors swirled around her mouth.

"I can heat it up for you," Jared said.

Katie shook her head. That would take too long.

While she ate, Jared flipped on an electric kettle and pulled a mug from the cabinet. Every move he made, Katie watched him close. She couldn't help it. He placed a tea bag inside his mug with a marijuana leaf on the tag, and Katie cocked her head to the side.

Jared followed her gaze, and she realized he was watching her too. "CBD," he said. "It helps my hand tremors." He took the side chair and sat in it. Tentatively, Katie took a seat, or rather perched, on the edge of his bed.

Breathe, she told herself. *It's Jared.*

As he added sugar to his cup, bits of white trembled out of the spoon.

"Your hands still shake?" she asked.

"Only when I'm nervous—which has been the whole time I've been here, but. . ." He tugged off his tie and tossed it into a vacant chair.

"What's your plan, Jared?" she asked. "You're trying to scare me. Why?"

Jared said nothing as he finished making his tea. "I'm not trying to scare you as much as get you to act afraid. You have to be afraid of me, Katie. That's the only way this will work."

"But you're doing more than just being intimidating. You're being…creepy."

For a moment or two, he sat there, moving his teabag around the mug. Finally, he said, "I needed an excuse to get you into my room."

Katie frowned at him, not fully understanding. Then the implication dawned on her. "Oh."

"I know you've never been in favor of people thinking we were sleeping together," he continued, "but I don't really know any other way to play this."

Katie's steak turned to rubber in her mouth. "You're turning me into Michelle."

Jared bit his thumbnail and nodded.

"I suppose there are worse things."

He snickered and looked away. It was a situation that he did not seem to enjoy either. What followed was an awkward silence with the only sound filling the space being Katie's chewing. Rubber or not, the steak was still food, and she wasn't about to waste it.

"Oh!" Jared exclaimed and grabbed his shoe from the floor. Katie jumped at the sudden motion, but he didn't seem to notice. Flipping the shoe upside down, he took out his pocket knife, slid it beneath the sole, and pried it up. "I have a note from your brother."

Katie set the take-out box aside and scooted closer to him. Jared extracted a zip-lock bag from the shoe, removed a folded-up piece of paper, and handed it to her. She flipped it open, her eyes burning as she scanned the page. For years there had been silence, and tears flooded her eyes as she read the note from Alec. She read it three times before the reality of the words penetrated her consciousness.

"Have you read this?" she asked and was surprised by the tremor in her voice. Jared shook his head. "Alec has been helping you?"

"He's been feeding me information from the FBI since the beginning. And he deleted my fingerprints from their database. Which was nice of him since I got arrested a week later."

She wrinkled her brow. "For what?"

"Possession with intent to distribute. The charges didn't stick though since they couldn't find the drugs. But if they had connected my real name, the guys I was running with would have killed me."

Katie folded the paper up and started to slip it into her pocket.

"You can't keep that," Jared said, and she frowned. "If they catch you with that…"

Katie unfolded the paper and read through it again, the tears coming to her eyes once more. She longed to be home so much it ached. But Jared was right. They would kill her—and him—if they found it. Instead, she studied it, trying to memorize every word. As she handed it back, she wiped a tear from her eye.

"It's not for forever," Jared said. "I promise."

"So, you have a plan?"

"I'm working on one."

Katie sighed and buried her face in her hands. She was so tired, and the clock on his nightstand read three-thirty. "I need to go back." She stood.

"Stay the night," Jared said. "Sleep in my bed. I'll sleep on the floor. What time do you need to get up?"

Katie laughed. "In an hour." Jared took her hand and brushed her hair from her face. He gestured to the bed, and Katie glanced at it tentatively. "I have lice," she said.

"I don't care." He rubbed his thumb over hers. When she still hesitated, Jared sighed. "Well, if you're not wiped, I am." He grabbed the pillow from his bed, tossed it onto the floor, and lay with his back to her. "Good night, Katie."

Katie stared at his back. Then she giggled at his false anger, and he smiled at her over his shoulder. That was the Jared she remembered. "Good night, Jared," she said and climbed into his bed.

As Katie ran the soft sheets smelling of lavender and laundry detergent against her cheek, she initially thought that she was at home. But the bed wasn't against the correct wall, and the lighting was wrong. And what was that other smell? Bacon?

She sat up rubbing her bleary eyes to find Jared in the kitchenette smiling at her. "Good morning," he greeted.

Katie bolted up and spun the alarm clock to face her. Four fifteen. She wasn't late—yet.

Jared took a plate from the microwave where four sausage patties sat. Not quite bacon, but her mouth watered, nonetheless.

"Did you sleep?" she asked, rubbing her head. "You were going to sleep when I laid down—"

"I'll sleep tonight. I hope you like turkey sausage. I would have liked to scramble you some eggs, but all I have is the microwave and mini-fridge. I'll pick up a griddle next time I'm in town."

Jared divided the round sausages onto two plates, and Katie snatched up hers and chewed them greedily. Vaguely, a voice in her head told her to take it easy. Had Jared given her this advice years ago? She went a little slower on the next patty. Jared barely picked at his, and Katie caught him watching her again. What must he be thinking about her right now?

"You've done a good job," he said as if reading her thoughts. "You've kept a low profile. Most of the Watchers don't even know you exist."

Katie laughed humorlessly. "Bullshit. I've turned into a coward."

"You're alive, aren't you?"

Katie dipped her head.

"When we're under threat, the body and brain have a way of protecting itself."

"Fight or flight," she muttered. "I know."

"Or freeze," he said. "If you can't run, your body slows down. Your blood pressure drops, your breathing slows, and you get dizzy—I recognized it in you the first day I was here."

"And what are you now, a doctor?"

"No," he said. "I was a victim. Now I'm a survivor."

"So how do I snap out of it, survivor man?"

He crumpled a napkin. "I don't want you to snap out of it. Not around them at least. I am going to do my best to protect you, Katie, but I'm still a minor player here. There is only so much I can do, especially at this early stage.

"You're saying you won't protect me."

"No," Jared said, "I will protect you any way I can. I'm saying it might not always work." She hugged herself, and Jared sat on the bed beside her. "I'm telling you this because you need to be prepared. When we step back out that door, I'm going to have to return to being Jack, the Watcher. And I'm going to be doing some things that will trigger your fear. Sometimes intentionally. But I swear to you, the moment we come in here, I will stop. You are safe here."

"Why do you have to trigger anything?"

"I have to convince the Watchers that I'm on their side." He took her hand. "No one can know that you're really my friend."

Friend. It was more than that, Katie knew. People didn't cross oceans for their *friends*. And with that thought, Katie grew suspicious once more. He wanted something from her. He was just working up the nerve to ask. And she might say yes.

*   *   *

Katie pushed the cleaning cart along the hall and entered the next room. Sheets littered the floor, and remnants of food and booze were scattered around. In nearly every room she entered, a white powdery substance was left on at least one if not multiple surfaces.

After she finished cleaning this room, Katie noted her supplies were running low and grumbled to herself as she pushed the cart to the service elevator. While she was in the basement, she stopped by the laundry to drop off her linens.

"Hey, Katie," Sally greeted and shoved a ball of linens into the washer. With dinner down to fifteen of Midas's goons, she had been sent from the kitchen until later. "Are you doing alright? I mean after last night."

Katie shrugged as she added her load of laundry to Sally's mountain.

"He's that bad, is he?" Sally asked.

"It could have been worse," Katie said then blushed. She felt guilty pretending that it was anything bad. Katie had received two full meals, some rest in a warm bed, and protection stronger than the armband. Katie considered elaborating her statement—and her lie, but Sally nodded, satisfied with the answer. Katie's guilt doubled.

After she had resupplied her cart, Katie headed back up the elevator, ignoring the ache in her throat caused by the guilt. Jared's presence was the best news any of them had ever heard and here she was keeping it to herself. Maybe she could at least tell Sally or Tucker.

As the doors opened onto the floor, Katie jumped upon seeing Stanton standing just outside. The reasons for keeping the secret came back in a flash. It wasn't her selfishness keeping the secret. It was her survival instincts.

"Here she is," Stanton said, and Jared stepped out of one of the rooms. "Girl, come here for a moment."

Katie pushed the cart to them, all while wishing to retreat down the elevator.

"A guest lost his phone last night. Have you seen it?" Stanton asked, and Katie shook her head. He asked Jared, "Which room did they say?"

"They didn't say."

"And you didn't ask? You at least caught their names, didn't you?"

"Uhm—" he said, and Katie cocked her head to the side. That didn't sound like him. Was he pretending to be less clever than he was?

Stanton rolled his eyes. "I give you photos and names for a reason. You should know each guest on sight." He turned to her. "Girl, which rooms have been cleaned?"

Katie swept her hand from the elevator to the room where Jared had just emerged. Four more were left.

"I'll look in this room," said Stanton. "You two search those others."

Upon entering the room, Katie shook the sheets onto the floor before moving to the couch and checking behind the cushions. A couple of years ago, stealing a phone would have been top priority to Katie, but now it was a useless box. No help would come in this corner of the world even if a call would go through.

Katie had just started searching behind picture frames on the dresser when she became aware of someone standing in the doorway. Jared was leering again.

"Find anything?" he asked, and she shook her head. She tried to step past him out the door, but he leaned his arm against the doorway, barring her path.

She knew what he was doing. Dammit, she knew, but the tightness in her chest returned, nonetheless. Finally, Jared raised his arm and indicated for her to duck under it. As she squeezed against his chest to exit, she blushed.

Stanton joined Jared to watch in the next doorway as she searched the room and said, "Okay, the body, sure, but the stench and the scar—"

Heat flooded Katie's cheeks. Instead of bending at the waist to pick the sheet off the floor, she squatted.

"But that's your problem Stanton," Jared said. "You always go for the tens."

"And why the hell wouldn't I?"

"Because the fat ones and the ugly ones are more appreciative."

Moisture sprang to Katie's eyes. *Come on, Katie,* she chided herself. *Let it go.* But the squeezing grew tighter. She wished to melt into the floorboards.

Stanton raised his brows, and a mischievous smile crossed Jared's face. Katie gave the sheet a final venomous shake, and the phone clattered to the floor.

"Hey!" Stanton said. "There it is. Last place we looked."

Last place I *looked,* Katie thought as Stanton picked it up.

"It's always in the last place you look," Jared said. "You don't keep looking after you've found it."

Stanton paused to take in his lame joke. "Yeah, I guess that's true." He handed Jared the phone. "Take this back down to the docks."

"Right, boss." Jared slid the phone into his pocket and lingered in the doorway.

"Oh, and once all the guests are gone, load the body into the speedster. There's a hidden hatch beneath the seats you can stow it in. I'll send Randall to the mainland to dump it."

"Uh, can do." Jared nodded and scratched the back of his head. Katie cast him a side look, and Jared looked away.

Stanton left for the stairs, and Katie went back to work. This time when Katie exited the room, Jared did not bar her path. She crammed her sheets into the cleaning cart.

"The body?" Katie asked.

"I didn't shoot him if that's your next question. Randall did. Long story."

Katie rolled her eyes and yanked out a bottle of cleaning spray.

"Are you okay?" Jared asked.

"Other than the whiplash I'm getting from your personality shifts? Sure, I'm peachy."

"Hang on, Katie. I have something for you. Wear this for about an hour, then take it off." He pressed a pendant necklace into the palm of her hand. Beneath a bead of glass was a yellow flower. A goldenrod.

"Why?"

"It will come into play later. Just do as I ask, please."

Katie ran her thumb over the glass, not really wanting to comply, but Jared had a plan. And she had promised to trust him.

"I—uh—gotta get back." Jared gestured to the door, but she only shrugged. Biting his lip once more, he turned to the elevator and disappeared behind the doors.

*   *   *

When the cleaning was done, Katie joined Sally in the kitchen. Her eyes blurred, something that happened whenever she was super tired. Between crying and cutting up onions, it felt like she viewed the world through water these days. Thankfully, once dinner was over, she would be allowed to go to her mat and sleep. She never had the energy to stay awake and scheme. This, she guessed, was by design. Starving, exhausted people weren't much of a threat.

Tucker joined her with a bowl of hard boiled eggs and removed the shells. Due to the guests still leaving, he had not been sent to the docks that day. They technically weren't supposed to be talking to each other, but if they kept their voices low enough and lips unmoving, they could manage a conversation. And even if they didn't talk, it was nice to work next to a friend.

The cook, who was watching some ridiculous high-action flick, let out a loud fart and swatted it away with her hand. Tucker and

Katie looked at each other with pinched faces, trying not to laugh. Then the smell hit them, and Tucker brought the boiled eggs to his nose. Katie clamped her hand over her mouth, holding in her laughter. But then Tucker's eyes widened, and he set down the bowl. Katie froze as well. A Watcher was behind her.

Hands rested on her shoulders and Katie tensed. "What are you two laughing about?" Jared asked.

Tucker and Katie stared at the table ahead. Of course, they couldn't tell him. Katie wasn't sure what he'd do, but an answer would demand action.

Jared took Katie's shoulder and turned her to face him. "Where's your necklace?"

"I uh…" Katie's finger fumbled as she brought it out of her pocket. "I thought…"

Jared brought his face near hers, and Katie shrank from him. "If I give you something to wear, you wear it, dammit."

Katie's hands trembled so much she dropped the necklace, and Jared bent to retrieve it. He shoved her to face the table and secured the necklace around her neck. "Ungrateful," he said as he dropped her hair back onto her neck. "I'd better not see you without it."

Katie shook as Jared marched back into the dining hall and swatted away tears. Tears of confusion, of anger—

Tucker placed his hand over hers. "I'm sorry," he whispered.

Katie pulled her hand away and shook her head. As she did so, she felt the necklace sway with the motion. She reached up to rip it off, but stopped. She needed to trust him.

Katie ran her thumb over the glass, eyeing the flower once more. Goldenrod. Goldie. Was that intentional? Inspecting the pendant further, Katie flipped it over and startled. Carved into the metal was the outline of the state of Tennessee. Both her and Jared's true home. Was the pendant a promise to get her home?

She looked through the serving window to see Jared sipping on a glass of water while his coworkers joked with each other. He said something she could not hear and the group roared with laughter even more.

A chill ran up her spine. He fit in so well. How could he not be one of them? Yet, the weight of the pendant hung heavy around her neck.

"Leave Tucker out of it," Katie said as the door to Jared's apartment closed behind her.

Jared locked the deadbolt and frowned. "I thought I did."

"You scared the crap out of him."

"Oh. Comes with the territory, I'm afraid." After chucking his shoes onto the floor, Jared pulled a pistol from his side holster. Katie startled. Noting her reaction, he dropped the mag, emptied the chamber, and set the weapon on top of the TV stand.

"I'm not scared of guns," Katie said. "My father's a cop."

"Hungry?" Jared asked, ignoring her statement.

"Of course."

"I need to go to the store," he muttered as he searched his cabinets and mini-fridge. "Unfortunately, my co-workers have quite the appetite for bar food, so most everything I have is dripping with oil."

"Doesn't matter. I'll eat it."

"I don't want to make you sick." He pulled out another Styrofoam box and sniffed the contents. "I'll do better next time to order something less—unhealthy. I shouldn't be eating this shit myself anyways."

"Going to lose that girlish figure?"

"When I first got out, I could barely eat. Now my nutritionist says I have a gorging tendency." He returned to the bed with half of a turkey club, a pack of crackers, and a banana.

"Your nutritionist?" Katie took a huge bite out of the sandwich.

"Stateside," he said. "I'm typically on a strict diet, although I've been off the wagon as of late. Speaking of which. . ." Jared moved to his nightstand and pulled out three pill bottles. "I forgot to take my vitamins this morning."

Katie laughed. "What are you? Some old geezer?"

"Laugh all you want, but after I got proper food in me, I gained three inches in the first year."

Katie raised her brows. That was indeed impressive.

Setting three pills in the corner of her to-go box, he said, "I'm going to share my vitamins with you."

"How tall *are* you now?"

"Five foot six."

So, he wouldn't be joining any basketball leagues, but he wasn't tiny either. Jared flipped on the kettle in the kitchenette, and Katie took the opportunity to study him while his back was turned. Not only had he grown in height, but he had been working out as well. Most of Midas's men did. And by the way he had handled his firearm, she could tell he knew what he was doing.

Jared's head had always been dangerous to the Watchers. Now every part of him was.

"How do you spend so much time with the people who ruined your life and not stab them in the throat?" Katie asked.

The kettle sang, and Jared made a cup of tea, dragged the chair from the table to the bed, and plopped into it. "I don't know. I've always done it in a way. I helped Clayton broker a deal with some cartel kingpin the morning after he dislocated my shoulder, hogtied me, and left me overnight in a trunk."

Katie slid the halved pickle spear around the to-go box. "I couldn't do that."

But Jared shrugged. "I was promised heaters in the huts if the deal went through, so I played nice and made him look good.

Afterwards, I vomited up some blood and won a day in my cell to sleep it off."

"You've never really had a chance to be yourself, have you? To do what you want, say what you think."

"Or maybe this is just who I am, Katie. A liar."

"Or it's what they made you."

Jared shrugged and sipped on his tea. When he got quiet like that, she knew he was done contributing to the conversation willingly. Since she wasn't in the mood to extract teeth, she changed the subject. "Does the beard feel strange?" She stroked her own chin.

"I've gotten used to it. It's just an extra layer of protection to keep Midas from recognizing me. I was considering colored contact lens—"

"I'm glad you didn't do that. Your eyes are the only thing that's the same about you, and I have a feeling Midas never saw much of those anyways."

"Probably true."

After this, they sat in silence for some time. Katie had a thousand questions, but didn't know how to ask them. Jared was, by nature, closed up, and no wonder, given his background. Any information she gleaned would need to be asked, but she struggled to find the best question for what she really wanted to know.

Jared set his mug on the table and grabbed the pamphlet lying beside it. "I have to do a little research tonight, but we have full streaming services. Do you want to watch something on TV?" Without waiting for her reply, he opened a drawer on the TV stand and fumbled inside.

"Jared, did you kill someone?" Katie asked, throwing diplomacy to the wind.

He paused for a moment, then closed the drawer and leaned against the cabinet. "I've buried sixty-two children," he said. "And I blamed myself for all of their deaths for a long time. In actuality, I've only killed two people, but I did not kill the woman Midas sent me to kill."

"Then what happened?"

"Alec edited the video to make it look like I had, and Bryan got new documents for Tonya and sent her to Europe."

"Bryan? So, he's okay?"

Jared tapped the pamphlet on his arm. "Yeah, it was rough for a bit, but he's doing fine now. I wouldn't have made it this far without him or Alec."

"So, you didn't kill the woman, but who did you kill?"

Jared retook his seat and ran a hand through his hair. "A drug dealer who was trying to burn me alive in a house," he said.

Katie nodded. That sounded reasonable.

"And I shoved one of my hut mates into an electric fence."

Her mouth popped open. "But—why?"

Jared ran his finger over the cover of the pamphlet. Katie expected him to shut down or change the subject like he did when he was younger and was surprised when he continued.

"He was a bully and a thief," he said, meeting her eye. "So, Bryan and I called him out on his shit. We got into a fight, and he ended up getting shoved into the fence."

"Oh," said Katie. Then she remembered Trevor staring up at her, struggling to breathe after Ben shoved him from the roof. "But he was one of your people."

"I didn't mean to push him into the fence," said Jared. "But I'm not sorry either. Kids were starving and freezing to death because of him."

Katie gulped. "Sometimes, Jared, you really scare me."

"I didn't grow up taking piano lessons or attending prep school," he said. "That life was stolen from me. But Bryan and I survived longer than anyone else there because we had what it took to make it."

A chill ran down her back, the same feeling earlier that evening as Jared joked and laughed with her captors. There had always been a sliver of ice in him, but she did not know how deep it ran.

Jared adjusted his glasses and thumbed through the pamphlet. "I'm not saying Bryan and I deserved to make it. A lot of good kids died. But we did make it. For better or worse, I don't know."

Part of her wanted to linger here, to ask more questions about his time in the camp before she came, but did she want to know?

She returned to less dangerous waters. "Jared, do you have a plan yet?"

He set the pamphlet on the TV stand. "I'm still working on that, but I'll show you what I've got so far. Stand up for a second, please."

Taking her to-go box with her, Katie stood against the wall as Jared propped the mattress up against the cabinets. He lifted the box spring, popped two of the staples attaching the batting to the wooden rim, and pulled out a cache of papers.

"Do they search your rooms or something?" Katie asked.

"Once a month, or so I hear." Lowering the box spring back in place, he set the papers on top and unfolded a page the size of a poster. At the top was Midas with lines coming down showing his lieutenants. Beneath this were their subordinates and so on and so forth. Half the words were in a curly, light hand while the others were shaky but legible.

"I'm here." Jared pointed to lower middle management.

"You have all of these names," Katie said. "Could you rat them to the cops?"

"This island is not in the jurisdiction of the US," Jared said. "If they were able to prove there were fugitives currently residing on the island, perhaps they could form an agreement with the locals regarding extradition. I'm pretty sure, however, that the local government officials are being paid off—or blackmailed—to stay away."

Jared stowed his papers and reset the bed. "I've been able to rise in the ranks so far by sabotaging my bosses or snitching on them to the Feds, but at this level, I'm going to have to play things a little more carefully." He fell into his chair and rubbed the bridge of his nose. "Especially since Jack Warner is now on the FBI's top one hundred most wanted list."

"Are you serious?"

"I'm a drug smuggler, murderer, and now a human trafficker working for one of the most elusive criminals on the planet. So far,

Agent Rogers hasn't told the FBI that Jack Warner is Jared Kelley, but if I keep ticking him off, he just might."

"So, if the US government won't help us, who do we have?"

"Bryan," Jared said. "And Alec."

"So—nobody."

Jared laughed. "I won't tell Alec you said that. Don't short sell your brother. And Bryan has been financing all this—"

"But we need actual help. Midas has over fifty guys coming in and out of this island—"

Jared shook his head. "He has more than that. This is just one base on one island in one country. He's rebuilding, and he's doing it fast."

"Kidnapping?"

"A little bit of everything, but his biggest thing right now is blackmail. Did you recognize any of our fancy guests the other night?"

Katie shook her head. She'd barely glanced at them.

"Politicians, royals, CEOs, you name it," he said. "He has cameras hidden in all the guest rooms filming them doing drugs and sleeping with underage kids—"

"They're like me?"

"Trafficking is more complicated than that," Jared said. "They've all been coerced into coming here, but they weren't kidnapped. But that's my point. It won't be enough just to get all of you off-island. We need to shut down Midas permanently. I'm hoping to figure out where the blackmail information is being kept. If we can cut off Midas from those protecting him, we might be able to take down his whole organization."

"And what about those who have gone along with his blackmail scheme?" Katie asked.

"I guess we will turn them over to the FBI." Jared shrugged. "After we get out, it won't really matter."

"It'll be dead on arrival," Katie scoffed. "You really think it's in the best interest of the agency to have their compromised agents exposed to the public?"

Jared ran his thumb over a chip in the table varnish. "Probably not."

"Midas was only able to operate because of the cowards who wished to save their own asses at the cost of the lives of hundreds of children. They're not getting away with this."

"You want to expose them."

"Don't you?" Katie stood, spreading her arms wide. "They're only on that stupid list because of doing stuff they shouldn't have done in the first place. Like sleeping with underaged kids for starters!"

Jared ran his thumbnail over the varnish chip repeatedly, causing it to click. "We'll start there then. I'll ask Alec to get with Sedonya and see if she has any high caliber connection with her alternative media site." Jared pulled open the cabinet doors of the TV stand. Connected to the TV was a gaming console, and he handed Katie a controller before sitting on the bed with his own.

Katie looked dumbly at the controller as Jared powered up the game.

"Ever played with the Falcon Brotherhood?" he asked.

"Alec's team?"

"I don't know if my communications are being monitored," Jared said, "so I can't let you talk to him, but see that user, ATMerlin93?"

Katie stared at the pixels. How many times had she seen that little avatar run across Alec's computer screen? Heck, she had been there when he designed it. But that was part of the past, a part of her life she barely brought to mind anymore. She smiled a half-smile at Jared, but only to appease him.

A grin spread across his face as he pulled a headset from the cabinet. "My man, AT. Whatcha up to tonight?" he set the headset/microphone combo between them and turned up the volume so Katie could hear.

"Not much, Jack, but what's up with you? Saw you hit the top one hundred."

Katie stared at the icon, visualizing her brother's face. Was that truly him? A sob caught in her throat and she clamped her hand over her mouth. Jared turned to her in question.

"Yeah, not quite the record I was shooting for," Jared said, still studying her curiously.

Top one hundred. Alec was talking about the FBI's most wanted list.

"Listen, I've got my girlfriend on the line over here," said Jared. "She's wanting to play a few rounds, but can't use the headset."

There was silence on the other end, and Katie held her breath. Was he gone? But the voice returned; shaky, but still Alec. "You managed to get a girlfriend? I can hardly believe that, Jack."

A choking laugh erupted from behind Katie's hand, and Jared wrapped his arm around her. "Yeah, yeah. I've heard it all before," he said.

"So t-tell me about this girl," Alec said. "What's she like?"

Katie pressed her hand over his microphone. "Don't tell him the truth. Tell him I'm fine."

Jared slid away her hand. "Aw, shucks, AT. Don't make me talk about her in front of you! But you know me. I don't go for anyone less than an eleven."

Katie closed her eyes and sighed. He couldn't tell the truth anyways. Not with the possible party line.

"Right," Alec muttered. "Of course."

Jared squeezed Katie's hand as tears fell freely. It was good to hear Alec's voice, but the wall was still up. Still hiding her from him. Her chest ached with longing for home.

"Tell you what, AT," Jared said, "she can't talk right now because she has laryngitis, but she wants to play a round with you. Would you like to do that?"

"Yes," Alec croaked. "I would like that very much."

For a couple of hours, Katie played games with her brother while Jared spoke into the headset. Katie sucked at the game, but it didn't matter. What mattered was that the little avatar on the screen was Alec. And playing with him was the closest she had come to her family in years. The ever-present, painful wall dimmed and she imagined she could see him at his own computer, playing with his clan.

She played as long as she could, but the late nights and early mornings of the past two days took their toll, and she started to nod. When she could hold her head up no longer, Jared took the controller back, and Katie slid beneath the sheets. She wasn't sure if she felt better or worse for the gesture, but wouldn't trade that time for the world.

*   *   *

Seating the headphones against his ears, Jared settled into the straight-back chair beside the bed. While Katie had played, he had brewed a fresh pot of coffee and nursed it now. He wondered if he could sneak off for a nap some time tomorrow, because tonight was going to be a long one.

"Alright, AT. Let's get down to business," said Jared. "I'm going to transfer you some items. Are you ready?"

"Ready and waiting," Alec sighed.

In the video game, Jared was able to transfer certain items back and forth to Alec. It was not the items that were important, but the numbers associated with them were part of a code they had set up ahead of time. It was a difficult but effective means of communication.

While he was on the line with Alec, Jared went ahead and requested information about Arhrit. Perhaps Arhrit's spy *was* looking for the drugs, but if he were going after the Comms, then perhaps an enemy of their enemy might be their friend.

After this, he and Alec switched to another game on a private server. The game was a player vs. environment, but the building part was what they were there for. Jared laid out the building blueprints to match the structures on the island: the marina, the mansion, and the various rooms in them. Only when Jared too could not keep his head up did he end things for the night.

ROSE-COLORED DANGERS

Jared sat on an overturned five-gallon bucket and flipped through various articles on his phone about boats. If Stanton did check his communications, he'd be impressed with how much time Jared had spent on these damn sites trying to fix this wiring mess. Or concerned by how clueless he was. Whoever had put the manual together did not speak English well, and Jared spent more time deciphering the words than learning anything about the machine.

Tucker sat cross-legged on the dock next to him with his head lowered. His shoulders raised and lowered rhythmically as he dozed. Jared should have kicked him over backwards into the water for such an offense, but he couldn't bring himself to do it. He didn't know Tucker's story, but Jared knew it was not a happy one. While Tucker's head was leaned forward, Jared could see the still-red pattern of scars on his back.

Movement caught the corner of Jared's eye as Stanton approached from the door. Jared nudged Tucker, and the boy nearly tossed himself into the water. Jared stood and stretched his back as the boss man's shoes tramped over the wooden boards.

"Figured out the problem yet?" Stanton nodded to the boat.

"I've got a few ideas," Jared said. In truth, he had one idea left to try, but this sounded less hopeful. Jared hopped over the side of the boat and lifted the motor cover. "I don't know—I just get the feeling this thing was hot-wired at some point."

"Well, you have this one to thank for that." Stanton's hand flew across Tucker's cheek, and Tucker stumbled back.

Jared's throat tightened as Tucker lowered his head once more and rubbed his arm. It took everything Jared had not to cower himself at the blow. Dammit, why had he brought that up? He thought Stanton's goons had stolen it. It never crossed his mind that the hot-wiring had been an escape attempt.

"So, is it fixable?" Stanton asked.

"I—uh—" Jared looked at Tucker. A trickle of blood ran from his cheek. "Yeah, I can fix it. That will be no problem. I was just wondering where the problem had come from." He hoped he could back up his words. Jared didn't want to see what would happen if Tucker's escape attempt had handicapped the vessel permanently. "Is there anything else I can do for you, boss? Or are you just checking in?"

"One of our supply boats just called. They're having some sort of mechanical failure and are stranded."

"Uh, boss—I hope you're not expecting *me* to—"

"No," Stanton said, "they have their own team of mechanics coming in, but there are certain…things…we need to get off the boat before the team shows up. You and Randall are going to go out and meet them."

Jared looked to the sun then remembered his watch. "How far out?"

"About four hours."

Jared nodded, but his stomach sank at the thought. He wouldn't get back in time to fetch Katie for the evening. Maybe Tucker would tell her where he went at least.

"I guess you'll take the kid to the house?" Jared asked.

"Kid's going with you," Stanton said. "He'll be helpful to load and unload. The other crew are familiar with how we run things."

Jared frowned at Tucker. He didn't know anything about Randall other than he was big and told dirty jokes, but Jared felt responsible for Tucker and was not thrilled by the prospect of taking him with them. Then again, there was nothing he could do about it.

*　　*　　*

Randall brought a case of beer on board and kicked his feet up while Jared undid the ropes. The boat was a small yacht with a storage area below deck and two sets of seats up top: eight behind the wheel and two up front.

"Go on, then," Jared nodded to Tucker, still standing on the dock. Tucker looked from the dock to the boat hesitantly but stepped on board and moved to the back—as far away from Randall as possible.

"Kid coming too, huh?" Randall asked. "He'll be good entertainment."

Tucker shrank further between the seats as Jared shoved the boat out with his foot and hopped aboard.

"Boy," Randall said, "stop hiding. Sit where I can see you and put your hands on the rail."

Begrudgingly, Tucker stood and moved to sit on the floor next to the railing across the way from Randall. Removing two zip-ties from his pocket, Randall secured Tucker's hands to the rail. He tousled his hair before sitting back down.

Jared fired up the engine and took off toward the GPS coordinates while Randall cracked open a beer and sipped on it as the wind ripped around them. They flew across the water, and the water sprayed up and over the sides of the boat, misting them, a nice relief from the heat of the afternoon sun. In fact, the wind and the spray made the temperature just right.

Jared decided he liked boats. When all this was over, maybe he would get one for himself. There was a lot of freedom in his hands, and he could go anywhere he liked.

The trip was uneventful. Randall drank beer and snacked, while Tucker sat huddled in his corner. In just under four hours, the supply boat came into view. Jared sidled up next to the larger vessel and tossed his lines to the men on board. They tethered the two boats together, and Jared climbed aboard while Randall cut Tucker's bonds.

The supplies in question were drugs, obviously. Jared grabbed one of the crates, but it was too heavy for him. "Tucker," he called, and the boy grabbed the other end.

"Huh," Randall muttered. "Didn't know the kid *had* a name."

Jared wanted to retort but kept his mouth shut. Besides that, everything went smoothly, or so Jared thought. He didn't at first catch the curious glances Tucker received until a sizable crowd had gathered to watch them.

"Is he worth the upkeep?" one of the men asked Randall as they returned for the last crate.

"Who? The kid?" Randall grabbed Tucker's shirt and hauled him over to the group. "What upkeep?" He poked him in the ribs, but Tucker kept his eyes on the deck.

The man crossed his arms. "Well, you still feed him something, don't you? Does he replace his value?"

"Of course he does," Randall said. "If not by work then as a punching bag." He landed a right hook into Tucker's cheek, and Tucker crashed to the ground.

Jared's fist tightened, but those around him jeered and laughed. Tucker stayed on the ground clutching his cheek. Internally, Jared commended the strategy. There would be no benefit to rising.

"Then again, he's a one and done sort of gimmick." Randall kicked him in the stomach, and Tucker flopped onto his side, pulling his legs to his chest. Jared's fingernails cut into the base of his palm.

Randall grabbed Tucker by the hair and pulled. With pain etched across his face, Tucker grabbed the handle and stood.

"But in truth," Randall continued, "he's not worth the air he breathes." Randall smashed his fist into Tucker's face, and the boy stumbled back. He tripped over a box and fell off the back of the boat.

Jared and the others ran to the rail to see if Tucker would surface, but only the ripples marked his entrance into the water.

"Dammit, Randall." Jared set his phone on the rail and dove in after Tucker. As he sank into the salty waters, he forced his eyes open, ignoring the burning. By sheer luck, his hand grazed Tucker's pant-leg. Jared wrapped his arm around his chest and kicked for the surface.

By the time they reached it, his lungs were bursting. A hand reached out and pulled Tucker on board, and Jared lifted himself out of the water after him. "Is he alive?" Jared asked as calmly as possible, although his heart pounded.

Tucker rolled to his side and coughed up sea water in reply. Jared pulled a pack of cigarettes from his back pocket to find them soaked through, and he used this as an excuse to glare at Randall.

Randall shrugged. "I didn't tell you to go in after him." He stepped past Jared and climbed back on their boat. Once Tucker stopped coughing, Jared grabbed his arm and followed Randall. After tying Tucker to the rail, he cranked the boat and drove away.

"What the hell was that?" Jared demanded once they were out of earshot from the other boat.

Randall shrugged and opened another beer. "Relax, Jack. It wasn't a big deal."

"Not a big deal…" He glanced over his shoulder to where Tucker shivered on the floor. He knew he should drop the whole conversation, but he was too furious not to say anything. "And what the hell was I supposed to tell Stanton when we came back without him? He's in my care, you know."

Randall howled with laughter. "Your care, huh? That's great." He crossed the boat to Tucker. With a flip of his wrist, he pulled a switchblade from his pocket and pressed the metal to the boy's throat. Tucker leaned as far as he could, but his bound hands held him in place. His eyes bulged as he stared at the glint of steel at the base of his throat. "I could slit this kid's throat in front of Stanton, and do you know what he'd say?"

Jared's throat went dry. He shook his head.

"Not a damn thing." Randall pressed the blade harder, and Tucker whimpered as a line of blood dripped from the point. "If it were up to Stanton, all of them would be dead now anyways. The only person who'd give a damn would be Midas. And if he didn't have this damn fetish, we'd have been rid of them long before now. In fact, we'd still be in the States, living like kings."

Randall folded the blade and retook his seat. "Don't worry about them, Jack. They're not long for this earth anyways."

Jared nodded as Randall spoke, but his gaze flitted to Tucker once more. Tears glided down his cheek, and he swatted them with his shoulder.

"Good to know."

The sun sank into the water long before they reached the island, and the temperature dropped considerably. Jared, who was still damp from his dive, found a few blankets in a storage compartment below deck and wrapped himself in them.

Randall leaned back in his seat, arms crossed over his chest, and closed his eyes. Tucker shivered where he hunched, hands fixed to the rails, and Jared rubbed his own wrists. The callouses had faded, but the skin was still tougher than normal. Doubtless, Tucker bore the same marks there as well.

After studying Randall for several minutes to ensure he was asleep, Jared walked silently to Tucker. As he placed a hand on Tucker's shoulder, the boy startled awake, and Jared wrapped the blanket around him. Tucker's mouth parted, but Jared, without a word, returned to the wheel and stared off into the ocean ahead.

A new, sleek, and aerodynamic boat was tethered at the marina when they returned. Before sidling into the adjacent slot, Jared slashed through Tucker's bonds with his blade and pulled him up by the arm. "Tether us to the docks."

Tucker walked to the end of the boat and hopped ashore, and Jared tossed him the rope. As Tucker secured them, Jared rolled the blanket left on the floor into a wad and tossed it in the driver's seat. Then he nudged Randall's leg.

The man let out a gurgling sound, and he knocked over his beer as he stood. "What's the time?" he asked, stretching his back.

"A little after one." Jared tossed the rope for the rear of the boat to Tucker. "Kid, start loading everything into the SUV."

"Hey, the boss man's here," Randall said, noting the new boat.

Jared straightened. "Midas?" His hands started shaking, and he ran them over his jeans.

"Haven't met him yet?" Randall stepped onto the dock. "He's a pretty cool dude—if you're not in his way."

Not how *he* would describe him.

Randall continued up the dock, and before Jared realized it, he was being left with the boat and a huge haul of drugs to bring to the house. "You're not gonna leave me down here with all the work, are you?"

"That's *your* job, dock man."

"Asshole," Jared muttered. A small laugh came from Tucker, and Jared quirked a brow at him. Tucker looked away, returning his attention to the crates. In silence, they carried the crates down the docks to the SUV.

Jared kept opening his mouth to say something to Tucker. Something reminiscent of "sorry Randall almost murdered you this afternoon—twice," but that would not do. Tucker, for his part, kept looking between the blanket and Jared. Jared could tell he was trying to process the gesture. It was something he never should have done yet did not regret in the slightest.

Once the crates were loaded, Jared gave Tucker a ride in the passenger seat back to the house. The kid sat still as a statue, not touching the dash, the armrest, or the door. His tension caused Jared's blood pressure to go up. More than anything, it reminded him too candidly of himself.

The hall behind the kitchen did not only serve to hide kidnapped children, but to stash other contraband as well. When they entered through the kitchen, Jared was surprised to see Katie still up, washing dishes. The cook, however, was nowhere to be found. On their way back with the first crate, Jared sent Tucker on for the next crate, stopped beside Katie, and plucked a glass from her clean section. "Are you okay?"

"Midas is here," she replied as she scrubbed out a pan.

"I know." He filled the glass from the tap. "Stay away. I don't want him to see us together." Jared downed the glass and tossed it into the soapy dish water. After taking a deep breath, he shoved his trembling hands into his pockets and entered the dining hall.

There he sat. Midas. The man who turned everything he touched into gold.

Jared forced his feet to cross the room to where Randall was already chatting with Stanton. As he approached, he lowered his eyes as his shoulders crept up toward his ears.

Then he stopped.

No. He was not Goldie or even Jared Kelley. He was Jack Warner, sociopath, human trafficker, and murderer. And Jack did not lower his eyes for anyone. Instead, he straightened his back and marched to the table.

"Warner," Stanton acknowledged as he approached. "Midas, this is our newest recruit."

Midas raised his head and smiled with his thin lips. Standing, he extended his hand, and Jack Warner gripped it firmly.

To Jared's surprise, meeting Midas's eye did not mean looking up. In fact, Jared's own shoulders were broader than Midas's. If Jared fought him right now, he was confident he could beat him.

Was this truly the man he had feared for so many years?

"You're the boss?" Jared asked.

"That's me." Midas smiled. "How are you settling in?"

Jared hesitated for exactly three seconds, taken aback by what seemed to be genuine interest. Then he shrugged. "Well enough." Jared pulled back an empty chair and plopped into the seat. "It's an interesting business you run here. I saw quite a few familiar faces yesterday. One of them a royal if I'm not mistaken."

"He's a friend, yes. As long as he stays in line."

"And if not, certain incriminating photos might surface."

Midas and Stanton exchanged a glance. "You said he was quick on the uptake," Midas said. "It seems that is true."

Jared motioned around the room. "The cameras are a bit of a giveaway. It worried me at first when I saw them in the guest rooms, but I didn't see any in my own quarters, so—"

"We don't film our employees," Stanton said.

"Of course not." Jared turned to him. "You already have enough on me from the little *job* that I did for you. Not that it bothers me. I knew what I was signing up for. I just wanted to make sure we were on the same page."

"Yes, well." Midas took a sip of wine and sat. "It's the best way I've found to do business. A man that takes a bribe will betray you for a higher bribe. But a man who knows what he has to lose…well…I wouldn't still be in business if it didn't work."

"Randall, Jack," Stanton said, "how did the job go?"

Randall shrugged and crossed his arms. "Fine. Nothing to report."

Except the near murder of a kid. Jared picked at a place on the tablecloth.

"Good, good. Anyone else feeling ice cream?" Midas asked. Without waiting on a reply, he called into the kitchen. "Katie Belle, be a dear and bring us some ice cream, will you?"

Jared winced. So far, Midas had not recognized him, but if he saw them now, side-by-side—

He tried to focus on the conversation at hand, something about getting wasted and banging women, but he could not engage. Instead, he said a small, silent prayer that Midas would not recognize him.

Katie emerged from the kitchen with three bowls of ice cream on a tray and set them before Midas, Randall, and Stanton.

She skipped Jared.

The tray didn't look too small. Was she not thinking of him as part of the group? He picked up his wine glass and leaned back, ignoring the missing bowl.

But Midas didn't. Katie was about to return to the kitchen when he grabbed her arm, pulled her back, and slapped her. "Can you not count?" He smacked her again.

With a deliberate motion, Jared set his glass down and reached for the blade in his right pocket. His head screamed to let this go, but his chest roared. If he slapped her again, he was going to kill him. Damn the consequences.

Midas shook her. Tears slid down Katie's red cheeks. "Where's Warner's bowl?"

"He…he's lactose intolerant," she croaked.

All eyes turned to him, and Jared leaned back in his seat and shrugged. That was a damn personal bit of information she knew, but they were supposed to be sleeping together. Nonetheless, his heart pounded as he prayed for Midas to accept this answer and move on.

Midas released Katie's arm. "My apologies, Katie Belle." With head lowered, she turned for the kitchen, but he called after her. "Not too fast! Bring more wine."

"Yes, sir," she whispered and scurried back into the kitchen.

Midas watched her go. "What the hell happened to her? She's looking…well."

Was she? She looked the same to him. Had something subtle changed about her? Had a good night's sleep and a couple of good meals made such a difference?

Stanton elbowed Jared. "Apparently, the ugly ones are more appreciative."

Midas raised his brow then laughed. The others did too, and Jared forced himself to chuckle. "Got herself a sponsor, did she?" Midas asked.

Jared shrugged. "Everyone has their own taste. I thought there might be something under all that, so I went for it."

"You weren't wrong," Midas said. "I remember that girl from years ago. She was quite the looker once. Until she got the scar that is."

"What happened?" Randall asked.

"Car accident. I told the son of a bitch not to ram them too hard, but I guess we had different definitions of *too hard*."

"She must have been important to make her memorable," Randall said.

Midas darkened. "Daughter of FBI Agent Peter Thompson."

Randall choked on his wine. "Peter Thompson? *The* Peter Thompson? I thought you killed her as payback."

"Killing her would be too good," Midas said. "After the raids, I raped her and sent Thompson the video."

Randall let out a low whistle, but Jared clawed his pant leg.

Katie returned with the wine, and Midas grabbed her around the middle, pulling her close. "It was a special night, wasn't it, Katie Belle?"

Jared took a long, deep breath and released it silently, forcing the vision of her crying alone in the corner from his mind. His eyes darted to Katie, but she stared at the floor. Midas brushed the hair from her face and looked down the table at Jared.

Suddenly, Jared realized what this was. A test. Jared squared his shoulders and met his eye.

I am Jack Warner, he reminded himself.

"Would you mind if I took another spin?" Midas asked.

Jared raised his glass to his lips and shrugged. "You're the boss."

A tear fell, gliding all the way down Katie's cheek. Jared felt as if his throat were going to close.

A grin crept across Midas's tight face. "She's not really my type." He shoved her away, and Katie retreated to the kitchen once more. "So tell me about yourself, Warner. Where'd you grow up?"

"I was bounced around the state of Tennessee for most of my childhood," said Jared.

"Oh? Parents move a lot?"

Jared cocked his head to the side. "Don't pretend you don't have a file on me. Hell, you probably even know the name of the goldfish I won at the fair when I was eight."

The others laughed, but Midas merely grinned. "I like to learn about a man from his own mouth rather than a piece of paper."

"Would you like me to tell you how many girlfriends I've been through too? Because that'd be easier to list for you than the number of foster families that ditched me."

"Just the highlights, if you don't mind."

Jared shrugged. "I grew up mainly in Tennessee, although I stayed with a family just over the Georgia line at one point. Never knew my parents. Dropped out of school, if not on paper then functionally, at fourteen. But I didn't want to end up in juvie, so I stayed with my foster parents until I turned eighteen. Worked the streets as a—" he cleared his throat. "Freelance whatever, doing odd jobs for odd people. Mostly slinging dope, but I worked a few B&E gigs as well. I had a couple of offers to jump in with a gang, but decided to set my scopes a bit higher. After working for Max Wilson, Emmanuel brought me on to work some jobs down in Richmond—"

"Max Wilson?" Midas interrupted and cast a look at Stanton.

Jared frowned, trying to decipher the meaning of the look. "Yeah, Wilson had an operation running out of—"

"I know all about Wilson's operations. I'm confused because I don't generally hire anyone at this level who has previously worked for my competitors."

"Well, I never really worked for Max Wilson. I worked for Emmanuel. I was your mole at the Richmond facility for—"

A coy smile lifted the corner of Midas mouth. "That was you, huh? I don't recall hearing that connection. That was some good work. Wilson is still rotting in the pen over that, isn't he?"

"Last I heard," Stanton said.

Jared bit his lip to hold back his feelings on that matter. Wilson and Anderson had been good to Jared, and he had traded them down the river to get in with Midas. Sure, they sold some less than legal products, but they had never hurt anyone Jared knew of. He washed the guilt down with another drink of wine.

"When you said you were looking for something higher than the gangs, you meant here?" Midas asked.

"Gang bangers usually top out on a local level," Jared said. "I was looking for an organization functioning at a global scale with power to shake the tree of this world and get whatever the hell I wanted out of it."

Stanton grinned at Midas. "Kid's got vision."

"And pretty words." Midas took another swallow. "Well, Warner, I can say with some truth that I'm glad to have you aboard."

He extended his hand across the table, and Jared shook it once more. As Jared picked up his wine glass again, however, he noted Katie watching him from the window. The scar running the length of her cheek looked more prominent than ever. Someone at that table had done that to her, and he had just won over their favor. They would choke on it before the end.

*   *   *

Tears fell freely down Katie's face as she returned to the kitchen. Tucker, who was putting away the clean dishes, asked if she was okay, but Katie shook her head and continued wiping down the countertops. Her cheek burned from Midas's blows, but that wasn't what gnawed at her stomach.

You're the boss. Jared's words kept running through her mind.

She looked through the serving window where Jared sat, leaned back in his seat, sipping wine like he'd been there the whole time.

Stop, she ordered herself. *Stop thinking like this!* But her thoughts just jumbled up further. Instincts meshed with higher reasoning and any attempt to discern between the two left her exhausted. She swiped at the air about her face as if she could swipe away the fog that remained in her brain.

Finally, the group in the dining hall migrated to the bar, and she and Tucker went to their room. Everyone else was already asleep, and she took her place among them.

She had been asleep for almost an hour when Jared came for her. Groggily, Katie followed him out of the room and into the hall. If he was going to come get her, she wished it would be sooner in the night, not after she had already gone to sleep.

She was blinking in the light of the hallway when Jared slid his hand around her head and pulled her into a kiss.

She pulled away tasting alcohol. "Jack!"

Moisture glistened in his eyes. "I love you. I loved you the first day you stepped into our camp."

"Jack—" Her gaze darted to the corner of the ceiling where a camera was mounted. "Shut up."

"I know you probably don't love me back, but that's okay," Jared blathered. "Because I'm going to get you home. I swore to your dad that I would. I swore to Alec."

"Jared!" Katie placed a hand to his face. "Shut the hell up, or you're going to get us both killed."

Jared sniffed and glanced at the camera as well.

"Let's go to your room and talk, but not out here."

Running a hand through his hair, Jared nodded. Then he took her hand and led her through the halls, weaving as he walked. Katie clutched his arm to keep him from colliding into a wall. What was wrong with him, getting plastered like this? Who knew what indiscretion could slip out when he didn't have his head? Would he even remember tonight? She prayed he hadn't gotten *that* hammered. Surely, the smartest kid she'd ever met hadn't been that stupid.

But the other part prayed he would not recall this and what he had just said. Because Katie did not love him back.

"What are you reading?" Katie asked Jared between bites of egg the following morning. When Midas's boat had come in, so had some of his personal packages. Now that he had a griddle to cook with, their food options expanded quite a bit.

"It's a boat manual." Jared turned the page in the pamphlet and rubbed his eyes. After a few minutes, he set the manual down and fetched some Tylenol from his footlocker to still the pounding in his head. He tried not to squint at the lights that wobbled and swirled in their mounts—or was that just his head wobbling?

Why the hell had he drunk so much?

"Jared, do you remember last night?"

The booklet vibrated in his hands. *I love you.*

Dammit! Why had he said that? He had promised himself he wouldn't do that. First off, it was unfair to put her in that position. Second, what kind of incel couldn't get over a girl he hadn't seen in two freakin' years? Sure, it was true he had pined over her for that long, but damn, that sounded downright desperate.

Or was it endearing?

Judging from Katie's expression across the table, or rather her avoidance of eye contact, it was not.

"I'm sorry," he said. "That was a huge mistake. I should never have drank so much."

That was an understatement. As drunk as he was last night, he was lucky he hadn't given everything away.

"At least he didn't recognize you," she muttered and took another bite of eggs.

They settled into silence for a time. Thank God. Another promise he had made to himself was not to lie to her. So far, it had been the hardest promise he had ever kept. Katie had a knack for asking questions he didn't want to answer, but she needed someone she could trust. And she couldn't trust him fully if he hid himself from her.

Katie rose to refill her plate, but Jared said, "I didn't make enough for seconds. If you'd like some toast or something, there's some bread in the footlocker."

She lifted the skillet still full of eggs. "You're going to eat *all* of this?"

Jared turned the page. "I'm bringing some for Tucker. I'm pretending to think he missed breakfast, and I'll feed him until someone corrects me." That was something else he knew he shouldn't be doing, but despite himself, Jared liked the kid. And he didn't like the fact that he could count each of Tucker's ribs through his shirt.

Katie shook her head but put the skillet back down.

Jared checked his watch. "It's about time. Are you ready?"

"No," Katie sighed, and Jared gave her a look of sympathy. It hadn't been a real question, just one of those things people said. Part of him was glad she was not ready. It meant she had begun to feel safe here with him. But he did hate having to kick her out to where just about anything could happen.

Katie trudged to the bathroom and brushed her teeth while Jared selected his clothes for the day. After changing his pants, he took off his shirt, set out his polo for later, and dug through his closet for an exercise shirt.

Katie re-entered the room while he was deep in his search. When he emerged from the closet, he caught her staring at his back.

Immediately, she turned away to dig a couple of granola bars out of his foot locker.

Instinctively, he wanted to stare her down to flip the self-consciousness on its head, but this would not do. Katie was not some federal agent or an over-curious medical person. She had once tended to his flogging scars, so if anyone had earned the right to study them, it was her.

So, ignoring her stares, he said, "One by one, each of my exercise shirts have gone missing. I'm not going to report this, but if you see them, can you redirect them back to my room?"

"Sure," Katie said with a mouth full of granola. "Nice tatt."

He glanced down at the fiery phoenix climbing up his side. "Thanks." Maybe she wasn't staring at his scars after all. She had, after all, probably seen many of them by now.

"You covered up the 'LIAR,'" Katie noted. "Did you ever think of covering up the flogging scars too?"

Jared shrugged a white undershirt over his head. "Most of the scars I acquired by doing the *right* thing rather than the wrong. They're part of who I am. The liar, however, while true, is not something I want to be defined by for the rest of my life."

"And what do you *want* to be defined by?"

Jared chuckled. "That's a rather existential question. I don't really know the answer to that one, Katie. God willing, something better than the role I'm in now, but…"

"God willing? You believe in God?"

Jared was caught off-guard by that remark. As far as he knew, Thompson and Alec did. He had just assumed that belief would have been inherited.

"I don't know," he replied. "I don't think about that stuff too much. I suppose I do sound a bit like my mom by saying it, but…yeah. I think there's a God."

"After everything that's happened to us, you, of all people, still think there's a God?"

Him of all people? Perhaps she was referring to his logical side, but the last time he had thought about that stuff was last year when

Mom dragged him to church after dropping by for Christmas. He was otherwise too busy for such things.

"I don't have answers for those sorts of questions," he said finally. "I don't know if there's a reason for the horrible things we've been through or if there's some sort of divine plan behind everything. I do know this: God didn't kidnap us or lock us up and leave us to die. Midas did that."

"But He could have stopped it."

Jared shrugged. "I suppose so. But if I've got my lore correct, He didn't keep his own kid from getting killed either."

Katie's brow depressed, as if this were an angle she had yet to consider. He wasn't really trying to convince her one way or the other on the topic. There was nothing wrong, however, with a little bit of faith. Many kids he knew took comfort in it—Bryan especially. For Jared's part, the belief that his actions had meaning—that doing the right thing over the wrong had merit—kept him closer to the straight and narrow than what would have otherwise been possible. Sure, his conscience was a bit dull to things such as stealing and lying, but he still knew which way was up for the most part.

At least most of the time.

Jared leaned forward into the mirror to study his hairline. "My roots are starting to come in."

"I'll help you fix it tonight."

He checked his watch once more. "I need to get going if I'm going to earn employee of the month."

"You mean brown-nose of the month," she said, and Jared chuckled.

*   *   *

Hands on his hips, Jared looked around the vehicle bay. All of the cars had been washed and the oil had been changed. Boat maintenance was up to date. The shop had been cleaned and swept. There was nothing else he could think of that needed doing.

"Am I missing something?" he asked Tucker, who stood near the door looking like he was going to bolt at any second. It was his perpetual neutral, but it continued to unnerve Jared, nonetheless.

"Missing what, sir?" Tucker asked.

"Any chores? Tasks? To-do lists that have been left undone?"

Tucker shrugged. That was helpful.

It was barely ten o'clock, and the thought of being idle for the rest of the day made Jared restless. If his hands were not busy, then he would be forced to be alone with his thoughts. But try as he might, there was nothing else he could think of doing.

"I guess we get the rest of the day off then," Jared muttered, and Tucker's face lightened.

What am I thinking? The kid probably needs a day off with as little sleep as they get. Jared, himself, was tired, but chronic insomnia was sort of *his* normal.

Jared led the way to the office where they could sit and relax, but as Tucker neared the room, he started rubbing his arm again.

Jared frowned. Was there something scary about his office?

As they entered, Tucker hesitated at the doorway and looked back at the warehouse with longing. Still continuing to act casual as he observed Tucker, Jared sat in the swivel chair and propped his feet up on the metal desk. Tucker sat on the floor in front of the frumpy couch, crunched his legs up to his chest, and looked to the door again.

The swivel chair was too high and too straight-backed for Jared's taste. He tried adjusting it, lowering it, reclining it, even raising it back up at one point, but any way he moved it, the position seemed worse. When the damn thing nearly pitched him out onto the floor, he stood abruptly to keep from toppling over.

Tucker pressed back against the couch, clawing at the sides.

Pretending not to notice, Jared knelt beside the chair and inspected the gears. Internally, he felt like his organs were melting, folding into themselves to form a molten lump. What had they done to this kid?

Maybe their day off would be better suited for the dock: a more public location, less tight quarters, and an easy escape by jumping into the ocean.

"You know, I'm going to give that hot-wired boat another once-over." Jared nodded to the door.

Tucker rose and led the way out of the office. Once at the boat, Jared turned over a five-gallon bucket and sat on it, leaning against a post. Meanwhile, Tucker sat on the dock beside him, looking down at the boards.

Instead of pulling up articles on boats, most of which he had already perused, Jared looked up his position on the FBI's Most Wanted List again.

Still only ninety-two.

He had made it onto the list the day after Tonya's "murder." The timing could not have been a coincidence. He assumed it was Midas's doing. A warning that he could never go back now that he was in. Being on the list unnerved him greatly. If, by some miracle, he made it out of everything alive, would this affect his ability to come home? Would he have to be on the run for the rest of his life? Or should he face the music?

Jared gritted his teeth. *See, this is what happens when you have too much time on your hands. You start worrying about shit you can't do anything about.*

"Should have taken that scholarship," he muttered to himself. Then he glanced at Tucker to see if the kid had heard, but Tucker's eyes were closed as he sat cross-legged beside Jared. His shoulders rose and fell steadily, and Jared smiled at him approvingly. The kid deserved a break. And at least here, Jared could still knock him into the water if anyone came by.

For the next two hours, Jared played on his phone while Tucker napped. In his current position, Jared was sure the kid would wake with a crick in the neck, but at least he got some more sleep.

"Warner?" a voice called from the warehouse.

"Yeah!" Jared hollered back, and Tucker's head bobbed. His eyes grew wide as he took in where he was and that he had been sleeping.

Lionel, one of the Watchers, ambled toward them down the dock. "I've got a run to go on, and Stanton told me to take you. To get your feet wet and all."

"Oh? Where are we going?"

"Myanmar," Lionel said. "Go ahead and lock up, and I'll give you the details on the way."

Hesitantly, Jared stood. He didn't quite know how long it would take to get to the mainland, but there was a good chance he'd get back after dark. There went dinner plans. "Is the kid going?"

"Hell, no," Lionel said, and Tucker visibly relaxed.

Good. Maybe this time Tucker could tell Katie where he went.

.

CRIMSON PULSE

Jared closed his eyes as the sea breeze flowed over him. There was a river in his hometown. Did people boat in that? He hadn't been around long enough to find out, but if he ever made it back, that was going to be one of his top priorities.

"Want a beer, Warner?" Lionel tapped the cold bottle to his arm. Jared accepted it and popped the cap with the bottle opener on his key ring. Lionel had come in with Midas the night before, and, while Midas was leaving this afternoon, Lionel was going to be staying.

Jared guessed him to be in his late forties. He was tall and broad in the shoulders, and Jared knew he'd lose to him in a fight. A tattoo of an anchor was drawn on his arm, but Randall told Jared he had been dishonorably discharged and arrested for human smuggling. It seemed the man's hobbies had not diverged much.

Jared did not know the details of their mission, only that he was supposed to drive to a port off the coast of Myanmar. The GPS on the dash had told him to drive in a straight line for three hours, and they had been traveling for two and a half. Keeping one hand on the wheel to keep it straight—he had yet to find an autopilot if such things existed on boats—he leaned back in his seat, kicked up his feet, and sipped on the beer.

It worried him a little bit, not knowing the details of this operation, but there was something about the ocean and the vastness that had cooled him down. There was so much freedom out here.

He was sure of it now. No matter where he settled down, it was going to be near water.

And he was going to have a boat.

If he survived.

Jared slowed as the shoreline came into view. "So, talk to me, Lionel. What's my role in all this?"

Lionel finished his beer and tossed the bottle on the floor for Tucker to clean up when they got home. "It's just a pick-up and delivery op. Keep the boat idling and your hand on your holster. Don't say anything, and if they shoot at us, shoot better."

Jared entered the bay, saw the dock, and turned the boat toward it. "Are we expecting hostility?"

"Always expect hostility." Lionel racked his pistol. "Then you'll never be surprised."

Not bad advice.

The dock was covered, and Jared parked the boat alongside it. Beyond the dock was a beach with a line of trees thirty yards back. An old, overturned boat lay half-buried in the sand.

Two men leaned against the posts of the awning, smoking. They tossed their cigarettes into the water and placed their hands on their holsters as Jared hopped onto the dock and secured the boat with a loose slip-knot.

"Afternoon, boys," Lionel said as he stepped out of the boat with a briefcase. "You look as cheery as usual. Do you have the stuff?"

The taller of the two nudged a black duffle bag with his foot, and Lionel eyed him before bending to open the bag. Jared let out a low whistle to find the bags filled to the seams with semi-automatic rifles. Lionel removed one of these and checked the serial number—it was filed off. After placing it into the bag with the others, he zipped the duffle up. Then, with a nudge of his foot, he slid the briefcase over.

The man picked up the briefcase and opened it, revealing several stacks of bills as Lionel rocked on the balls of his feet. "So, do we have a deal?"

"We have a deal." The man extended his hand, and Lionel smiled as he took it.

"FREEZE!" From the treeline burst men in dark tactical gear, weapons raised. Only one had shouted the English word while the others burst ahead shouting in a language Jared did not understand.

"Shit!" Lionel drew his weapon and fired it into the sellers' chest before shooting at the guys running at them. "Get down!" he ordered Jared as return fire erupted from the beach.

Jared took cover from behind one of the posts and looked over his shoulder to the men now hiding behind the overturned boat on shore. Although there were no insignias, Jared was pretty sure they were cops. He didn't want to shoot cops. He could try shooting over their heads, but feared hitting one by accident.

"Get the bag!" Lionel shouted as he grabbed the suitcase and tossed it into the boat.

Jared slung the bag over his shoulder, and his bad shoulder nearly ripped out of the socket, it was so heavy. He dropped the bag into the boat and dove in after it as bullets peppered the side of the vessel. Lionel bounced off the seats and hit the floor behind him. Jared tugged on the slip knot, threw the boat into gear, and swerved away from the dock.

As they reached the exit of the bay, a gray boat with "Myanmar Police Force" written in white letters next to a scrawling language met them. Jared hit the floor and bullets shattered the windshield. Keeping low, he steered away from the vessel and shoved theirs into full throttle.

The boat leaned precariously on its side. As they passed the nose of the boat, Jared swerved alongside, and the men on board raced to fire on them from the other side of the boat. As he had guess-timated, their boat zipped past the police boat in the opposite direction before they could get an accurate shot, and the bullets struck the boat instead of him.

Jared shot off from the shoreline into the vast ocean at top speed. The other boat was bigger than their own. Would the weight slow them down? Or would they have stronger engines? Did they have radar? Would they call in for help?

Jared turned back to Lionel with these questions in mind to see him lying on the floor, clutching his thigh.

"How bad is it?" Jared asked, determined not to let up speed. He didn't come all this way to get locked up in a jail in Myanmar.

Lionel growled in response as he slid his belt from his pants and wrapped it around his leg. Jared rubbed his own shoulder. Damn, that bag had really torqued it.

Taking a bit of rope from the side compartment, he tethered the wheel in the direction of home. Evasive maneuvers were useless out here and would only burn up gas. Getting into international waters was their safest bet. Where that was, he did not know. Damn Lionel for not giving him more information.

Once he was satisfied the boat would not veer off course, Jared knelt next to Lionel and took in the bloody pant leg.

"How bad is yours?" Lionel asked, and Jared frowned. Lionel pointed to Jared's shoulder, and Jared did a double-take to see blood on his shirt. He hadn't nearly dislocated his shoulder. He had been shot.

Jared touched the spot, and pain roared from it, but Lionel lifted his hand and blood spurted from his leg. Either way, he was better off than Lionel.

Jared grabbed a towel and pressed it against Lionel's leg. "It might have hit the femoral artery," he said. "If it's only a nick, we might make it back in time."

"Did that fountain look like a nick to you?" Lionel snarled. "What the hell was that back there? You forget how to fire a gun or something?"

"It misfired."

"Misfired my ass! You panicked, didn't you? Freaking newbies. I was told you were the iceman! Calm and cool. Don't tell me that cops are your kryptonite."

"It misfired, Lionel," Jared said. "I'm not lying to you."

"What'd it do? Misfire at the floor? You didn't even raise your freaking weapon! I'm almost surprised you didn't shoot *me* to help the cops along!" Then Lionel's eyes widened.

Jared looked away as he continued to hold pressure, and beads of sweat broke on his brow. His hands shook violently.

"What the hell are you man?" Lionel asked. "Are you a cop?"

"I am no cop," Jared said, but Lionel sneered. His hands went for his pistol, but Jared grabbed it first and tossed it out of the boat.

"You son of a bitch!" Lionel shouted and grabbed Jared's arm, but Jared elbowed him in the nose and backed away. Lionel grabbed for Jared's ankle, but Jared stepped out of reach. "Get back here! I'll kill you!"

"No," Jared said. "I don't think you will."

Lionel shuffled toward him still holding his leg. As he swatted at Jared, blood poured out from beneath his palm. He moaned and cursed at Jared. But blood continued to pour out and color left his face. In less than a minute, Lionel leaned back and gazed up at the sky.

BLOOD OF TRAITORS

As Katie raked fresh dirt into the flowerbed, she caught herself humming.

Immediately, she stopped and glanced around to see if anyone else had noticed. No one had, but she berated herself on her carelessness. Her life was supposed to be more hell than ever. She couldn't be caught humming.

Hope and a friend—it was amazing how much of a change these two factors had caused. Even if her friend had multiple personalities and a gray moral compass.

Katie dusted off her hands and stood. She had already trimmed back the hedges and removed the clippings and dead plants. Now she was shoveling fresh garden soil onto the beds from a flat-bed trailer. Several cases of flowers waited to be planted when the soil was in place.

Two young ones worked with her, an eight-year-old and a six-year-old, so the bulk of the work was on her. Whatever wasn't finished by dinner would have to wait for tomorrow. The odds were fifty-fifty as to whether the Watchers would act rationally about this or not. Either way, it was out of her hands and she decided not to think about it.

Tucker had stopped by for a little while until he was poached for a job in the house. He told her Jack Warner had been sent off island again on a job. Katie didn't know what the job was. Honestly, she didn't want to.

Katie paused to take a sip from the plastic water bottle that had grown warm in the sun and called the young ones over to drink as well.

"Katie, look what I caught!" Lenny, the eight-year-old, dangled a grasshopper in her face. The thing was a whopper, one of the biggest she'd seen. The poor creature wiggled and fought as the small fingers of the child held him by the leg.

"That's great, Lenny."

"This is the third one I've caught today! Do you want him?"

Katie considered the bulging eyes of the terrified insect. "Do you want him, Selena?" she asked the six-year-old.

Selena licked her lips and nodded fervently. Lenny held the bug out to her, and Selena took hold of the other leg. With wide, expectant eyes, Selena ripped the wings off one-by-one then tore away the legs. Once the creature was nothing but a thick, green cylinder, she popped it into her mouth and swallowed it down.

"Good job, Lenny." Katie petted his matted, greasy hair. "And thank you for sharing."

Lenny's proud smile filled his face. "Maybe I can find some more!" He knelt in the grass along the edge of the bushes and pushed back branches and leaves. "Come on, Selena. Help me!"

A knot filled Katie's stomach the size of the steak Jared had brought her as she watched them.

A gentle rumble accompanied the normal sound of waves lapping on the shores, and Katie raised a hand to her eyes. The outline of a boat, nothing more than a silhouette as the sun sank into the ocean, approached. Purple clouds stretched across the red and orange sky reflecting off the water rolling in on the beach. Too bad such an extraordinarily beautiful place was coated in such darkness.

She started back to work, but continued to keep an eye on the incoming boat. Was it Jared coming in from the job? She hoped so. Each time he left the island, she feared he would never come back.

As the boat came to dock, someone started yelling. The Watchers nearby ran to the boat, and the silhouette of a body was raised and set on the docks.

Katie's throat nearly closed. She should have continued working, ignoring what was taking place, but she could not. One man knelt next on the docks then stood while the others stared at the form. If he were injured, they would be doing something, not staring. Someone was dead.

God, please let it not be Jared. If it was Jared. . .

If it was Jared, Katie might use that piece of broken glass on something more important than her cheek.

One of the men left the docks and trudged up the walk. As he drew near, Katie saw it was Jared and released her breath. But he was covered in blood and pale—deathly so.

His eyes caught hers. "You!" He pointed at her. "Get towels and some cleaning supplies and get down to the docks."

"Uhm," Katie mumbled, and his brow furrowed. She gestured with her head to the kids working with her. It was a bad idea to leave the young ones unattended and unprotected.

"The rest of you," Jared said, "go to the kitchen."

Katie nodded, dropped her trowel, and followed Jared inside. While he continued up the stairs, she entered the laundry for the towels before going to the docks as ordered.

The dock and boat were painted red with the man's blood. Katie recognized Lionel lying pale on the wooden planks but turned away, unable to take in the sight of his white, open-eyed face.

Randall stood leaning against the dock digging dirt from his nail with his pocket knife. "Should have brought a shower curtain," he muttered.

Katie moved to the edge of the boat and stared at the blood already drying on the floors and seats. This was an impossible task. The blood would never come up. But she laid the towels on the floors and set to wiping the vinyl seats.

Jared returned with Stanton, and they stood silently around the body. Finally, Stanton sighed and scratched his nose. "I guess I'll let Midas know…" He turned to go.

"Better tell him about your mole," Jared muttered, and Stanton stopped, turning back to him. "They knew we were coming."

"Could have been the sellers who tipped them off," Stanton said.

Jared gritted his teeth. "They were as surprised as we were."

"I'll look into it—"

"You sure as hell better!" Jared squared up to the man, their chests nearly touching. "And the next time you send me on one of your damn missions, I want the whole story. I don't want just guesses as to what we're buying or selling. You brought me into this and swore I had a seat at the table—"

Stanton held up his hand. "You're upset. And I understand why—" Jared chuckled darkly, and Stanton frowned. "Go shower and change your clothes." He nodded to Katie. "Hell, go burn off some steam."

"You think a whore and a shower—"

"We'll talk later, Warner. We will, but we've got a pile of shit on our doorstep and I don't need you flying off the handle right now."

Jared's lip curled as he looked back at Lionel. Then he grabbed Katie's arm and pulled her out of the boat. "Walk," he ordered and shoved her in her back.

Once they entered the mansion, Jared walked in-step with her, and Katie noticed his left arm hanging at his side. Although his entire shirt was smattered in blood, the part around the shoulder appeared wetter than the rest, and blood dripped from his fingers onto the floor.

"Jared," she whispered, touching his sleeve, but he shook his head and stared ahead. Once they reached his room, however, his face pinched into a grimace.

He turned his back to her. "Is there an exit wound?"

She touched his shoulder. "Yes, there's another hole."

Jared winced as Katie rolled his shirt up and over his head. One bloody hole was seated just above his clavicle, and the other next to his shoulder blade. Katie pressed his shirt to them. "Come over to the bed."

"Let me hold pressure. Get the med kit from beneath my bed."

Katie fetched it and set it next to him while he sat on the bed. The box was full of bandages, Neosporin, iodine, and IV supplies.

"Those white pouches are coagulants." He pointed to them. "Pour one into the wound to staunch the bleeding."

"Why didn't you have them patch you up?" she asked.

"I can't let them see my scars."

"Geez, Jared. Your cover is as thin as an egg shell."

"I know." He groaned as she pressed the cloth back to the wound.

"You shouldn't have come here."

"Too late for that," he muttered. "I have a suture kit in my closet. Oh, and there's some vodka in there too." Katie brought back both and placed the vodka to his lips, but he turned away. "No, in the wound."

Katie doused the wound, and he nearly came off the bed. Jared pounded his good fist into the mattress. "That'll wake you up. Damn, it's been a while."

Katie opened up the suture kit. "Any lidocaine?"

"Just some numbing spray, but I don't think it'll do much good here. Do you need instructions on putting in stitches?"

"I've seen it done once." Then Katie smiled.

Jared tried to match it, but it came out more as a sneer. Without much further ado, Katie inserted the needle into his skin, and Jared gritted his teeth. Carefully, with tongue protruding, Katie made little knots until the wound was sealed up. Finding some gauze in the kit, she taped it to the wound. "You're going to need to be more careful."

Jared took the bottle of vodka and drank a swallow.

"Do you really think there's a mole?"

He shook his head. "No. The sellers set us up. But they're dead, so there's no one to disagree with me, and I thought it was a good opportunity to spread a little paranoia around. Paranoia makes people stupid." With trembling fingers, Jared pulled a pack of cigarettes from his pocket and lit one. He took several long puffs before he leaned his head against the headboard and closed his eyes.

Katie climbed onto the bed next to him and leaned her head on his good shoulder. Jared looked down on her, then placed his head on hers. He trembled ever so slightly and Katie knew he was shaken up more than he let on.

*   *   *

About an hour later, a knock sounded on the door. Once Katie was set, Jared opened the door and all Stanton saw of her was her ankle as she entered the bathroom. The sound of water running came from the next room. A wad of girl clothes lay on the floor next to bed sheets, and John McClane was busy feeling like a TV dinner on the flat screen. All traces of blood had been removed.

Jared leaned against the doorframe, his shirt untucked, hair messed. "Did you speak to Midas?"

"I did."

"Does he have any idea what tipped the pigs off?"

Stanton shook his head. "He's looking into it. But listen—I want to commend you on your work today. When shit goes sideways like that, it can be hard to keep one's head. You managed not only to get the shipment back to us, but also the cash."

Jared lit a cigarette. "Thank my lucky stars."

"You're right," Stanton said. "I should have read you in. But that's not something you're going to need to worry about anymore. Thing is, a business like this never stops moving. When I picked you for the job, I checked in with your old crew. All of them spoke favorably of you. Said you were quick on your feet, always coming up with some scheme or the other, reliable, driven. And let's just say, I've seen all of those things even in the short time you've been here. You've got promise, Jack." Stanton slapped Jared on the shoulder, and Jared nearly screamed. He blinked a couple of times to settle his face and puffed hard on his cigarette.

"You're moving up a rung," Stanton continued. "Come see me in my office tomorrow for the details."

"Thank you, sir. I—I *am* honored."

"But…"

"Sir, Lionel's not even in the ground yet. It would seem…"

"Too soon, huh? How about this then: I promote you, but to the rest of the crew, I tell them you're subbing on a temporary basis. After a couple of weeks, when you've proven yourself, we'll make it more permanent. Or you can turn it down. Your choice."

Jared pretended to deliberate for a moment. "Alright, that sounds agreeable."

Stanton smiled at him. "See? Smart. That's what we need more of around here. Oh, by the way, you got a package." Stanton lifted a cardboard box from the floor beside Jared's door. "And some commercial ads." He handed him a stack of advertisements labeled for Jack Warner.

"How in the hell?"

Stanton laughed. "You know the saying there are only two things for certain in life: death and taxes? They should have added junk mail to that list. Feel free to take the rest of the day off. And have fun." Stanton winked at this last part.

Have fun? Jared glared at him as he sauntered away. Sometimes pretending to be a sociopath was tough. Oddly, if he were a sociopath, he wouldn't feel such a strong urge to stab Stanton in the back.

After pulling the door closed with his foot, Jared set the box on the bed and winced once more as he felt his shoulder. There didn't seem to be further damage done. He knocked twice on the bathroom door, and the water shut off.

Katie stepped out of the bathroom still fully clothed. "What did he say?"

"I just got promoted," Jared muttered as he studied the package. "Said I had promise. Told me I was smart."

"That's a good thing, isn't it?"

Jared laughed. "I wanted to be smart, but not like, noticeably smart. I was shooting for a 110 IQ."

"What's in the box?"

Jared flipped open his pocket knife and slit through the packaging tape. Buried beneath a couple of layers of packing peanuts was a toaster oven.

Katie looked to the kitchenette already starting to overflow with small kitchen appliances. "Planning on making a lot of toast, are we?"

"Your brother's gifts are rarely *just* appliances." He showed her the box flap. "See the postmark? Mailed from Atlanta, Georgia. Alec probably planned the package and got Bryan to send it. And pay for it."

Jared flipped the toaster oven upside down and pulled out his multi-tool to unscrew the back panel. Tucked behind the heating coils was a black, rectangular box with an antenna. "Bingo." After a little finagling, Jared dislodged the device.

A note was taped to the back:

> "This is a satellite phone with end-to-end encryption. As long as Midas doesn't know about it, we should be able to talk without being traced.
>
> --AT"

"We can call him?" Katie exclaimed. "Jared, does this mean we can call him?"

"Seems so," he said.

Katie clutched his arm as a smile spread across her face. Her smile was sufficiently infectious, and Jared returned it. This would truly be better than playing video games across the world. But if Stanton found out about it, they were dead. Another thing to keep secret.

"Well, what are we waiting for? Call him, Jared!"

Jared punched in Alec's number and waited on the ring. Halfway through the first one, Alec picked up. "Jared?"

"Uh, not just me, Alec."

"Katie?"

A sob erupted from Katie as she snatched the phone from Jared. "Alec?" Tears filled Katie's eyes as she clutched the phone to her ear.

Jared looked away, feeling as if he were intruding on such a personal moment. He stood and fetched another cup of tea while Katie wept on the phone with her brother. Some conversations between family deserved to stay private, and Jared tried his best not to eavesdrop. After a few minutes, however, he rejoined her.

"I don't want to cut you off, Katie, but—"

Katie sniffled. "Uhm, Alec, Jared needs to talk to you too."

Jared switched the phone to speaker. "Hey, did you find that dossier I asked for on Arhrit?"

"Yeah," Alec chuckled. "He's a peach. Wanted for smuggling drugs and weapons mostly. My dad called in a few favors from some friends in Interpol. Apparently, Arhrit runs most of the drug trade in Thailand, Laos, and Cambodia with ties to some bigwigs in China. He's recently been trying to inch his way into Myanmar, which is probably the source of the conflict between him and Midas."

"Your dad's helping now too?" Jared asked. "Didn't think he was on board with this."

"Let's just say I left out a few details, but he now knows I've been helping you. You went out of my league the moment you stepped off American soil, so I had to read him in. Since then, he's been going through bottles of Pepto-Bismol left and right, so you'd better make it home in one piece."

Katie's petite mouth arched downwards. "He sounds more worried about Jared than me."

"When you were taken, Katie, Dad almost ended up in the hospital with a stomach ulcer. There's no comparison."

Katie looked pleased by this bit of information.

"You didn't tell *my* mom I was in Myanmar, did you?" Jared asked.

"Hell, no. But from what Leida says, she's still worried sick. You two have people who care about you here, so don't leave us hanging, alright?"

Jared grabbed an ice pack from the freezer and pressed it to his shoulder. "We're working on a plan. I'll keep you up to speed as it develops."

STAINED RED

Jared stared down at the bloody boat as visions of Lionel sputtering and bleeding to death played on repeat. He barely knew Lionel, so why did he feel so bad about his dying? Sure, he hadn't rendered aid, but he hadn't shot him either.

Tucker jostled the cleaning bucket as he set it on the boat, and Jared shook his head to clear his thoughts. "Where are your gloves?" he asked.

Tucker looked down at his hands and shrugged.

"Hang on," Jared said. He found a box of gloves in his office desk and donned a pair before handing Tucker another set. He had seen how these Watchers lived. No sense in possibly exposing Tucker to a deadly illness to cover up a murder.

Tucker grabbed a sponge out of his bucket and looked between it and the stained carpet and upholstery. He scratched his head. Words could not have conveyed the sentiment better.

"There's no salvaging the carpet," Jared said as he stepped into the boat. "Maybe not even the vinyl seats. I'll have to research that." He pulled out his knife and pried away the carpet from the floor. "Grab a corner and let's get this up."

After piling the soiled carpet on the docks, Jared dragged a lawn chair near, kicked his leg up on one of the dock posts, and read articles on how to remove blood stains from vinyl. He had told Stanton the odds of getting the blood out were low at breakfast, but Stanton still wanted them to try. Jared resisted an eye roll when he had told him that. If they could afford Mercedes golf carts, they could afford to re-upholster the damn seats. But he didn't argue.

Perhaps he should have. Warner probably would have.

Tucker dangled his legs off the dock and leaned back with his eyes closed. This was no act of accidental dozing. Finally, the kid relaxed around him.

"I don't feel like going all the way up to the house for lunch," Jared said. Tucker glanced up at him, but Jared kept his eyes on his phone. From the corner of his eye, however, he saw the disappointment on his face as Tucker stared back out at the ocean ahead.

Jared stood and stretched. "Come on. I'm probably not supposed to do this, but I'm going to feed you lunch. I don't want to wait on you to get back."

Tucker's brow crinkled, but once again, he said nothing. As Jared walked back to the office, however, Tucker was right on his heels.

Jared tossed a couple of frozen dinners into the microwave in the office, and Tucker licked his lips as he stood at the doorway. When the microwave dinged, Jared said, "I think we left the bucket out by the dock. Go fetch it."

Tucker's lip curled, but only for a second as he left the office for the bucket. Once he was gone, Jared pulled a packet of powdered vitamins from his pocket, dumped it onto Tucker's meal, and stirred up. The meal was already full of vegetables, proteins, and fats—it was marketed for elders who had trouble getting enough nutrients. Jared had bought the frozen dinners and vitamins just for this purpose, but hadn't been able to find an excuse to use them yet. He was flirting dangerously close to arousing Tucker's suspicions, but couldn't help himself.

When Tucker returned, Jared shoved the food across the desk, propped his legs up, and drove his fork into the meal pretending to pay the kid no mind. Tucker sat on the floor next to the couch and dug in. A look of delight filled Tucker's face, and Jared pulled out his phone to hide his smile.

For a few minutes, they enjoyed the silence between them, then a bump sounded in the garage. Jared dropped his legs from the desk and rounded it. He ripped the food from Tucker's hands—there was only a bite or two left—and slid it under the couch. Jared then pressed a finger to his lips, and Tucker's brows disappeared into this hair they shot up so high.

Jared entered the garage. "Randall? What's up?"

Randall ran his finger over one of the vehicles, leaving a line of oil on the shiny panel. Jared resisted a sneer.

"Squeaky clean," Randall said. "Impressive."

Jared shrugged. It *was*.

"I need to borrow your kid to bring a load up from the shed on the east side of the island," Randall said.

Jared looked behind him, expecting Tucker to have slunk out of the office, but he still sat on the floor by the couch, legs against his chest, looking like he wished to disappear. "We're cleaning the boat today," Jared said.

Randall laughed. "You take your job too seriously, Warner. The boat can wait, but Midas wants this stuff moved *today*."

Jared bit the inside of his cheek but nodded. "Tucker—"

Tucker rubbed his arm as he rose from the floor and stepped hesitantly from the office. His shoulders were tense again. Jared didn't want to let him go, but he wasn't his to keep. As Tucker left the garage, he glanced longingly over his shoulder at him.

Was Tucker figuring it out? Or was Randall just that bad?

Jared walked back down the dock to the bloody boat. A couple of the articles he had read recommended a few products he could try. Granted, most of these articles were trying to remove small amounts of blood from nose bleeds or unfortunate menstrual accidents. The interior of the boat, however, looked to be the site of a hog slaughter.

What he needed to do was run some tests. The hardest thing about blood was its coagulopathy—its tendency to stick to everything. He wondered if a straight emulsifier like soap would be most effective. Jared considered removing a flap of fabric from the seat and carrying it up to the house, but couldn't find a good sample. So, he unbolted the base, hauled it down the dock, and loaded it up in the SUV.

Randall was right. Jared cared too much about his island jobs, but getting the seat clean was not just something that needed to be done. It was an opportunity to go see Katie.

Sure enough, when Jared arrived at the Big House, he found Katie in the laundry. After gathering some cleaning supplies, they went back to the SUV to work on the stain removal process. The work achieved on the seats was minimal, but it gave them a chance to brainstorm on how to get off this rock.

*　　*　　*

Tucker stared at the ground in concentration as his arm wavered from the weight of the black duffle bag. Randall, however, smiled as he gazed over his shoulder at him. For his own load, Randall carried an overnight bag.

Tucker hated it when Randall was in town. The other Watchers were bad enough, but Randall was the worst.

At least he had gotten a good meal from Jack—that was snatched and hidden. He still didn't get that. Was Jack really that scared of getting caught feeding him? It was strange, but Jack was sort of weird anyway. He wouldn't have despised him as much if he weren't treating Katie like his personal whore. That enough made him want to rip his guts out. And the fact that his cowardice kept him from doing just that made him feel like scum. Katie was the strongest girl he had ever met to have taken this blow from Warner in stride.

Randall typed the code to his apartment and ushered Tucker inside. "Set it on the bed," he said as Tucker stumbled on through.

With a heft, Tucker dropped the bag on the bed, nearly falling forward from the effort. After extricating his palms from the strap, he stood against the wall, praying to be dismissed.

"Don't you wonder what you were carrying?" Randall asked.

Tucker kept his eyes on the floor. *No. I don't give a crap.* All he cared about was the clock on Randall's nightstand that read ten minutes until dinner. He had been hauling shit like this all over the island for Randall for the past several hours. First, they had moved the entire drug cache out of the room, down to the docks, and into hidden compartments on three of the boats. Now there was this monster they had brought up from the warehouse.

Randall unzipped the bag and raised the corner to expose a cache of weapons inside. He lifted an AR-15 from the bag and racked the slide. Sweat dripped down Tucker's neck.

"Is there something else you need, sir?" he asked breathlessly. Randall was trying to scare him. And it was working.

"I'll tell you when you're dismissed!"

Tucker's eyes flew to the floor, and he forced his curled lip down to neutral. What he'd give to wrap his hands around this man's thick neck…

Randall pulled a full magazine from his pocket and shoved it into the gun, and Tucker's eyes went wide. Randall turned the gun on Tucker, and he backed against the TV stand, fingers scrambling against the smooth surface. Randall pressed the barrel of the gun against his chest, and Tucker swallowed hard.

"I've been thinking about you. Ever since I had my blade on your throat." Randall petted the trigger. "It's been a while since I've killed anyone. I miss the look in their eyes as life drains out of them." He twisted the barrel against Tucker's chest. "After you are dead, do you know what will happen to you? We'll toss your body in the ocean and that will be the end of you. A forgotten lost boy eaten by little fishes."

Tucker's legs wobbled. He knew the score, dammit! Why was he doing this?

A knock sounded at the door, and Tucker nearly fainted, thinking the trigger had been pulled.

Randall winked at Tucker. "Saved by the bell." He lowered the weapon and answered the door. "Yes, boss?"

"It's the first Tuesday of the month," Stanton said. "Clear out for an hour."

Randall nodded. "Just finishing up anyway. Boy, get out of here."

Tucker sped out of the room and down the corridor. He walked the halls aimlessly for some time as his heart pounded and his chest ached. He couldn't remember what his next job was supposed to be or where he was supposed to go, but he knew if he were found being idle, someone would snitch on him.

Not sure how, he stumbled his way into the kitchen. Sally was preparing drinks on a metal cart, and he joined her.

"Are you alright?" Sally whispered to him, placing her hand over his. Tucker pulled it away. He didn't want sympathy from the girls. He was a guy after all. Wasn't he supposed to be the brave one?

"Isn't it your night to collect laundry?" she said.

Tucker closed his eyes tight. During dinner, the staff would leave baskets of laundry in the hall for them. He was already late collecting them.

Tucker left the kitchen for the staff quarters once more, but as he entered the hall, tightness clutched his throat. He stood there, sweating, staring at the carpet while his brain screamed for him to move. With a shudder, he forced himself forward. Going down the line, Tucker stacked the baskets on top of the other until he couldn't carry any more and took them to the laundry. He was on his last round when the sound of a knob turning came from down the hall.

Randall's door.

Heart pounding, Tucker tried the knobs as he moved down the hall. To his surprise, one of the doors opened, and he dropped the baskets and entered just in time.

Tucker leaned against the door, his breaths coming in heaves. Peeking through the peephole, he saw Randall go down the hall and sighed. He would give him a couple of moments to leave the hallway before venturing out once more. Most of the staff would be eating, and hopefully not be back any time soon.

Tucker brushed sweat from his brow as he glanced around the room. Whoever stayed here kept a tidy place, but a bag of beef jerky sat on the table, and his mouth watered once more. Tucker stole a couple of strips from the bag and tucked them in his pockets. Next to the table sat a footlocker, and Tucker stole a few granola bars from there too.

The door beeped, and Tucker whipped his head around. Someone was unlocking the keypad.

Tucker scampered into the closet, surrounding himself with clothes reeking of laundry detergent and men's deodorant. The door opened, and the occupant entered with muted steps. Tucker prayed for them to leave again. If he was found here, he doubted flogging would satisfy their rage.

"What'll he send this time? A blender?" a girl asked, and Tucker frowned. Was that Katie's voice? Had he taken shelter in Jack's room?

"I don't know. It'll depend on how small of a device he can hide it in. Or even if this plan works. Are you sure—" Jack stopped mid-sentence, and Tucker slipped further into the closet behind the hanging clothes until his back was against the wall.

"What is it?" Katie said.

"Shh!"

Tucker's heart drummed. Had he left something out? Jack knew he was here. Somehow, he knew…

"We're clear," Jack said, and Tucker pressed against the wall to stay standing.

"What was that?" Katie asked.

"It sweeps for listening devices. Another present from your brother."

Her brother?

"Someone's been in here," Jack said. "Probably Stanton. He searches our quarters once a month." The springs on the bed creaked and a thump sounded on the floor. "Anyways, I'll ask Alec if he can build a virus like that, but are you sure that installing a virus via memory stick is actually a thing? Or is that just something you saw in a movie?"

Installing a virus? On whose laptop? Who was this guy?

"I dunno," she said. "But now that we can talk with him through the satellite phone—"

The door to the closet ripped open, and Jack slid the clothes to the side.

"Shit!" Jack scrambled away, and Katie screamed. Tucker flattened against the wall as they stared back at him.

"Tucker! What the hell are you doing?" Katie exclaimed.

Tucker clutched his hair and shielded his face with his forearms. "I'm sorry," he cried. "I'm so sorry. It was an accident—"

"You broke into my room?" Jack looked between him and Katie. "Shit!"

"Th-the door was open," Tucker said. "When you came back-"

"I never leave my door open," Jack snarled.

"Stanton must have," Katie said. "When they checked your room."

"I'm sorry." Tucker crashed to his knees. "I didn't mean anything by it. Please! Please, don't hurt me." Jack pulled his gun from his belt, and Tucker let out a moan.

"Jared, what are you doing?" cried Katie.

"He heard everything, Katie. If he's a snitch—"

"He's not a snitch!"

"We can't risk it."

Clutching his head, Tucker let out another moan.

"You would do this?" Katie's voice caught. "You would betray your own people? Kill them to save your ass—"

"Katie—"

"If you do this, Jared, I will *never* forgive you."

Jack sneered at her, tugged on the slide, and pressed the gun into Tucker's scalp. Tucker clutched his stomach and rocked back and forth. So, this was it. This was how it would end.

But the gun rattled in Jack's hand.

"Please—" A tear slid down Tucker's cheek. "Please, just do it. I can't take this anymore. Please."

Jack swore and lowered his weapon. "Dammit, kid."

Tucker gasped and fell forward. His eyes blurred as he buried his fingers into the carpet. Katie placed a hand on his shoulder, but he could not focus her in his vision.

Jack flopped down into the armchair and tossed his pistol onto the table. "I hope you're right, Katie," he said. "Because if not, we're all dead."

*   *   *

A cup of chamomile and lavender tea cooled in Tucker's hands while Katie explained who Jared was and why he was here. All the while, Jared sat with his hands peaked, observing Tucker and his stolen glances.

Jared still wondered if he should have fired the bullet. From what he had seen of the kid's life, it would seem almost merciful. Now everything hinged on the better nature of this boy, including Tucker's own survival. But would he have the strength to see that? Would he be able to see past a warm bowl of soup to eventual freedom? Would the pellagra let him?

Why hadn't he just done it? Why hadn't he pulled that trigger knowing that it could save them all?

But the answer was obvious. It was for the same damn reason he'd been feeding this kid when he knew he shouldn't have. Tucker was one of his people, and more than that, he was a reflection of Jared himself. To kill him would be to kill part of himself.

"Have I lost you anywhere, Tucker?" Katie said. "Do you understand?"

Tucker set the mug on the table and rubbed his eyes. He glanced at Jared, but quickly looked away.

"You may speak, if that's what you're waiting for," Jared said, but Tucker stared at the table in front of him. "Give me something, kid. Your silence is unnerving."

"I don't trust you," Tucker said, barely audible.

"No shit," Jared said then sighed. "I don't expect you to, Tucker, but do you trust Katie?"

"I did," he muttered.

"I'm not lying to you, Tucker," Katie said. "Why would I lie about this?"

"Because the truth is unfathomable," Jared said. "So, the alternative is that we're lying."

"You're a murderer…and a rapist," Tucker said.

Katie shook her head. "He's not a rapist."

"Murderer's not bad enough?"

"I haven't killed anyone you'd care about," Jared said. "And if you tell me there's no one whom you'd like to shank yourself, I'd call you a liar."

Tucker looked away. "A guy like you couldn't possibly know what—"

Jared, who knew where this was going, stood and removed his shirt showing the carnage on his back. Tucker's mouth parted.

"As you were saying?" Jared pulled the shirt back over his head. Tucker returned to silence, and Jared lit a cigarette with his trembling fingers. Smoke puffed around him and collected on the ceiling.

"What do you want from me?" Tucker said.

"I need you to keep your mouth shut," Jared said. "Something you've been good at for the past twenty minutes."

"Twenty minutes?" Tucker sat up. "Shit. I'm late—"

"What excuse do you need?" Jared said.

"Excuse? There's nothing I can say that will—"

Jared stood and checked his watch. "I brought up one of the bloody seats from the boat. Katie and I got nowhere on it today.

Let's you and I go check it out. Katie, you finish…whatever job Tucker was going to do, and tell them I poached him."

"That should work." Katie smiled at Tucker and patted his shoulder, but Jared's stomach was too sour to share the sentiment.

"Come with me, Tucker." Jared walked to the door.

For a moment, Tucker hesitated, but then joined Katie and him. After checking both ways, Jared led them out of the apartment. Katie picked up the laundry baskets outside the door, and Tucker followed Jared to the back entrance.

Tucker kept his eyes to the floor, but continued to sneak occasional glances in Jared's direction. Whether for good or for ill, he was stuck with Tucker. If he had to pick between him and Katie, however, the choice was clear. He hoped it wouldn't come to that.

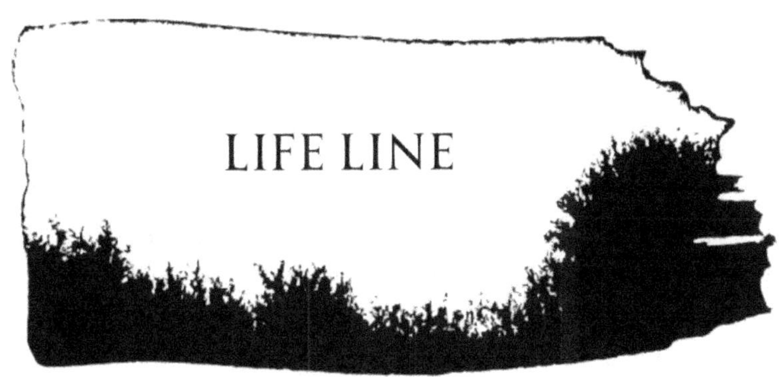

LIFE LINE

By the time the movie of the night ended, Jared was asleep, his head resting on the headboard. Katie smiled at him, glad to see him so peaceful. Although the beard had added quite a bit of age to his features, Katie could still see her friend if she looked close enough. If she guessed his age now, she would say twenty-eight or twenty-nine. To think he was barely out of his teens…

Katie pulled the covers up around both of their necks and rested her head on his shoulder. Soon, sleep overtook her as well.

Some hours later, Jared bolted straight up, and Katie slid off his chest. "Hmm?" she muttered, glancing around the room. Jared stared down at her with wide eyes, and his fists clenched and unclenched the sheets.

She straightened. "What is it?"

Jared leaped from the bed and paced the floor. Sweat formed on his brow, and he folded and unfolded his hands. Grunting loudly, he closed his eyes tight.

"Jared?"

"I'm fine," he snapped then pinched the bridge of his nose. "It's a panic attack. It will pass." He paced back and forth, wringing his hands and running them repeatedly through his hair. Katie slid from the bed and placed a hand on his shoulder.

"Don't touch me!" He swatted her hand away then winced. "Please."

Katie backed away with her hands up. "Okay."

Jared retrieved a mug from the cabinet, but his hands shook, and the mug teetered wildly. As he attempted to fill it at the tap, water sloshed out of the sides, and Katie took it from him.

"Microwave it. One minute." Jared smashed the button on a strange round machine beside the griddle, and a cloud of mist spewed out the top. The smell of lavender filled the room, and he returned to pacing.

When the timer beeped, Jared rummaged through his footlocker and brought out a bag of tea. Katie submerged the packet and handed the mug to him. Hot water spilled out the sides, and she took it back.

Jared sat on the floor, leaned his back against the bed, and brought his knees to his chest. With his eyes closed, he took deep, ragged breaths and held them. "Dammit!" he interjected here and there before continuing with his breaths. His fingers dug into the carpet.

Katie took a seat at the table and watched with interest. He acted so calm most of the time. Like stone. His hands did not shake as much, and sometimes Katie forgot how terrified he was.

After a few minutes, Jared was able to take the tea from Katie and sipped on it slowly. Katie slid down to the floor beside him. "Can I help?"

Jared shook his head. "Just stay with me, please."

"You had a nightmare, didn't you?" she asked, and he nodded fervently. "Do you want to talk about it?"

"No," he said firmly. "Not…not now."

"Okay." Katie folded and unfolded her hands; his anxiety jarred her own nerves. Ever so slowly, the shaking in his hands diminished as he sipped on his tea.

Finally, Jared slid his hand into hers and caressed it lightly. "I'm sorry."

Katie frowned. "For what?"

"For freaking you out."

Katie laughed half-heartedly. "It takes more than that to freak me out." He squeezed her hand. "Would you like to talk about it now?" she asked.

Jared stared down at the tea bag swimming in the water. "I almost shot Tucker tonight."

"But you didn't."

"I came really close, Katie," Jared said. "I *really* did. I just…" He ran his hands over his face. "I've been walking in the dark, out here on my own for so long, I don't even know what's right and wrong anymore. I'm really screwed up…"

"But you did the right thing in the end," she said, and, as he looked at her, his eyes misted.

Abruptly, Jared checked his watch and stood. "I'm not going to sleep much for the rest of the night, but you should go ahead and try." He grabbed his cigarettes from the table, slid open the sliding glass door, and stepped into the courtyard.

Katie hesitated, wondering if she should get him to come back so she could comfort him some more. But if he wanted that, he wouldn't have stepped outside. There were only a couple more hours left in the night for her to get some rest, so she climbed back in bed.

Through a slit in the curtains, she saw the glow of Jared's cigarette rise and fall. What had he dreamed about? Somehow, he had still managed not to tell her. Something about Tucker—did he dream he killed him?

Katie liked Tucker. He was one of her people. But what if Jared's initial instinct had been correct? What if all this fell apart because of Tucker? They really would all be dead.

*   *   *

After his morning run, Jared cleaned up and made his way back down to the garage to find Tucker sitting by the door. The boy looked up at him with a scowl as Jared unlocked the padlock and lifted the bay door. With a jerk of the head, Jared indicated for him to enter, and Tucker rose slowly and dusted the dirt from his pants.

"I've given up on the seats," Jared said. "Stanton's going to order some new ones. Can you think of anything else that needs to be done?"

Tucker shrugged. His scowl remained fixed.

What crawled up his butt and died?

Jared could have shot him last night, but didn't. That should mean something. Or was he just making his distrust of him loud and clear?

Jared walked to the beginning of the dock and looked out over the ocean. The waves lapped against the sides of the wooden posts. It was as if the world itself was breathing in and breathing out with each roll. He didn't think there were any listening devices in the bay, but just in case, he walked to the end of the dock where the ocean would interfere with any such device.

Tucker hesitated at the beginning of the dock, but when Jared gestured for him to follow once more, he continued on. Jared sat and dangled his legs off the end, and Tucker sat cross-legged next to him.

"I know you don't trust me," Jared said. "And I can't blame you either. But since I'm your only shot off this God-forsaken island, you might want to consider it."

"You may have Katie fooled," Tucker said, "but I've been around you long enough to know you're not one of the good guys."

"I never claimed to be a good guy. But I came here to bring Katie home and destroy Midas. You can get on board that train, but only if you keep your mouth shut. If you get in the way, Tucker, I will kill you."

Tucker sneered and faced the ocean. "I have enough information to have you killed first."

Jared's brows rose. *So that's how he is going to play it.*

"Fair enough. But if you do, you will never leave this island. And the next time Randall knocks you off a boat, there won't be anyone jumping in after you."

Tucker's mouth parted, and he turned to Jared. For the first time, he met Jared's eyes.

Jared cleared his throat, uncomfortable with the sustained look. "Look, I can't say I'm thrilled about this situation either. And I think that if you were going to turn me in, you would have done it by now. So, I'm prepared to roll with our current status quo if you are."

After checking behind himself just to be sure there were no observers, Jared pulled out a foil package and handed it to Tucker.

As the boy unwrapped it, the smell of sausage and egg from the breakfast burrito wafted up. Tucker did not devour it immediately as he had previously done but stared at the morsel instead. Then a sob erupted from his throat, and Jared whipped his head around. Tears collected in Tucker's eyes.

Is he seriously about to cry?

Jared checked over his shoulder once more, but there was no one coming from the garage. "What the hell, kid?"

Tucker hugged himself and rocked. "You—you jumped in after me. But you said. . ."

"You need to cool it," Jared said. "If somebody comes…"

Tucker smacked his hand across his mouth and stifled another sob.

Jared stared, mouth agape. It was just a little food, just the absence of abuse. He considered sending him to the bathroom, but Tucker would have to walk facing the door. If anyone saw him in such a state, they might ask questions. But he didn't know what to do about him either.

He couldn't put his arm around him to comfort him, but if anyone came by, he could always shove Tucker into the water. That would stop the crying. So, Jared stared out into the ocean and let him weep.

*   *   *

That evening, Katie walked in-step with Sally as they left the kitchen for the night and entered their room in the back hallway. "I have something," she whispered as she pressed two granola bars into Sally's hand. "Can you help me distribute them?"

"Yes, ma'am," Sally said with a grin. The bars disappeared into her pockets, but not without the eyes of watchful children taking note first.

Once inside, Sally sat on her mat surrounded by the young ones. She pulled her blanket over her lap and broke the bars beneath the cover before slipping pieces into their expectant hands.

"I have some too," Katie whispered. She fluffed her mat, sat, and wrapped the blanket around her, distributing the food in similar fashion.

"Four bars," Sally marveled. "How'd you get such a score?"

"I stole them from Warner."

Tucker glanced at her then away, but Sally's mouth popped open. "You took four bars from him? In one go? Katie, that's reckless!"

She shrugged and slipped out the last of the bars to Selena. If the six-year-old thought a grasshopper was a treat, she'd think the granola bar a banquet. Jared hadn't given Katie the snacks, but she didn't think he would mind. And if he did, it wasn't like he was going to turn her in to the Watchers for it.

Tucker took his spot beside her and leaned against the wall. "Katie's the best thief here, Sally. I think she'll be fine."

Sally shook her head but said nothing else, choosing to attend to a young one with a splinter instead of arguing.

"Why aren't you keeping Jack company tonight?" Tucker whispered.

"He's playing poker with some of the Watchers," Katie answered. She lay on her back and folded her hands across her middle. Then she flipped to her side. Had the floor always been so uncomfortable?

"We haven't had a chance to talk much. How are you dealing with all this stuff?" she asked Tucker.

He rolled on his side to face her. "Well, I figured out why he's been feeding me this whole time. I should have picked up on it, but—"

"You weren't expecting it," Katie finished, and he nodded.

"What's his plan in all this? How's he going to get us out?"

Katie looked around at the others. They had been talking low enough for no one else to hear and most of the others were drifting off to sleep already. "My brother is building a computer virus on a memory stick that he's sending to us through the mail. Once it gets here, we just need to plug it into Stanton's computer. After that, my brother will be able to access his files remotely."

"But—how does that help us get off the island?"

"Well, that's just part of the issue," Katie said. "Jared wants to shut Midas down completely. Destroy him so no one else ends up like us."

"I just want to go home."

She smiled and took his hand. "Jared knows what he's doing. Just trust him. His loyalty to us comes first."

Tucker nodded, but his brow remained creased. As he lay back on his mat, Katie could tell he still wasn't sure, but time would show him.

Tucker and the others were asleep in minutes, but Katie continued to toss and turn. Had she become spoiled by sleeping in a bed? Or was it the better food that left her with more energy? But as she lay there not sleeping, her eyes kept wandering to the little red light on the surveillance camera.

When she had first come to the island, the little cameras everywhere had bothered her, but now she accepted them. The only place where there weren't cameras were the staff quarters. She guessed Midas's staff wouldn't like being spied on.

Katie sat up bolt straight. Of course, they wouldn't like that. No one would. What's more, it would be insulting to be surveyed so closely. An idea started forming in her mind, and she spent the rest of the night mulling it over.

Randall gaped at Jared. "You've *never* played poker?"

Jared's hand lay splayed before him on the table: a jack, queen, king, ace, and ten of hearts. "No, I've never played before."

Stanton laughed around his cigar and leaned back in his chair. "I think he's bluffing."

Jared shrugged and pulled the pot to himself. It was one of the rare times since he had been there that he wasn't lying. That was probably what was throwing them off.

"I'm gonna get another drink," Jared said, standing. "Anybody else want one?"

Randall and Tom raised their glasses, and Jared took them by the rims.

Stanton's apartment was larger than Jared's with the bedroom separate from the sitting room. He had pushed his couch against the wall and brought in a table and chairs from the bar. Stanton had fewer small appliances than Jared, preferring to eat the communal food rather than fix any meals himself, and his kitchenette counter was lined with glass decanters of assorted alcohols instead.

Jared set the glasses on the counter and glanced over his shoulder. The others were busy lighting new smokes or chatting.

Jared slid the small scotch tape dispenser from his pocket and eyed Tom's glass. A nice thumb print stood out along the side. Jared tore a bit of tape and pressed it against the print, then folded a bit of clean adhesive over it to preserve it. He had never taken prints without first applying some sort of powder before, and prayed this would work.

Randall's glass did not have a clear print, but that was fine because lingering much longer would cause suspicion. Instead, Jared poured the drinks, loading his own with ice to dilute the alcohol, and brought them back to the table.

"Bluffing or not, just know that I intend to rob you blind tonight, Warner," Randall said, accepting the glass.

Jared shrugged. "We'll see." There was no way in hell they would be able to read him tonight. He was nervous, sure, but not about any cards that may or may not be in his hand. *They* made him nervous. That coupled with the fact that Jared did not give a shit whether he won or lost made him indecipherable.

"Warner, there's another reason I asked you, Tom, and Randall to come by here tonight." Stanton set his cigar on the ashtray. "We found the source of the leak."

Jared paused with his hand on the cards. Had they found out he lied?

"One of our guys in the Myanmar Police Force said the tip originated from Arhrit's guys. The leak came from a mole in the seller's crew, not ours."

Jared's limbs thawed and he picked up his cards. They knew the truth, but his statement was not accusatory. "That's good to know."

"It certainly is. In a situation like this, however, a response is required. We've managed to secure a few moles of our own in Arhrit's crew, and now it's time to show Arhrit who's the boss in Myanmar. We're planning on making a move soon."

Jared took a drag off his cigarette and let out a puff of smoke. "So we're going to war with another operation?"

"If we do *this* right," Randall said, "there won't be an operation left to go to war with. We're planning a precision strike that will bring the operation to its knees."

Jared inclined his head in understanding but resisted the urge to gulp. If this were a hit of some sort, Jared wasn't sure he could stomach it. "An assassination?"

Stanton shook his head. "Nah, nothing *that* extreme. More like a raid. We got wind of a stash house just over the Thai border. A drought hit Arhrit's drugs earlier this season, so another loss of product might be enough to take him out. And, hopefully, it will make his bosses in China pissed off enough that they'll drop him and go for us."

"Won't his bosses be a little concerned that it was us causing the problem to begin with?"

"Half this business is security," Randall said. "If you can't keep what's yours, then you have no business owning it to begin with."

"Midas has an exceptional record for keeping his goods," Stanton said. "One that you preserved the other day with Lionel. It's why you're moving up."

Exceptional record minus the 224 kids he lost.

"Alright, so what does that mean for me?" Jared took a sip of his brandy.

"It means we get to work together." Randall grinned and smacked him on the shoulder.

"You and Randall are going to plan this operation, and then *you're* going to lead it."

Jared choked on the drink.

"Aw, you've scared him, Stanton!" Randall smirked. "Don't worry, kid. I'm going to be with you just in case. But if you're going to be part of this team, it's time we gave you some *real* responsibility."

Jared laughed nervously.

"So, whatcha think?" Stanton asked.

Jared set down the glass and looked at each of the Watchers in turn. "Yeah. Yeah, I'm in."

Stanton smiled. "Good to hear it. Now Randall, deal us another round. And this time, send the good cards to me!"

*　　　*　　　*

Jared set his pistol on top of the TV stand and collapsed into a nearby chair. Shaking his head, he replied, "No. It's too risky," to Katie's idea as he kicked his shoes off into a corner.

Katie bounced as she sat on his bed. "You did the same thing only a couple of years back!"

"Yeah," Jared said, "and it was a dumb idea then too. What if the air ducts collapse? You'd be caught in another room. They will kill you."

"I'll be careful. And you'll be there to back me up."

Jared ran his hands over his eyes. Not only did he have this little operation to run with Randall, now he had to deal with *this* hair brained scheme.

"I can always break into Stanton's office and plant the little virus—"

"No," Jared balked. "Hell, no. I don't even know if *I'll* be able to do that one."

Katie stood, arms wide. "Then let me do this! I want to help!"

"It's not your job to help. It's your job to survive."

"That's bullshit, Jared! I have as much right to take down Midas as you do!"

Jared sneered at her as he floundered for a good comeback. The plan wasn't a bad one, but the risk was still too high—for Katie. "Look, if anyone is going to do it, it's going to be me."

After fumbling through the TV stand drawer, he pulled out a webcam and dragged a chair beneath the air duct between the bathroom and the TV stand. Using his multi-tool, he unscrewed the grate and peered into the black hole.

Katie placed a hand on her hip. "You're never going to fit. You've grown too much."

Ignoring her, Jared grabbed the vent with his fingertips and pulled up. He pressed his palms on either side of the duct and tried to wiggle inside, but his shoulders were lodged at the entrance. He dropped back into the chair. Damn bar food.

"May I try?" Katie's huffy, feminine voice asked over his shoulder.

Jared's lip curled as he turned back to her. *This is a bad idea*, played over in his mind again, but no better idea replaced it. "If the vents sag even a little bit, you're coming back."

Katie snatched the camera and stepped up to the chair, as if barely resisting the urge to knock him from it. With a final mumbled complaint, Jared stepped off the chair and allowed her to take his place. As she gripped the edges of the vent, however, Jared took hold of her calf.

"If you get caught," he said, "I'm not going to let them flog you. I will kill them before that happens. Which means we'll probably both die. Don't. Get. Caught."

Katie's brow furrowed. "You know I've already been flogged, don't you?"

An image of her screaming in pain tore through his mind. "Doesn't matter," he said hoarsely. "I'm not going to stand by and watch that."

"You would screw us both for—"

"Yes," he snarled. "So don't get caught."

Katie's mouth parted at his adamant response. Then, with a deep breath, she turned back to the vent, jumped, and pulled herself through. Jared took her legs and eased her in.

*   *   *

Dust shifted as Katie slid through the shaft, and she buried her face into her arm to stifle a sneeze. She doubted a couple of years ago *she* would have been able to fit either. It was amazing how much weight-loss she had endured, but she shoved these thoughts away. She had a mission to complete.

They only had the one webcam, so this was only going to be a test run for the actual plan. The air duct merged with a line of larger ducts, but the turn was sharp, and Katie's side caught on the corner of the vent. It took quite a bit of squirming, but she was finally through. Katie quickly found out that the ducts did not cross the hallway but stayed only on this side of the staff quarters. Perhaps they could get away with only half of the rooms having cameras? If she went far enough through the ducts, would she be able to loop back to the other side?

Then after that, would they be able to map out the whole building? Then they could enter any room they chose in this manner! Why hadn't she thought of this before?

Immediately, she knew why. Because she had been so tired and hungry before. And there had been no reason to plan or hope.

Katie took a left at the end of the hall. As she pulled up to the grate, she immediately regretted doing so. The video on the TV screen was not something she ever wanted to see. Katie set the camera at the edge of the grate peering in and backed away.

Katie returned to Jared's room, but as she reached the grate, the sound of a door shutting echoed through the vents.

"Warner—" Stanton said, and Katie froze. "I need to run something by you."

"Oh?" Jared said. "Whatcha got?"

Katie's eyes widened as she stared ahead at the open grate. Would he question that? As quietly as she could, she slid backwards. She didn't make the turn for fear of causing some sort of noise. Instead, she moved back until her feet hit the wall. *Please don't look,* she prayed.

"I brought you the house schematics for the job we were talking about last night. I've given the other copy to Randall, but he's going off-island tonight. Go ahead and get familiar with it though, then you two can brainstorm on how you want to hit this place, alright?"

"Three floors. That's a lot of rooms."

"You don't have to memorize it or anything," Stanton said. "Just get familiar with it."

Katie smiled. Jared could probably have an entire neighborhood memorized by the time Randall got back.

"Why is your vent open?" Stanton asked, and a knot formed in Katie's throat.

Come on Jared. Lie!

"I was looking for a place to stash my gun," Jared said, and Katie heard a scrape—probably as he pulled the pistol off the TV stand. She relaxed a little. Sometimes she envied his ability to lie like that.

"That's a hard place to get it from if you ever needed it quickly," Stanton said.

"That would be true—if it were my only piece laying around."

Stanton laughed. "Alright, then. But don't forget, you have a Comm in here pretty often. Just make sure to keep your toys put away so she can't get them."

And just how far did he think she'd get with a gun? All of his men carried one. She would never be able to shoot her way off this island.

"Will do, boss," Jared said, and Stanton left, closing the door behind him.

After a few moments, Jared whispered, "Katie!" into the hole, and Katie squirmed on through and out into his arms.

"Robert now has a private TV channel," she said as she dusted herself off. "But after seeing his choice in shows, I'd rather not watch it."

"We'll see if Alec can send us some more cameras."

"Soooo—" Katie said, "are you going to say it or what? I did good, didn't I?"

"Yes, you did." He patted her on the head. "Good, Katie."

She swatted the hand away but smiled. "Jerk."

Jared laughed, and Katie climbed onto his bed and leaned against the headboard. He joined her. "Would you like to watch a movie tonight? Or are you too tired?"

"Go ahead and put one on," she said. "If I fall asleep, I fall asleep. Do you want to finish *Die Hard?*"

"Eh, too close to real life," Jared said. "How about something lighter. Disney?"

Jared selected *Beauty and the Beast*, and they sat watching the movie together for some time. As the romance grew between Belle and the Beast, Katie's thoughts regarding herself and the boy next to her tumbled around in her head. Was Jared her Beast? Minus the hair of course. He was a decidedly unattractive boy as they grew up, but he had blossomed into something else. She considered her contribution to this transformation minimal, but it left her scratching her head.

It was incredible, what he had done by coming for her. Even if she thought he had survived, she never would have imagined him doing so. And he hadn't asked anything of her after all.

Or was he still working up the nerve?

"Thank you," Katie said, and Jared peered down at her in question. "For coming for me."

He took her hand and squeezed it. "Of course. You are one of my people."

Katie bit her lip. And because he loved her. He had said it whether or not he was going to admit it again. She knew what he wanted too, whether or not he was going to admit that either.

Katie returned the squeeze, placed a hand on his cheek, and pulled him into a kiss. His eyes pinched closed as he returned the gesture, and Katie recalled their first kiss. Alone in the safehouse with Clayton just outside the door. His mouth had tasted of cigarettes then too, but this time, she found it less offensive. She kissed him again, and Jared slid his hand beneath her hair, drawing her closer.

A shiver tore up Katie's spine. A flashback changed Jared into Midas, but Katie forced herself to ignore it. Another flash, and Katie pressed her lips firmer against Jared's, trying to drive the image out. She slid her hand under his shirt.

Jared's eyes flitted open as her hands ran against his bare skin, and she kissed him again, her lips running against his neck. If she kept going, if she distracted herself from the flashes, they would go away, wouldn't they? After all, she was the one running this show. She was in control. Katie slid her hand against the inside of his upper thigh.

Jared grabbed her wrist, and Katie froze. Her breath caught, and Midas's face came into view. His hands clutched her wrists, pinning them above her head—

"Katie," Jared's voice came softly, shattering the illusion. A gentle hand rested on her cheek, raising her face to his own, but she would not meet his eyes. "Katie, that's a bit fast, don't you think?"

She stole a glance at his face to find his brow pinched. Was that anger? A sob caught in her throat. "Don't be angry."

"What?" His scowl deepened, and Katie wrapped her arms around herself. Her chest felt like fire as her breaths came fast and shallow.

"I'm sorry!" she cried. "I'm sorry. I thought…but of course, not after everything. I'm stupid. I'm just so stupid…of course you don't want me."

Jared took her hands into his own shaking hands and inhaled a quivering breath. "Katie, I am not angry at you. Please, just look at my face and you'll see that I'm not."

With deliberate effort, Katie raised her eyes to his before hiding them beneath her hands.

"This has nothing to do with what *I* want," Jared said. "I just think we might need to slow things down, okay? In fact, I'm sorry I let things get as far as they did."

Katie frowned as she peered up through the tangles of hair that had fallen across her eyes. *He* was sorry? But that didn't make any sense. None of this made sense.

"Katie, do you love me?" he asked, and Katie's mouth fell open. "Hell, do you even like me?"

Katie stared at the sheets. Did that matter? He had come to save her. What did he want her to say? Yes?

Would he know if she were lying?

Jared rubbed her hand with his thumb. "You don't owe me anything. If you feel that you do, then—"

What?

Fire boiled within her chest. "You arrogant son of a bitch."

"Katie—"

"If you don't want me, then just say that you don't want me." She slid off the bed. "Don't pretend that this—"

"That's not what I'm saying."

"What are you doing here anyway, Jared? It's not your job to save me. You've come all this way to find me, and now what? I don't meet your standards? Well, sorry, but life hasn't exactly been good to me, you know? And if you want to talk about standards, let's talk about standards. When I first met you, you were a scrawny piece of nothing who couldn't even write his own name. I was repulsed by you and your stinking breath and everything else about you. So how dare you? How dare you treat me like some old whore?"

Jared stared at the bed. His shoulders rose and fell with deliberation. Abruptly, he stood, marched to the sliding door, and slammed it shut behind him

Katie stared after him with mouth ajar. Had she really just said all of that? Why had she said that? He was her only hope and—

Jared opened the door again and slid it closed quietly behind him. The hand at his side clenched and unclenched as he kept his eyes on the floor. "If we are ever to be together, Katie…" He met her eyes with his piercing green. "It will not be on this island." Then he stepped out into the courtyard once more.

With trembling hands, she reached behind her for the wall and slid down against it. Tears poured down her cheeks as Belle and the Beast danced a tale as old as time.

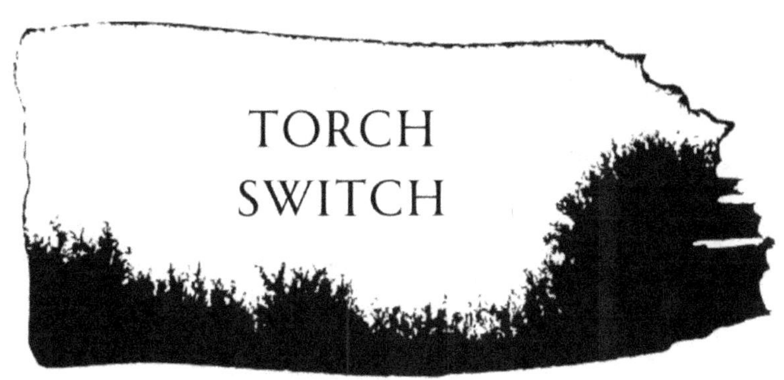

Tucker stared off into the ocean, his legs dangling above the water as he sat on the docks next to Jared. "You said Katie could fit. Why can't she do it?"

"Because I don't have a good excuse to be in the house with her during the day," Jared said.

A little over a week had passed since the air duct plan had come into play, and the video cameras had arrived in the mail that morning. If Katie knew about them, she'd have demanded to be the one to install them all—even the ones across the hall. But Jared wasn't going to risk that.

Instead, Jared came to Tucker. That's what boys were supposed to do, right? Take the risky jobs so the girls wouldn't have to? At least, that's how he had always reasoned it. It was why he chose Dakota as a hut leader rather than Leida. He had made Olivia a hut leader only because they were short on boys. Hut leaders were flogged more often than the others, and he despised watching girls get whipped. But he wasn't going to tell Tucker that. He might disagree, and Jared needed his cooperation.

The waves curled and collapsed onto themselves before shattering on the dock, again shielding them from prying ears.

Tucker was slow in answering, but Jared remained patient. A forced answer would probably be a negative one, so he waited.

"You'll have my back, right?" Tucker asked. "If I fall through the vent shafts—"

"I'll be right there," Jared said. What he was going to do right then and there, he had no idea. But he'd be there alright.

"Fine," Tucker whispered. "Fine, I'll do it."

Jared clamped his hand on the boy's shoulder. "This will be another step closer to home for you too."

Tucker smiled uneasily.

Before they went up to the house, Jared stepped in a camera blind spot in the corner of the garage and sloshed oil on his teal shirt.

"What'd you do that for?" Tucker asked.

"We need a reason to go back to the house," Jared said.

Jared led the way back up the path to the mansion. No one questioned them when they turned into the staff quarters. More often than not, people wouldn't, but it was never a bad idea to play it safe. Once inside his room, Jared set the chair beneath the grate and unscrewed it once more.

"Don't take any risks," Jared said. "If any part of the vent shaft feels too unstable, just come out."

The cameras were small, about two inches by two inches. Jared had considered getting something a bit bigger—and more noticeable, but multiple trips would have been required with something so bulky.

Once loaded up, Tucker began to rub his arm once more, and Jared bit the inside of his cheek. He really shouldn't be asking this of Tucker, but it was a decent plan.

He shook his head, removing all sentimentalities. "Alright then. Off you go."

Tucker was taller than Katie, but still thin enough to slide inside. The Watcher diet did wonders on those trying to sneak into air ducts. Once Tucker was inside, Jared stepped into the hall and lit a cigarette. No one else was around at that time. Half the guys were off-island while the other half were doing their side job—or having the kids do it for them.

Jared strained his ears for any sounds of disturbance coming from the other rooms in that hall but heard nothing. In his mind, he tracked Tucker's projected path and the estimated timing for the job to be completed. As he finished his second cigarette, he heard a knock coming from his own room and stepped back inside.

Jared locked the deadbolt before moving to the vent shaft. Tucker, whose face was covered in dust, peered out at him from the hole in the wall. Grabbing his arms, Jared pulled him out of the vent. He was a bit heavier than Katie, however, and the weight threw him off balance. The chair toppled and they landed with Jared on his back and Tucker on top of him, face-to-face.

Tucker rolled away and coughed, and Jared straightened his collar before standing. That would have been sexy had it been Katie. Jared wasn't sure if that would have been better or worse considering the ice that had settled over their relationship since the other night.

"Ready for part two?" Jared asked.

"Not really. Are you sure he's gone?"

"Supposed to be off-island until tomorrow," Jared said. "You saw him leave this morning yourself."

Tucker shook his head. "I don't like this, man—"

"I've got your back, remember?" Jared knelt next to the bed and slid an envelope out from a hidden pocket in the mattress where he had stashed Tom's fingerprint. "And remember, 7-5-6-2-5." The fingerprint he had collected on poker night, and the numbers he had observed Tom punching in the other night after dinner.

Tucker mumbled the number under his breath and nodded.

"For freedom," Jared said, and Tucker's face crinkled in resolve. Taking a deep breath, the boy marched to the glass sliding door and stepped outside.

Damn, Jared hoped this worked.

Jared watched from the peephole to see Tucker arrive back in the hallway from his trip around the courtyard. Once he was at Tom's door, Jared left through the backdoor as well. The courtyard had a stone floor and a concrete fountain in the center. He had taken many smoke breaks lounging in the chairs on the nights he couldn't sleep and didn't want to wake Katie.

Upon entering the courtyard, Jared took a left and entered a back hall. Here, he passed by the private laundry and an ice machine. Midas's paradise island was a legitimate hotel before it was a blackmail factory, and the courtyard for the apartments on the other side of the hall had a pool area with a Tiki bar and a hot tub. No one was there at this time of day, but Jared spotted a security camera at the corner of the building.

Jared strolled as casually as possible to Tom's door and tapped twice on the glass. Tucker slid the door open just a crack, and Jared brought a cigarette to his mouth and covered it with his hand to light it. "All good?"

"So far," Tucker whispered.

Jared took a puff and looked out over the pool area. "Then hurry."

"Right."

Jared glanced inside, taking in the room as quickly as possible. It was quite the mess, and a strange smell wafted from the door. At first, Jared thought it was pot, but that wasn't quite it. Above the unmade bed was the grate, and Tucker set to unscrewing it as quickly as possible. Soon, he scampered up inside the vent and disappeared.

Jared leaned against the glass door and smoked. His hands shook, and sweat rolled down his forehead. *Come on, kid.*

After what seemed an eternity, a bump sounded from inside the room, and Jared glanced back into the darkness. Tucker pushed himself out onto the bed and flopped with as much grace as a seal. He gave Jared a thumbs-up as he dusted the grime off his shirt and hair.

"See you in my room." Dropping the cigarette onto the concrete slabs, Jared fast-walked to the end of the pool area and back through the door. As he re-entered his room, he heard shouting from the other side of the door. *Shit!*

In the hallway, Stanton had Tucker pinned up against the wall. "I'm sorry!" Tucker cried. "Th-the door was open—"

"What the hell happened?" Jared asked.

"Where were you?" Stanton demanded.

"Taking a shit. I told him to wait in the hall—"

Stanton smacked Tucker against the ear. "Little thief!"

"Well, what did he steal?"

Stanton backed away as Jared approached, and Tucker looked up at Jared pleadingly.

Jared forced his face to remain neutral. Uninvolved. Jack Warner didn't care about Tucker. Instead, he grabbed Tucker's shirt collar and shoved him face first against the wall.

"Please," Tucker mumbled. "Please—"

"Shut up." Jared reached into Tucker's front pocket and pulled out a granola bar. Tucker's eyes widened in awe—it hadn't been there before Jared pulled it out.

Jared purposefully ignored the rectangle-shaped bulge around Tucker's belt line. He knew a hidden knife when he saw one. With a little sleight of hand, he managed to find another granola bar in the other pocket as well.

Turning Tucker around, Jared pressed his palm to his chest to pin him there. "Just food as far as I can tell."

"Please…" Tucker fell to his knees. "Please, I was just so hungry. And…and the door was open—"

Stanton smacked him. "I ought to kill you where you stand."

"I thought you flogged them for stealing," blurted Jared.

Stanton stopped for a moment, considering Jared. "You haven't ever seen that, have you, Warner?"

Jared swallowed hard and forced his face to remain neutral. *Better than dead,* he told himself. But the look on Tucker's face was one of utter betrayal.

"Nope, I haven't," he told Stanton.

"No!" Tucker cried, but Stanton jerked his arm, dragging him along to the door. "No—please—Jack! Jack, come on!"

Jared followed behind mechanically.

Stanton dragged Tucker out the front walk and to a palm tree right off the path. Ignoring Tucker's pleas and protests, he stripped him of his shirt and tied his hands to the trunk. The whip he fetched from a hook on the wall hidden behind a bush.

"Jack," Tucker said, tears in his eyes. "Jack, please—"

But Jared stood there, jaw clenched. There was nothing he could do now.

When the first strike came down, Jared jumped. But then he widened his stance and folded his shaking hands behind his back. This had always been a possibility. It was why he had chosen Tucker in the first place.

When the next blow came, Tucker screamed and slumped against his bonds.

It was only temporary. Either Tucker was to endure this, or they would all die. He'd thank him later. Once he was free.

Maybe.

Was he lying to himself now too?

His hands shook violently, and he lit another cigarette.

The blows continued while Jared watched, sucking on his cigarette. In his quest to find something else to watch, anything else to watch, he glanced over his shoulder to find Katie standing by the door. Her mouth was parted, her eyes wide as she looked at Jared.

Jared ripped his eyes away from her. She would understand later. Not today. Not tomorrow even, but later. When the ends justified the means.

Jared glanced at the security camera in the hall as he opened the door to the Comm room. Another camera hung on the wall next to the door, and he pushed it away with the barrel of his pistol.

Tucker glanced over his shoulder as he approached, then closed his eyes tight and scrunched his pillow. "What do you want?" the boy asked with a trembling voice. The red, bloody stripes on his back shimmered in the overhead light.

Jared knelt beside him and placed his black duffle bag on the floor. "I'm going to take a look at your wounds."

"Just leave me alone, asshole." A tear slid down his cheek. "Haven't you done enough to me?"

Ignoring the internal monologue of self-loathing he had been reciting to himself for the past hour, Jared pulled an aerosol can from the bag and shook it. "This is going to be cold, but it will help."

Tucker groaned as he sprayed the can onto the wounds, but after a few seconds, he loosened his grip on the pillow. "What is that stuff?"

"Numbing spray. It won't help entirely, but maybe it will take the edge off. Here, take this pain pill." Jared placed the tablet on the edge of Tucker's lips.

The boy scowled at him but opened his mouth.

"I'm putting two more in your pocket. Take them four hours apart. I'll send more with Katie later." Jared wetted a handful of gauze with a plastic bottle of saline, then doused Tucker's back liberally with the solution.

Tucker tensed. "Wow, that's cold."

As gently as possible, Jared dabbed at the wounds. Tears still filled Tucker's eyes, but not nearly as many as there would have been before. After drying his back with a towel, Jared applied a slick cream. "I'm going to put on a clean dressing pad, but it'll be a dead giveaway that I was here if it is seen, so keep it covered with your blanket."

"You moved the camera. Isn't that a sign enough?"

"If anyone was watching at the time, sure. But it was worth the risk. I'm sorry."

"You betrayed me," Tucker said. "You swore you'd protect me and—"

"I kept you from getting shot, Tucker," Jared said. "I kept Stanton from finding the cameras—"

"To save your own ass. Why are you here, Jack? To save us, or to kill Midas?"

"Both."

Tucker balled his pillow up tighter. "Yeah, and if it comes down to one or the other, which will you pick?"

"I'm going to end all this, Tucker. I promise."

Tucker looked less than convinced, but it was all Jared had to offer.

*   *   *

Katie slipped away from the kitchen while the others were cleaning up so she could tend to Tucker before the others arrived.

As she entered the room, she glanced up at the camera which had been returned to its usual position.

Tucker's mouth was open and his face relaxed as he breathed heavily in his sleep. Katie hated to disturb him and bring him back to the pain, but they didn't have much time before the others returned. She nudged him gently, and pain scrawled across Tucker's face once more.

"I need to clean your wounds," Katie whispered. Keeping the blanket over him, she rolled up the dressing draped across his back and slid it under his mat.

"Your boyfriend is a piece of work, you know that?" Tucker sneered.

Katie brought out a washcloth she had snuck from the bathroom and dabbed at the cuts. Tucker reared up and clutched his pillow tight.

"I'm sorry," she whispered. "Jack's only doing what he has to."

In truth, Katie was furious at Jared, but they still needed Tucker, and divulging her personal feelings about the matter would not inspire Tucker's confidence. She still wasn't sure how she was going to bring it up to Jared herself. After her move on him the other night, their conversation had stilted even further. He spoke when he had to, and not much more. Katie, for her part, was too embarrassed to attempt further conversation as she lay in his bed, ate his food, and shared his toothbrush.

"You say he's here to save us," Tucker hissed through clenched teeth. "If that were true, wouldn't he have done it by now?"

"He's taking Midas out too," Katie said. "You just have to trust him. He's just looking at the big picture."

Tucker snickered. "The big picture. Face it Katie, in the big picture, we mean nothing. If the big picture is taking out Midas, then we're just collateral damage."

Jared had made it clear where he drew the line concerning her, but Tucker *was* collateral damage. How much collateral damage was tolerable to Jared? She honestly didn't know. She realized there was very little she knew about what was going on in that head of his.

"Jared's a good kid," Katie said. "He forgets it sometimes, but when it counts, he'll be there for us. Okay?"

Or at least he'll be there for me.

Tucker opened his mouth to retort, but the door opened and Sally entered with the other little ones. The older girl joined them, sitting cross-legged next to Tucker and petting his hair. "I'm sorry, Tucker," she whispered.

"I'll be fine," Tucker muttered and stared into a corner.

"Stanton and Jack are bastards!" Sally said. "I'd like to rip their throats out!"

Tucker glared at Katie. "Wouldn't we all, Sally."

CRIMSON MUTINY

"Hey, Warner!" Jared winced as Tom called him from down the hall. With a shuddering breath, he pulled his door closed and turned to the Watcher with a neutral face.

"What's up?" Jared asked as Tom trudged down the hall to him.

"Did you hear anything about that kid breaking into my room?"

Sweat dripped down the back of Jared's neck, and he reached to wipe it away, but stopped midway up, returning his hand to his side, not wishing for Tom to know he was nervous.

"Uh, yeah," Jared said. "Look, man, I'm sorry about that. I had to take a shit and left the kid outside my room and—"

Tom crossed his arms. "Stanton said my door was open. I never leave my door open."

Jared shrugged, but his heart pounded like a jackhammer. "I don't know, man. I didn't see it go down."

"And you didn't find anything on him but food?"

"You missing something else?"

Tom looked down the hall one way then the next. "It's not what's missing. Come with me."

Blood drained from Jared's face, but thankfully, Tom had turned back to his room. He had found the camera—sooner than Jared had hoped. After the incident yesterday with Tucker, he hoped no one would find it for about a week. Finding it now would put suspicion on Tucker and subsequently him.

Jared forced his legs to follow Tom. He had to come up with a lie—to explain everything without involving Tucker. But what?

Sure enough, on Tom's bed sat the little camera, but Jared scratched the back of his head and looked around the room instead, pretending not to notice it. He sniffed the air, and his nose crinkled at the smell of molding food. The place had probably not been cleaned since Tom's arrival. A giant pile of clothes filled the corner next to the bathroom. The sheets were half-scattered on the floor and off one corner of the mattress. Jared counted seventeen visible Styrofoam take-out boxes—probably the source of the smell.

Jared laughed. "You're not going to tell me the kid did all this, are you?"

"I found this in my air duct." Tom picked up the camera and tossed it to Jared.

Jared brought the camera up to his eye. "Who's watching you?"

"Who the hell do you think?" Tom sneered and lowered his voice. "Stanton says *he* caught the kid in here, but I think it was the other way around. More than once I've come back to my room after a search and found my damn door open. So, what I think happened—Stanton came in here to plant this shit or change the batteries but left the door open. The kid peeks in and catches him, so Stanton spins the story on the kid. I don't keep granola bars in my room. The kid probably *did* steal those, but not from here." Tom snatched the camera back and slammed it onto the bed as Jared stood gaping.

He couldn't have come up with a better lie if he had tried.

"Let's check your room." Tom grazed past Jared as he stepped back into the hallway. "And we'll see if I'm the only one Stanton's got his eyes on."

Jared followed him out into the hall, put in his code, and opened the door for Tom. The man entered as if it were his own place but stopped at the end of the entry.

"You OCD or something?" He laughed. "Damn, this is the cleanest apartment I've ever seen."

Jared laughed half-heartedly. He said this as if it were an insult, and Jared wasn't sure how to take that.

Tom dragged a chair from the table over to the vent and shined a flashlight through the grate. He clicked it off and turned to Jared, mouth straight and brows raised.

"Shit," Jared said. "Are you serious?"

Tom dropped down from the chair and handed him the flashlight. Jared went through the motions of finding the small camera inside and acting surprised about it.

"I betcha every damn one of these rooms is being surveilled," Tom said. "And I don't know about you, Warner, but I'm not going to tolerate this bullshit." He pulled the radio from his belt and jammed the button down. "Stanton, you're needed in the staff quarters. And if any one of you dickheads care about your damn privacy, you should come too."

Soon, the hall was filled with the other Watchers, and Tom showed off his camera to them. When they heard, each man went to his own room and soon returned with camera in hand. Meanwhile, Jared leaned against the wall and watched, doing his best to suppress the smile trying to creep across his face. Could his plan truly be working this well?

"Now, hold on, hold on." Randall made a placating motion. "Here comes Stanton now! I'm sure he has a good explanation."

"I know nothing about these cameras," Stanton said. His subordinates groaned and turned from him. "Listen! I have always respected your privacy here. I would never—"

"Shut it, Stanton!" Tom shouted. "You really expect us to believe you? You work in blackmail!"

"That's right!" Randall said above the others. "We work in blackmail, Tom. All of your movements are already on camera. With the setbacks the boss has been having lately, is it any wonder he felt the need to put cameras in the rooms? They're for our protection, you dipshit—"

Tom swiped his hand and turned his back to Randall. "I'm done with this shit. Anyone else with me?"

Several voices of ascent rose up from the crowd.

"What?" Stanton said. "Where are you going? You can't just leave."

Tom drew his pistol and raised it at Stanton. "And you're going to stop me, are you?" Stanton's eyes grew huge as he raised his arms in surrender.

"Tom," Jared said, "the boat in Dock 2 is fueled and ready." He tossed him the key. "Take it and go."

Tom glared at Stanton for a long minute before lowering the weapon. "Come on, boys. Pack your bags. We're headed home." One by one, they dispersed to their rooms.

"I'll have you know," Stanton said to Jared, "that's not your boat to give."

"The boat in Dock 2 is the one the kid sabotaged," Jared told him in a lowered voice. "No way in hell it will make it to the mainland. They'll get what mutineers deserve."

That was a lie. If they managed to get it started, they should make it to Myanmar just fine, but the lie felt appropriate to his cover.

The corner of Stanton's mouth raised, and he glanced sideways to Randall. "Told ya he was a good find, didn't I?" Stanton stepped past them shaking his head, but Randall narrowed his eyes at Jared before following the boss.

FUEL THE FIRE

Katie stiffened as the warm pressure of a hand slid about her waist. Incredible. Even knowing who he was and why he was there, she could not help but have that reaction every time Jack Warner approached her. As he brushed her hair behind her ear, Katie cringed.

"How's Tucker?" Jared asked.

Katie glanced to the back of the bar, but Louie was nowhere to be seen. Jared would keep up the act, however, since the bar was located by the front door. Anyone could walk by.

"He's doing some better," she said. "But what's going on with the Watchers? Was someone talking about mutiny?"

"The count is up to thirteen right now." Jared twirled a strand of hair around his finger. "Our little camera scheme worked."

She turned to him, brows raised, and he took a step back. "Thirteen of Midas's guys just quit? Just like that?"

Jared glanced to the back of the bar. "Keep your voice down," he hissed through unmoving lips.

"That…that's incredible," she whispered. "Jared—"

"Jack," he corrected, and Katie winced. He continued, "We'll talk later. I just wanted you to—"

"Warner!" Stanton called from the door, and Jared spun to face him. "Come with me, please."

Stanton kept going past the bar and up the stairs while Katie's heart nearly beat out of her chest. Had Stanton overheard? Surely not! He was too far away. It was something else. It had to be.

Jared glanced back at her, his lip white from where he bit it. He shoved his shaking hands into his pockets as he followed Stanton up the stairs.

*　　　*　　　*

"Close the door," Stanton ordered as he collapsed into the chair behind his desk.

Jared did as he was told then took the seat across the desk. Upon setting his hands on the armrests, he noted their shaking and quickly set them back into his lap. He needed to calm down now. Jack Warner wouldn't act like this. Taking a subtle deep breath, he refocused.

Stanton pinched the bridge of his nose. "As you can see, we've had some openings come up."

"Bunch of pussies," Jared muttered. "Couldn't take a little videography. I mean, what the hell? At this level, I'm surprised I haven't found a camera in the men's room. They're just a bunch of children that don't know how the real world works."

Stanton slid a paper around his desk. "Yes, well, I suppose that's one way of looking at it. But I didn't put the cameras in the room."

Jared cocked his head to the side. "But—"

"Did you see how quick Randall was to throw me under the bus?" Stanton leaned back in his chair and propped his feet up on the desk. "If you had to choose who to follow, would you choose me or Randall?"

Jared's mouth fell open. "I…uh—"

"I don't know if Midas is looking to replace me or what. It's possible Randall went rogue on that one, but I doubt it. Randall's good at following orders, but not so much at coming up with them himself. And it wouldn't be the first time Midas gave Randall orders he didn't tell me about."

Jared had never thought about the Watchers at the highest level being suspicious of each other. The operation had always seemed well-oiled. Machine like. But with a master manipulator like Midas at the helm, did anyone truly know what was going on?

"I am loyal to Midas." Stanton slammed his fist onto the desk, causing Jared to jump. "But I will not be loyal to that oaf if he ever makes a play for my job. How about you, Warner?"

Jared swallowed hard and looked around the room for an answer. "I…uh…to be honest, I prefer you a hell of a lot more than Randall. But my orders come from Midas first and foremost."

Until it's time for me to kill him.

"Of course, of course." Stanton waved his hand. "Listen, I brought you up here to warn you. This job you're working with Randall—there's something up about it. I don't know exactly what."

"Do you think I'm in danger?"

"No, I don't think so, but there's something more to this than I'm being told. Just keep your eyes open, alright?"

"Will do, boss," Jared said. "And thanks for the heads-up."

Stanton flipped open the lid of his laptop, and Jared glanced at the USB port. Perhaps Stanton bringing him into his confidence was a good sign. Maybe it meant more chances at getting access to the files. The flash drive hidden in the secret pocket of his pants grew heavy.

*   *   *

"You didn't send for me last night," Katie said as she tugged firmly on the knob behind her, making sure it closed all the way.

Jared glanced at her over his shoulder as he made his way to the mini fridge. "I knew what you were going to say."

"About Tucker?"

Jared grabbed an Ensure from the fridge and tossed it to her. "Yes, about Tucker. You know I didn't want that to happen, right?"

Katie broke the seal of the milkshake. "So, why am I here tonight?"

"When I go to Myanmar tomorrow, I've arranged an in-person rendezvous with Bryan. If you want to write Alec and your dad a note, I can smuggle it out to them through him."

"Are you changing the subject? Trying to win my favor so that I'll forget about Tucker?"

Jared's shoulders sagged. "Maybe. A little, yeah."

"You stood there and watched him get flogged, Jared! You did nothing while they ripped open his back and—"

Jared slid his finger between the curtains and peered into the courtyard.

"Am I boring you?"

Jared dropped the curtain and turned back to her. "A little, yeah. You don't think I feel bad? I know the taste of the whip probably more than any of you combined. But Tucker's sacrifice…I mean hell, look how much good it's done already. Half of Midas's crew just walked off in one afternoon. Stanton is scrambling to find guys to do his operations. This is a big win for us!"

"And what about Tucker?" she demanded. "He's the one bleeding. Have you asked *him* how he feels about this?"

Jared waved her off. "What's done is done. There's no point arguing about what already happened, and if that's all you're wanting to do tonight, then I can always send you back."

Katie clenched her fists. Her gaze fell upon his warm bed and soft sheets. To the mini fridge stocked with food. "There's no need to send me back, Jared. I'll go there myself." Setting the Ensure on the TV stand, Katie turned to the door.

"Katie," Jared called as he stood. "Katie, wait—"

But Katie yanked open the door and stepped outside.

My turn to say no, Jared Kelley.

BLOOD OF BROTHERS

"So, what's good here?" Jared asked as he slid into the seat next to the only other American in the place. Then again, at eleven in the morning, the place wasn't exactly hopping. The bar was dim with the primary lights coming from beer racks on the wall behind the counter. The set up was surprisingly familiar, like most American bars Jared had been in.

With a curled lip, Bryan picked up a round spiky creature on his plate. "If you find out, let me know."

The bartender came by for Jared's order, and he requested rum and Coke. "I'm glad you got my message," Jared said once he was gone. "I don't know when I'll be heading to the mainland again."

"It was a hell of a message. You're lucky I was able to find this place since most cab drivers around here don't navigate by longitude and latitude."

"What'd your mother say about you coming to Thailand?"

"My mother? I'm almost nineteen now!" Jared eyed him incredulously, and, after a long drink, Bryan admitted, "She thinks I'm on vacation in Hawaii."

That sounded more likely.

Bryan made a face as he scooped out a hunk of sea urchin. "Slimy."

"If you don't like it, why are you eating it?"

"Don't want to waste it."

"Access to over a million dollars and—"

"Like you'd be any different. We've starved too much to leave food on our plates," he said as he plopped another bite into his mouth. "Perhaps you could tell me why I'm in Thailand?"

The bartender returned with Jared's drink, and they waited until he was gone before Jared said, "I've been whittling down Midas's team since I've been there. Right now, he has an average of fifteen of his guys on the island at a time."

"Fifteen guys is a lot for just you and me to handle. I could try to hire a private security team, but that's going to require some heavy equipment: guns, boats, maybe a helicopter. My pockets are deep, but they might not be *that* deep."

"Go ahead and get the team together but wait for my signal. I'm going to need a bit more time to get the virus Alec made for me installed, but once I do, we'll have all of Midas's blackmail victims."

"What about Katie and the others? Does your extortion plan include an escape route for them too?"

"As soon as we get things set, we'll get them on a boat and off the island."

"You have those capabilities now?" Bryan asked.

"I could probably swing it, yeah."

"Then why haven't you done it?"

"Because I can't maintain my cover and do that."

"Those children are in danger. You *know* this. Every day they spend on that island—"

"Is unfortunate, but unavoidable." Jared glanced at the barkeeper who was busy shining glasses and lowered his voice even further. "Midas is rebuilding. You would not believe the amount of dirt he has on people in how many countries. If we raid the base now and capture him, he'll use his blackmail and be out of jail by the next day. Then he'll go off and build back everything we've worked so hard to destroy. There will be more camps. More kids taken. More lives destroyed. We've got one shot at ending all this, Bryan, and I'm not going to screw it up."

Bryan tilted his glass from side to side, allowing the light to stream through the liquid and ice.

"I need you to trust me, Bryan," Jared said.

"I trust you, Jared. I've always trusted you, but I don't have to like it. What else do you need from me?"

"Once I get the kids on the boat, we're going to need a rally point. A place where we can meet with you and smuggle these kids back to the States."

"I'll make some calls." Bryan finished his drink. "Wrap this up, Jared. Sooner rather than later."

"It's almost over, Bryan. I promise."

*　　*　　*

Jared peered through the heat-sensing binoculars once more to confirm the hostiles were in the same positions as before. Most were located in the lower levels of the two-story house, but a couple were poised upstairs. According to their information, one or two members of the household staff were present, but the family was gone for the day. Arhrit did not usually store his wares at home, but pressure from Midas had caused shipping delays, forcing this less than typical mode of operation. At least, that's what their information told them.

"Is your team ready to go?" Jared asked.

Randall glanced at Jared in the rearview mirror from his place in the driver's seat before continuing to scrape dirt from beneath his fingernails with his pocket knife. "Locked and loaded, Warner."

"And your guys know to guard the south side perimeter and--"

"They're my guys, Warner," he said with a sigh. "Of course, they know the plan."

Jared checked his watch again and gulped. Five minutes until go time.

"Damn, son, you need to relax," Randall said.

"There are seven armed security guards in there." Jared pointed toward the towering white mansion across the street surrounded by a brick wall. "I just want to make sure everything goes according to plan. We don't have room for mistakes."

"Nothing will go wrong," Randall said. "I've done this shit a million times. Just do what we talked about and everything will be fine. I'll be out here waiting for you if things get spicy."

Jared met Randall's eye in the rearview with a tense smile. The bastard was a mean son-of-a-bitch, but he did know his stuff. Jared was glad to have him watching his back.

A white delivery truck rolled down the street toward them, and Jared checked his watch. Right on time. As a security guard exited his station at the gate, Jared pulled on a New York Mets ball cap, stepped out of the vehicle, and crossed the street.

The driver of the van handed the security guard a clipboard all while talking and motioning with his hands. They spoke in Thai, so Jared did not understand the words of the animated conversations, but it seemed intense enough to keep the guard's attention.

When Jared was close enough to the guard, he pulled a needle from his pocket and inserted it into the man's neck. The guard fell limp into Jared's arms, and Jared dragged him into the guard shack.

Jared pulled his overshirt off and tossed it into the corner. Quickly, he changed into the guard's uniform. He kept his own undershirt on, not risking any of his team seeing his scars. The gray uniform was a touch baggie, but it would do. Jared pressed the button to open the gate and waved the truck in.

The truck continued up the driveway and parked in the loop at the front door. Another staff member, disguised as a butler but outed by the weapon bulge on his side, stepped out to meet them.

Jared fired a tranquilizer dart at the man, and he went down. Randall had wanted to go in with lethal force, but Jared had insisted they didn't want that much heat. It had worked—this time.

While Jared was dragging the man behind some bushes, the backdoor of the truck opened, and five of his crew exited. Now they officially had security outnumbered. The team led the way into the house, and Jared followed behind, his tranq-gun still drawn.

A maid in the room to the left screamed, dropped her duster, and pulled out her phone as they rushed past. Jared shot her with another dart, and the phone fell to the ground with her.

Jared counted the rooms as he passed. His objective was the third room on the left, across from the stairs. By the time he reached it, the lock on the door had been shot off, and his guys were tearing the room apart—flipping couch cushions, ripping open drawers.

One of his men waved him over to a hole in the wall where a bag of powder stuck out from between the studs. Jared nodded, and the Watcher ripped open the drywall pane. The plastic bags fell to the floor with a thud.

"Load them up," Jared said. "Two minutes."

As Jared returned to the door of the office to cover their exit, a *bang!* erupted from the stairs. Jared dropped low as bullets struck the door. Another shot followed with a different- sounding bullet, and Jared peered out to see the guard fall. Randall peeked down at him from the second floor. The guard who had opened fire tumbled down the stairs before him.

"What the hell, Randall?" Jared asked. "I thought you were going to be in the car."

Randall continued down the stairs, stepping over the body and clutching the arm of a fifteen-year-old girl. Her face was pale as she tugged with bound hands against Randall in a futile effort to escape. Muffled screams came from behind the duct tape across her mouth.

"I've got one final lesson for you, Warner," Randall said. "Plans change."

Sirens wailed in the distance as Jared exited the house, tranq-gun at his side. The guys were finishing up loading the trunk with the dope. Everything had gone according to plan. Just as Randall had said.

Except you just helped kidnap a girl.

Randall guided the girl to his car parked behind the truck and opened the trunk with his key fob. The girl disappeared inside, and the lid slammed down above her.

Jared yanked open the passenger-side door and sat in the vehicle. He clenched and unclenched his fingers, dispersing the tremors before turning on the baby monitor set upon the console. The screen came to life, showing Arhrit's daughter screaming through her gag and banging against the walls of the trunk.

"What are you doing, Warner?" Randall asked as he took the driver's seat. "You're supposed to go in the truck."

"Change of plans," he sneered. "Your guys know how to get the drugs back to Midas without me. You're going to tell me what the hell this is all about."

Randall grinned, his fat teeth spreading across his face. "Alright then. Fasten your seatbelt."

Jared complied, setting the monitor in the cupholder facing himself as he did, and Randall followed the truck out of the driveway. Just as both vehicles turned the corner, the police vehicles arrived on the scene. At the next street, the truck took a left while Randall took a right.

As they drove through the streets of Bangkok, Jared slid down in his seat as the other cars zoomed past them, feeling as if every car they passed, or each motorcycle that passed them, knew what they had done.

The girl thrashed against the walls of the trunk. Randall had shut off the sound miles back, but Jared could still hear it in his mind. Finally, she curled into a ball as her shoulders heaved.

Jared stared at the screen with such intensity, he didn't notice at first when they left the city, taking an old, one-lane road out to who knew where. He had to do something but could think of nothing. Maybe he could attack Randall, kill him if need be, and take the girl back home? Or he could contact the police. What was the equivalent of 9-1-1 here anyways?

But what about Katie? He would never see her again.

But he couldn't kidnap this girl.

Could he?

Jared stared ahead at the pothole-filled road as they continued on. The drug-filled truck was on its way to a safe house to be divided and shipped to Midas's stash houses over the next few days, and Randall's shipment was supposed to leave tomorrow morning. The contents of the shipment had changed—not that Midas's people would bat an eye at this.

Randall turned onto a dirt road. The wildlife grew across the road in places and the roof of the sedan scraped beneath the vines. The trees were similar to the ones on the island, but the forest here was much denser. Occasionally they would pass a field growing who the hell knew what.

Jared gripped the handle above the door as they bounced along. The girl on the screen bounced too, but her hands were tied in front of her and she couldn't brace against the bumps properly. She smacked her head more than once on the floor, and Jared cringed, knowing exactly how that felt.

"Why didn't you tell me Arhrit's daughter was the real target?" Jared asked.

Randall glanced in Jared's direction before shifting gears and turning onto an even narrower road. "Midas's orders."

"I was supposed to lead this job! Stanton said—!"

"Stanton's got a soft spot for you, kid. I don't know why the hell that is, but as for the rest of us, well let's just say we're not quite sure about the company you keep."

"What the hell is that supposed to mean?"

"The girl, Warner."

Jared balked. "Th-the girl?"

"Little Miss Scarface. You know if it were just the occasional tail, I'd get it, but that bitch is with you almost every night. All night. You got feelings for her?"

The tremor started in Jared's hand, but he forced himself to ignore it. Bringing Randall's attention to it would be no good here. Instead, he mustered up the best sneer he had.

"This is some bullshit. You think that I came all this way to work with the big leagues to waste it on some bitch? I have jumped through all of your damn hoops, passed every one of Midas's stupid tests, and now you're going to doubt me because of her?"

"Midas brings in whores every week, and not once have you gone for them. If it were just about tail—"

"You know what? Screw it. You wanna know why I go for the girl? Because I have this thing about sharing. The way you guys share girls, it's gross. But I didn't want to step on any toes, so I didn't go for the prettier one. I went for the one no one else wanted. And yeah, I keep her with me most nights. If she's with me, then she's not with anyone else."

Randall continued to peer at Jared with incredulity, but then he barked a laugh and shook his head.

"What?" Jared demanded.

"No, it's just—damn, son. We all knew you were a little OCD. I just didn't realize it was *that* bad." He laughed aloud.

"Yeah, well, laugh all you want, but *I've* never had to get a shot in my ass."

Randall stopped laughing, cleared his throat, and straightened in his seat. "Fair enough."

Now that the interrogation had ended, Jared turned his attention once more to the girl trapped in their trunk. He had thought often about his motives with Katie being questioned, but now that it was happening, the presence of their guest trumped that worry. He still could not wrap his mind around the fact that she was back there. The car was eerily quiet due to the soundproofing of the trunk.

The branches above them slapped the roof of the car as they continued on the narrow road. The car bounced with ferocity, and Jared hoped they wouldn't break an axle. After a few more miles, Randall turned onto a road Jared would have missed entirely. Around the next turn, they reached a small shack, and Randall flipped off the ignition.

Jared reached for the door handle, but Randall grabbed his sleeve. "Check for squatters. If you find any, shoot them. With your real gun this time."

The area around the shack was still overgrown, but a clearing had been cut up to the door. Jared's shoes sank into the red mud as he stepped out of the vehicle, pistol drawn. The birds sang a long, sad song; a rhythmic trill that set his nerves on edge. Jared approached the plywood and bamboo shack and listened intently at the door. Nothing but the sound of the forest. He yanked the door open.

The inside of the shack was dark and dusty. To the right were a few crates and an old hand pump sink. The left had a fireplace, and in the center of the shack was a lopsided queen-sized bed with a gray, rat-chewed mattress.

Randall kicked the door open further as he dragged in the girl. She was resisting, of course. Jared could have told her it was pointless but knew saying so would also have been pointless.

Randall tossed her onto the bed, and a cloud of dust puffed around her. Taking her arms, he dragged her to the metal frame at the head of the bed and secured her hands there with another zip-tie. She thrashed at him with her feet.

She was pretty, Jared reflected. Which was not a bonus considering the situation. How long would she fight? How much could she resist until they broke her? How much would he let them?

"You gonna help me, Warner, or just stand there?"

Jared swallowed hard. Now was not the time for this. He'd have to wait for a better moment to get her to safety.

Jared grabbed the girl's feet, holding them together while she bucked and pulled. Randall handed him two thick, black zip-ties, and he secured her ankles to the bed frame. Her ankles were thin and dainty. Jared made sure to leave a finger's-breadth of space between them and the hard plastic.

Randall brushed his thick fingers against her cheek, and she pulled away from him, her eyes glaring. "Aren't you a pretty one?" he said, echoing Jared's earlier reflection.

A knot formed in Jared's throat. The ransomed girls were not to be touched: Midas's rules. But Jared was not deluded enough to believe the rule was not broken. He needed a distraction.

There was a light switch on the wall beside the door, and Jared flipped it a couple of times. As expected, nothing happened. "Are there any lights?"

"There's a generator in the corner by the sink," Randall said as he continued to pet the girl's face.

The paint on the generator was still shiny. Clearly, it had been brought here for this purpose. "And how do you turn it on?"

"Flip on the fuel valve, set the choke, and turn the ignition."

Jared scratched his head. "Dude…"

Randall sighed as he turned from the girl. "You're supposed to be our mechanic."

Jared laughed. "I was told not to take my island job too seriously."

Whoever had put the thing there hadn't filled it with gas either, but there was a stash out back. Jared was able to keep Randall away from the girl while working on this until the sun started sinking behind the trees. All the while, however, she watched them, her hands slowly yet stubbornly tugging at the restraints, trying to weasel her way out.

Once the generator was up and running, they were able to see with the single bare bulb on the ceiling. By then, Randall was seemingly out of the mood. He pulled up a chair, leaned back against it, and propped his feet up on the generator.

"What about food?" Jared said.

Randall sighed again. "Do I have to do everything? There's a town just up the road. Go find a store and bring us something back."

"I don't know where the hell I am, Randall. I'm more likely to get lost than bring us back shit."

Randall considered Jared, and under the weight of his stare, Jared felt himself shrinking. "Listen, kid. I want to believe you're on the level, but I'll just say this so we're on the same page: out there is nothing but miles and miles of jungle. If you try anything funny with the girl, you'll both get lost out there and die."

"Really? Are we back to that?" Jared attempted a laugh, but it came out weak and thin.

"I sure as hell hope not," said Randall, but then he checked his watch and dropped his feet to the floor. "I'll be back in an hour."

"And I'll be here," Jared muttered.

Randall lumbered past Jared to the door, his hand resting on the firearm at his hip as he did so. But he did not stop. He did not turn back. Randall stepped out of the shack, and soon the car engine started.

Meanwhile, Jared turned his attention to the girl who watched him silently with those dark eyes of hers. She had yet to make a fraction of progress on the restraints, although the tape across her mouth had peeled up some. What the hell was he going to do with her?

Part of him, the part that had rationalized every moment up to this point, argued that she deserved what came to her. She was the daughter of a drug dealer after all. Her dad was a bad guy and she was probably no better. But that argument collapsed in short order. At least twenty-five percent of Jared's people had been born to shady parents. It didn't make them any less victims. This girl, Malai if he recalled her name correctly from his research, was just a fifteen-year-old school girl. While at a certain point in her future she might be expected to partake in her father's business, she was still far from that time in her life.

"What are you going to do?" whispered Malai, and Jared startled. How long had he been staring at her? He could only guess what she thought he was thinking in those moments. His efforts to get her alone had most likely been noticed. What else was a girl in such a situation to think?

Jared chose not to answer, electing to earn good faith rather than to assure it. He fetched his water bottle from his backpack and sat on the edge of the bed beside her. The girl pulled away from him as far as she could—which was maybe six inches.

"This is going to sting for a second." Jared grabbed the edge of the duct tape and ripped it off. She squeaked in pain, but taking it off slower would have just extended the time of the pain. "Water?" he asked, bringing it near.

Malai looked between him and the bottle with wide, questioning eyes.

"I'm not going to hurt you," he said and cracked the lid and took a sip himself. Again, he pressed the rim up to her mouth, and this time she received it, drinking it down to half.

"I have food too. Granola bar?" He held up the silver package. There was never a time when he went without at least one of these on his person.

"Yes," she said hesitantly. "Please." Her accent had a British lilt to it, but was quite clear.

"You speak English," he noted.

"Yes, I learned it in school."

Jared nodded in acknowledgement before feeding her the granola bar piece-by-piece. Once finished, Jared took a seat on the floor beside the bed and leaned his head against the mattress.

Damn it. What am I going to do?

Randall was probably right. If they tried to make it out of here in the dark, they were goners. Jared didn't know what sort of wildlife was around, but surely something deadly.

He should have done more research on Myanmar before now. He was living on an island just off the coast after all. Of course, his smartphone had no signal for him to look up anything about this place now—or phone Bryan. He had left the satellite phone back on the island, afraid to be caught with it.

"You are American," Malai stated. "Where in America?"

She was a brave girl if she was trying to make conversation. That and smart. Smart for humanizing herself, brave for opening her mouth. He scooted over to lean against the wall and see her better.

"Here and there," Jared answered.

"I have been to America," she said. "Los Angeles—"

"Yes," Jared said. "I lived there for a few months."

Malai tried to sit, but the restraints on her legs prevented such a motion. With a flick of his knife, Jared freed her feet. It wasn't like she was going anywhere without her hands. She could try to kick him or, if she were really talented, put him in a lock of some sort. He decided to take his chances.

"You stole from my father," Malai said once she was seated with her bond hands at her hips. "And you kidnapped me. Why?"

"To be honest, I don't know. I knew we were coming for the drugs, but I didn't know you were a target. I'm sorry you're wrapped up in all this. I really am."

"Then let me go."

Jared glanced at her face but couldn't meet her eyes. Shaking his head he said, "It's not that simple."

"These people, don't you know what they will do to me? They will kill me—"

"No." Jared ran his hands over his face. "No, they won't kill you."

"You are a liar!"

"Yes," Jared told her. "I am a liar. But not in this. While you are valuable, you will be protected. Then once you are not, you will be used as a slave."

"And this is better than death?"

He shook his head. "Not by a long shot."

Her lip trembled, then a sob erupted from her throat. Jared let her cry and made no attempt to comfort her. There was, after all, no comfort to be had.

A half-hour passed before Randall's headlights flashed outside. By this time, Malai's tears had been exhausted, and she had resumed tugging at the bonds. Jared had warned her about cutting her wrists by doing that, but she had ignored him. So, he had ignored her, choosing to wallow in his own miserable thoughts beside her. But when the lights lit up the woods just outside the open window, he ordered her, "Lay down."

Malai frowned at him, confused.

"I'm the only thing between you and my boss. Get me in trouble…get me shot, and you're on your own out here, understand?"

Hesitantly at first then with a bit more speed, Malai slid her legs back down to their original place. Jared took some of the zip-ties Randall had left in his chair, secured her legs, and duct taped her mouth closed. He returned to his seat and pulled up a game on his phone just as Randall came through the door.

The window for escape had passed.

Malai was theirs.

RED TRAITOR

The island grew steadily larger on the horizon. Jared should have been glad to see it. To be near Katie again after having survived another mission, but the horror of kidnapping Malai canceled out any positive feelings, leaving him in a state of numb ambiguity.

"Swap with me," Randall said, approaching the wheel. "I'll bring us in. Go get the girl and bring her topside."

Jared entered the below-deck sleeping compartment, tossed the mattress and everything aside, and raised the lid. Malai curled up tighter upon seeing him, but he was numb even to this.

"We're coming into port," he told her flatly. "I'm going to take you to your room. You'll meet some of our…er…your people there. They will explain the rules to you. Now, come on."

But Malai's spirit had not yet been replaced with one of submission. She did not budge.

Jared tugged on her arm, trying to pull her out of the small space, but she hooked her leg on the side. He grabbed her about the middle and dragged her out of the hold, but her kicking and thrashing caused him to drop her. She landed on her back in the discarded linens. She kicked at his face, but he caught her legs and dragged her close.

"Stop this," he hissed, but she thrashed her head about. He cupped her around the back of the head, forcing her to look at him. "Stop."

Her eyes glared at him, speaking more words than her gagged mouth ever could.

"You're about to get hurt," he told her. Ignoring him, she tried to make another go at it. Jared shook her hard. "Stop! I'm serious! I don't want to hurt you, Malai, but I have to do my job. And if you keep thrashing around like this, you're going to get dropped again or worse. Do you understand?"

Again, he received a look of sheer venom, but she had stopped thrashing.

"Everything okay down there, Warner?" called Randall.

"Everything's fine!" he shouted back. "Now, Malai, I'm going to undo your legs, but listen close, you're on a boat in the middle of the ocean. There is literally nowhere to run. And once you get ashore, you'll be on an island. I understand your determination here, but seriously, the way things are going, I'm afraid you're going to pitch yourself into the sea."

"Maybe that's what I want," she garbled through the gag.

"No, I don't think you do," answered Jared, understanding her perfectly. She cocked her head to the side, and Jared rolled his eyes. "Yes, I understand you. It's a weird gift. Now, come on. There will be time for suicide later. At least take a day or two to get your bearings." And with that, he hoisted her to her feet and led her to the top level.

The island had grown much closer by the time they returned topside, and Jared led Malai to a seat behind Randall. He secured her hands to the rail there if for no other reason than to remove the temptation of an afternoon swim.

"Thought you might have gotten lost down there!" said Randall.

"Well, I was considering taking a nap, but didn't want you to get your panties in a twist." Jared took a beer from the cooler and pried off the cap with the boat rail. He fell into a seat beside Malai and checked the sun. Four hours until sunset. The clouds in the distance and the smell mixing with the salt in the air suggested rain. Malai's ever-watchful eyes fell upon him, and he resisted the urge to look back.

Randall steered the boat into port and parked the yacht into an empty slot. "Home again, home again, eh Warner?"

Jared, who was not feeling very conversational, hopped ashore and grabbed the ropes. Randall leaned against the boat wheel sipping on his beer. He was eyeing Malai again, but there was nothing Jared could do to stop that.

"I thought you might be getting a bit of a feel down there," Randall said. "You know, before the rest of us got the chance to."

"The hinge on the smuggler's hold is faulty. It got stuck. I'll fix it—"

"I wouldn't have begrudged you none if you had. No, after what you've been screwing, I wouldn't have blamed you a bit. Hey! You know, once this business is done with this girl, you could claim *her* as your own. It'd be a bit of an upgrade."

Malai gazed wildly between them, understanding in part but not in whole. Jared resisted a sneer and merely moved to tie the stern.

Randall slit the ties holding Malai to the boat and yanked her to her feet. He was about to shove her onto the docks, but Jared grabbed her beneath the arms, lifted her out of the boat, and set her down on the wooden planks, keeping her knees from being dragged over the rough wood. Taking her arm, he started the trek to the bay.

Randall chuckled again as he joined them onto the docks. "She's less bony than your current girl. Hell, she'd probably cry less too."

Jared froze mid-step. His grip tightened on Malai, and she squirmed beneath his nails. His nostrils flared and his hands shook while his insides burned with rage. Slowly, he turned on his heel—

"Warner!" Stanton hollered down the docks, and Jared stalled. Stanton's shoes clopped along the wooden boards as he approached, and Jared bit the inside of his cheek until he tasted metal. Avenging Katie needed to wait, but the rage needed an outlet. Fast.

Jared shoved Malai to the side and stomped to Stanton. "What the hell did you send me on?"

"I'm sorry," Stanton said. "I tried to warn you, but Midas—"

Jared slammed his fist into the man's face. He raised his fist again, but Stanton blocked the punch and socked Jared in the gut. Jared reeled momentarily then took another swing, but Randall grabbed his arm, pulling him back.

"Whoa!" cried Randall. "Let it go, Warner!"

"You want to fight me?" Stanton shouted. "I'm as mad about this as you are!"

"Get off me!" Jared shouted. Randall released him, and Jared balanced on the balls of his feet, fists clenched, ready to go again. It was a rage that had been growing in him for years, and now that it had a taste of freedom, he wished to release it all at once.

"You gonna hit me too, Warner?" Randall asked, then laughed. "Get a grip, kid. Midas is the boss and doesn't have to tell you shit." Grabbing Malai's arm, Randall led her down the docks. "And that goes for you too, Stanton."

"Warner is *my* guy!" Stanton argued. "I had a right to know where he was being sent and he had the right to know too."

"Well, boo-hoo," Randall growled as he turned back to them. Malai stumbled as she was yanked back by his abrupt turn. "You two can bitch and moan about this all day, but I'm going to do my damn job and secure the prisoner first. Is that alright with you two?"

Stanton adopted a sheepish look. Jared continued to burn with rage, but the lull had cleared away the red. At least in part.

"Put her in the back room, Warner," said Stanton. "Then meet in the dining hall. We'll go over this bit of *business* there."

*   *   *

Katie heard the door to the house open and resisted the urge to run to it right away.

Jared had been away for three nights now, and each day her fear that he would not return increased. But then, as she was scraping up peanut shells from the barroom floor, she heard Jared's voice on Stanton's radio announcing their imminent arrival. A woozy haze of relief had settled over her at the sound, although she dared not let Stanton see it.

While rushing to the door and wrapping her arms around Jared was not an option, she paused in sweeping as they passed by. Jared glanced into the room as he passed, but instead of providing his customary wink, his mouth formed a line. In his hand was the arm of a terrified girl with brown eyes. Those eyes locked with Katie's as they went past, pleading for help. The girl tried to linger in the doorway, but Jared yanked her forward, causing her to whimper.

Jared, what have you done?

Randall went by next, followed by Stanton who nursed a bloody lip with a tissue. That bit she could not make sense of.

Louie stepped in from the back, and Katie set to sweeping again, but the tightness in her throat was back. A warm wetness rolled down her cheek, and she realized she was crying.

No. There has to be an explanation. Jared would never—
Or would he?

As soon as the floor was mopped, Katie made for the kitchen. Preparations for dinner would be needed soon, and it would give her a good excuse to stop by their room. If they were keeping a hostage, it would be there.

As she stopped by the dining hall, she saw Jared sitting at a table with Stanton and Randall, folding and unfolding his hands. When he saw Katie, he paled, bit his lip, and looked away. The fist around Katie's throat tightened.

Tucker was already in the kitchen when she entered. As she walked to the back of the kitchen en route for their hallway, he laid his knife on his cutting board and followed her to it.

"What the hell, Katie?" he whispered.

"I know, Tucker, but I don't have any other information. I'm sure there's an explanation." Tucker was clearly unhappy with this statement, but what else was she supposed to say? He turned to go, but she stopped him with a hand on his shoulder. "I'm going to go check on her and will need you to let me back out of the room."

As they entered the back hallway, the sound of pounding and screaming met them. The screams were in a different language mostly, but English was thrown in here and there giving the words a bit of context: "Let me out! I'll kill all of you!"

"Are you sure you'll be able to handle her on your own?" Tucker asked.

"I'll be fine," she bluffed and slipped inside. Malai rushed at the door, but Katie managed to get it closed behind her before the girl could burst through. It was a cruel but kind gesture. Nothing good would come of her running around in this state. But it instantly gave Malai the wrong idea.

"Stay away from me!" she shouted, stumbling over the blankets littering the floor. She retreated to the back wall and pressed her palms against the cinderblock.

Katie made no attempt to soothe her. She was, after all, not in a state to listen. Instead, she just sat down on the floor.

Malai continued to watch her, wide-eyed and ready to fight, but after a few moments of silence, she ventured, "What do you want?"

"I certainly don't want to hurt you," said Katie, "but there's a lot for you to know, so have a seat and let's talk."

Malai glanced at the pile of blankets then back at the crazy girl across the way. She clearly had no interest in sitting at this time—not that Katie was surprised by this. The girl's heart was probably racing and that nervous energy was not so easily tamed.

"My name's Katie," she said instead. "I'm a prisoner here like you."

Malai swallowed hard. "What—what's going on here?"

"You've been kidnapped, Malai. Which is something you probably already knew, but it's helpful to lay that out for new people anyways."

"Wh-where am I?"

"On an island off the coast of Myanmar." Katie took a pillow from one of the young one's beds and hugged it as she spoke. It had been a while since she met anyone new, and explaining all this brought back the memories and feelings of what it was like to be kidnapped. She wanted to ease her fears, comfort her, but after being back on mostly normal rations for three days and sleeping on the hard floor once more, she really didn't have the energy to even try.

"Are you hungry?" Katie asked instead.

Hesitantly, Malai nodded, and Katie stood and pulled out a granola bar from a hidden pants pocket. It was her last one, and she had been holding onto it until Jared's return. But now that he was back, she could part with it. Within seconds of handing it over, the bar had disappeared.

"They didn't feed you, I take it," Katie muttered bitterly.

"The one guy did," Malai said with a full mouth. "The smaller one with the glasses. He gave me granola bars like this when the big one wasn't watching."

"Jack Warner," Katie found herself saying.

"Sounds right," said Malai. "The big one called him Warner. He's a bit off, that one."

"What do you mean?"

"He was pathetic. He kept telling me how sorry he was. How he didn't want to be there. I mean, don't get me wrong, it was better for *me* that way, but if you're going to be in this business, you've got to own it. Ya know?"

"Yeah, he can be weird sometimes," she said. "Listen, I'll make sure you get some food this evening. It's not the greatest, but it's better than nothing. But before I go, I'll give you the run down. While you're here, you are going to be expected to work. It's just menial work. Cooking, cleaning, but you have to do as you're told in order not to be punished. Since you are a hostage, you are going to be protected until the kidnappers get what they want. Do you understand?"

Malai crumpled up the wrapper in her hand. "And after they get what they want—the kidnapper, Warner, said I was going to be a slave?"

Jared hadn't sugarcoated it for her. "Yes, I'm afraid the kidnappers have no intention of giving you back."

Malai took the information with a curt nod, and Katie had to give it to her, she was stronger than she looked. Two knocks sounded on the door, and Tucker's face appeared in the doorway. Malai sat up straight, clutching her knees.

"It's okay," Katie said. "Tucker's one of us."

"Katie, we're needed in the kitchen." He nodded to the hall.

"But, what about me?" Malai asked.

"Stay in here, Malai," Katie said. "Believe it or not, it's one of the safest rooms in this God-forsaken place."

Jared tossed his bag onto his bed, sank into the chair by the table, and pressed his hands to his face.

Well, that went to shit.

He wanted to tear apart his room, toss the mattress from the bed, knock over the TV stand, but knew none of those outlets for his rage would be conducive to his cover. Instead, he sat picking at a chip in the table varnish until his nail fractured and bled.

You knew the risks, he told himself. *You signed up to work for one of the most well-known human traffickers in modern history. This was always a possibility.*

A lot of things had been possible when he had signed up for this gig. Some things he didn't give two shits about—like dealing dope and stealing, which he had been doing since childhood—but this?

The faces of the newcomers to Camp 1 flashed through his mind one after the other. During his time as Goldie, he had been the first to greet them. The first to tell them the horrible truth. The first to commiserate about their captors and their fate. How many had he buried shortly after such introductions?

Four other kids had been present when Jared and Leida were first taken. When Liam, one of the four, had died, Jared had counted two other graves when he went out under guard to bury him. That meant of the sixty-eight kids buried in the woods around Camp 1, he personally knew sixty-six of them. And he had dug each of their graves.

Was Malai going to be another one of those faces? Another one of the bodies for him to spill into the dirt? The others, he could blame Midas for, but this one? How could he not be culpable?

It's not going to happen again, he told himself. *Nobody else—at least none of your people—are going to die. You're going to get them out. You're nearly there. You just need a little more time.*

Jared stood abruptly, mounted the chair, and unscrewed the light fixture over the table. Hidden in the wiring was the satellite phone. He dialed Bryan's number while he sucked on his bloody finger. He'd have to come up with a story about the injury. Thankfully, no one but Katie would be around to see the blood now staining the freshly exposed wood. A quarter of the table was now absent of varnish and his nail was bound to fall off in a day or two.

It took three rings for the phone to be answered, but the voice saying "hello" on the other end was most welcome.

"It's me," said Jared. "I made it back to the island in one piece."

"Glad to hear it," Bryan said. "But you didn't have anything to do with that little kidnapping job I heard about this afternoon, did you?"

"Things got complicated."

"Shit! Do you know what you've done?"

"Do I know what I've done? Dammit, Bryan, you know who you're talking to, right?"

"No, I don't think I do. Not anymore. You just kidnapped a girl, Jared. What the hell were you thinking?"

The screaming in his mind started up once more as the faces flashed before him. Jared closed his eyes and grabbed his head as if he were pressing a pillow to his ears to silence it.

Shut up! Shut up!

"I will protect her," he told Bryan, forcing the tremor out of his voice. "I will keep her safe. Minimize the trauma until we get off this rock."

"Minimize the trauma?" Bryan laughed. "Do you think she'll ever be the same after this? You came to her home, dragged her out of her room. Nothing will ever feel safe to her anymore. She will wake up with the same nightmares you and I both have about getting snatched from our homes and—"

"Dammit, Bryan!" Jared shouted. "I know. But what the hell else was I supposed to do? If I blew this op, I'd never see Katie again. She'd be gone forever if not outright murdered."

"Get them out of there, Jared. Now."

Jared pinched the bridge of his nose. The panic was rising. He could feel it crushing his chest, squeezing it like a vise. In the kitchenette, he fumbled a mug and sloshed in some water from the tap. "How's it coming with the private security team?"

"I'm working on it."

Think. Think. You have a plan. Tell him then get off and panic. You have to get this done.

"I just found out there's supposed to be a party coming up at the end of the week," said Jared. "Stanton will be busy with the guests, and I might be able to plant the virus then. Midas usually comes up before the party to set up then a couple of days after to review the collected information. I'll let you know when he does and we can plan a strike then."

"Are you sure we need this blackmail? Because—"

"Yes, we need the blackmail, Bryan! If we want this thing to truly end, we need it."

Bryan paused for a moment, then muttered, "Fine. But you'd better get this done, Jared, before this whole thing spirals further out of control."

Jared pressed the end button and sank to the floor. The memories returned in full, and the sound of his own thoughts drowned out every other sound in the room.

"That won't happen this time," Jared promised himself. But the shakes took over, and he made no effort to stop them.

*　　　*　　　*

Katie was distracted talking to Sally when she yanked on the doorknob to their room, and did not consider the possible actions of the terrified girl trapped inside. Malai, however, who had been waiting for this moment, leaped from the floor screaming and charged them. She slammed Katie against the back wall and knocked Sally and Tucker away before sprinting down the hall.

"Malai! Wait!" Katie called, chasing after her.

That did as much good as expected, and Malai burst through the exterior door at top speed. Katie halted as the door hung open, revealing the darkness outside, not daring to follow and be accused of attempting an escape. Slowly, the door closer began the door's journey back, but before it finished, it swung open again. Jared entered, Malai's arm caught tight in his fist. Cursing, she pulled against him, but he held on as if unaffected by her resistance.

"Who let her out?" he demanded.

He was angry. Furious really. At whom, she couldn't really tell. His hand, the one around Malai's wrist, was bandaged, and a shadow of blood was visible around the fingertip. Something he had picked up on the mainland?

Meekly, Katie raised her hand—something she probably would have done guilty or not considering the inquisitor. "It was an accident," she mumbled, not wishing to agitate him further.

A guttural grumble came from Jared, probably a curse word beneath his breath, as he dragged Malai back down the hall. "Open the door."

Sally held the door for him as he dragged Malai back into the storeroom. The others followed, and when the door shut, Jared released Malai's arm. She spun around and tried to smack him, but Jared caught her wrist and shoved her to the ground. "Stay!" he ordered, then to Katie, "Why didn't you explain it to her?"

"I did. Greenies aren't good listeners, remember?" Katie replied, and Sally's mouth popped open at the retort. Katie was not sure why she had sassed him like that, or even if it was meant to be an insolent remark. She was echoing an answer Dakota had given regarding a similar question years ago.

Jared, too, hesitated as if unsure of what to say. "Are we going to have a problem?" he asked finally.

"No, sir," she said, shaking her head. "That did not come out as intended. I explained it to her as best as I could. I'm just saying that, as a new person, such things can be hard to hear."

"If you think I'm not going to try and escape, then you're crazy!" cried Malai.

"You," Jared said, pointing to Tucker, who had seated himself on a mat in the corner away from everything. Although he had been listening intently, he dropped his head at Jared's attention. "Come here."

Sluggishly, Tucker complied. As he drew near, however, Jared grabbed his shirt and yanked him to himself. Tucker whimpered at the action as his shirt pulled tight against his wounds. Keeping Tucker close, almost in an embrace, Jared raised the kid's tattered tee. He did so slowly, gently, exposing the now scabbed over scars. It was a strange combination, the roughness and near tenderness so closely intertwined. Had Malai not been horrified by the damage, perhaps she would have noticed the opposing actions. As it was, she recoiled at the sight of the wounds and shuffled backward over the floor, scattering blankets in her wake, to get away from the sight.

"If your ears don't work, then maybe your eyes will," said Jared. "Do as you're told, Malai. This is your final warning." He released Tucker, allowing the boy to stumble back. "As for the rest of you, those of you who *have* seen and heard, who know the rules—" He looked pointedly to Katie, "—and still neglected them, I should have you all flogged. As it stands, I'm too tired to bother with such things. So, consider it your lucky day. Katie—" He jerked his head to the door, and Katie lowered her head in acknowledgment. Jared pressed his thumb onto the door lock, and it popped open.

"Where's she going?" Katie heard Malai ask behind her before the door clicked closed. A pang of embarrassment came over her, but she quickly dismissed it. There were things of greater concern to be dealt with.

"This is getting increasingly complicated," Jared muttered when they entered his room.

"No shit," Katie replied. "What the hell, Jared? You said it was a drug heist!"

"Randall had second orders I was not aware of," Jared said, collapsing into the upholstered chair by his bed. "Apparently, I am not as close to Midas's inner circle as I thought."

"But what does that mean? Are they on to us?"

"I don't know, Katie. I don't think so, but…"

"Well, what about Bryan? Is he ready to bust us out?"

"He's working on it. Cash flow may be an obstacle, but he'll figure something out. Our focus needs to be on securing the blackmail files. I can break into the office during the party at the end of the week—"

"What about the cameras? Your cover will be blown."

"If anyone is watching the cameras at that time." Jared pressed his hands to his eyes. "It's the only idea I have at the moment." His exhaustion was evident as he sat hunched over in his chair. He probably had not slept the whole trip. She knew she shouldn't pepper him with questions now, but the weight of what had just happened pushed her onward.

"Stanton's office gets cleaned once a week," she said. "I can assign myself to that job. I'll come by while you're in a meeting with him. He's got an expensive-looking vase on the bookshelf by the door. I'll break that and distract him while you—"

"No," Jared groaned, "I don't want you to get in trouble."

"He'll probably just hit me. I don't think I'll get flogged over that."

"It doesn't matter. We're not making any plays that put you at risk."

"Jared, walking through the halls here puts me at risk."

"Katie," he insisted, "I'll break into his office and plant the virus. The hardest part will be getting his fingerprint, and I have an idea for—"

"If your cover gets blown, we're all dead."

"I'm not letting anyone else touch you!" Jared shouted. Instinctively, Katie ducked and retreated against the wall. "I'm sorry!" he said. "I didn't mean to—"

"It's fine," Katie dismissed, her cheeks warming from embarrassment about her over-reaction to a little raise in volume. She took one of the dining room chairs and drew it nearer to his, hoping that by sitting close, she would provide in some way a comfort to them both. "Jared, I know you're trying to protect me, but I want to bring Midas down too. Let me be a part of this."

"You have a right to revenge as well, Katie. I know that. But you've suffered enough. I don't want you to suffer anymore."

Katie slipped her hand into his. "You spent ten years getting the crap beaten out of you by Midas and his goons."

Gently, he took her hand into his own, running his thumb over the back of it. "It is because I know the full extent of your suffering that I don't want you to endure it any longer. Nobody should have to survive the things we have. Nobody should have to say, 'oh, it'll be fine; I'll just probably get smacked around a bit.' Nobody should have to endure the violation of their body at the hands of another."

"This isn't what should or shouldn't be experienced," argued Katie. "This is about what needs to happen next."

"Up to this point, I have had no way of protecting you, Katie, but now I do." He patted the gun at his hip.

"That gun won't plant the files."

"But it will end anyone who comes near you again." He cupped his hand against her cheek, stroking the elevated scar. "I'm going to destroy them, Katie. Everyone who has ever touched you is going to feel my knife. And I'm going to carve up the face of the one who cut you—"

Katie laid her hand upon his, covering the scar entirely. "There's just one problem, Jared. *I'm* the one who cut up my face." Jared paused, his face crunched in confusion. "It makes me less of a target," she explained. "I did it to survive. You wish to protect me and to achieve retribution, but ending Midas, getting those blackmail files and destroying anyone who ever helped him, that's what I must now do to keep on surviving. Surely, you understand this. You are, after all, here."

The moment the words left her mouth, Katie knew they had landed.

Yes, he had come for her and the others. Yes, he desired to protect her, but there were other ways to help this outcome to be achieved. More sane ways than jumping in both feet to this mess to be certain. But he was here personally because it was, in fact, personal. Killing Midas was the only way to truly escape. The only way to survive this horror and live again.

"I don't like this," he said finally, and Katie laughed aloud.

"When was the last time you did *anything* you liked?"

Katie moaned as the *beep-beep-beep* of the alarm clock ripped her away from the juicy sixteen-ounce sirloin steak just inches away from her watering mouth back to the drab interior of Midas's luxurious prison. Katie smacked the clock with more venom than necessary as she swiveled to a sit and dangled her legs off the side of the bed.

A bendable desk lamp illuminated the silver internals of Jared's pistol on the table as he cleaned it, but his face was shrouded in darkness above the light. "Sleep well?" he asked.

Katie slid her fingers into her hair and instantly regretted the motion as her fingers became trapped in the matted tangles. Once she had extracted her digits, she clicked on the lamp beside the bed, bringing light to the whole room. "Well enough? Yes. Long enough? No."

Jared set the pistol pieces down, poured a cup of coffee, and slid the mug to her side of the table next to the plate of scrambled eggs, sausage, toast, and apple slices. His plate had exactly half of the portions left on it, a habit Katie had noticed more than once, usually when the refrigerator was running short on leftovers. It didn't matter that the kitchen and the bar were right down the hall. Some habits were hard to kill.

Jared picked up a thin brass rod with a cloth dipped in cleaning fluid at the end and ran it through the barrel. The previously white cloth came out black. Had he fired his pistol during the raid?

I don't want to know, Katie thought as she sank into her chair. But her gaze kept coming back to the weapon and the bullets lying beside it.

"Targets," Jared said, noting her gaze. "Randall insisted on doing a little target practice before the raid. I used a tranq-gun during the actual job."

"I didn't ask you," Katie said before plopping a bit of egg into her mouth.

Jared slid the barrel and spring into the slide, attached the slide to the frame, and racked it back. "I'm going to make another pot of coffee. Do you want any more?"

Katie shook her head and nibbled on another apple. Jared jammed the loaded magazine home and racked the slide again before tucking the weapon into his shoulder holster. The coffee pot had only a cup left at the bottom, and Jared always made a full pot. How long had he been awake?

"We probably need to contact Alec or Bryan tonight to get a status on the security force Bryan is supposed to be hiring," Jared said. "If things go sideways on the blackmail plan, we're going to need a speedy extraction."

A smile tugged at the corner of Katie's lips as the thought of contacting her brother warmed her more than the coffee.

"We're in the end game here, Katie," Jared said. "So, keep your head down and play it safe, alright? We don't need any hiccups."

"When do I not do that?"

Jared's mouth formed a line, but he said nothing in reply. A glance at the clock showed that Katie had ten minutes left, so she shoved the last piece of toast in her mouth, grabbed a pair of granola bars from Jared's foot locker, and headed to the bathroom to brush her teeth.

Jared entered behind her, and the hair on Katie's neck leapt to attention. But he merely grabbed his electric razor and ran the head over his neck. Katie checked him continually in the mirror as he leaned over the sink to see the coarse hairs. When his red, tired eyes met hers, she looked away immediately and cursed internally.

Would she ever be able to be normal around him again? Around anyone?

When she finished, Jared walked her to the door and held it open for her. It was this part where most couples would kiss, tell each other good luck, stay safe, and that they loved them. Jared said nothing, for there was nothing to say, no words of comfort for the world she was about to step into. But he gave her his now familiar confident nod.

As someone who had by now doled out a number of these well-meaning but ultimately nonsensical nods, the gesture only upset the butterflies gathered in her gut.

Katie's steps were silent on the carpeted hallway of the staff quarters, and she kept her head lowered as she passed the rooms of the sleeping Watchers. Only when she entered the hall behind the kitchen to find her friends sitting against the walls eating gruel did she feel like she could breathe again. To her surprise, she saw Malai among them, staring at her bowl of gruel with a look of disdain as it dripped from her spoon.

"I guess she's on board with everything now, huh?" Katie asked Tucker.

Tucker glanced at Malai. "Stanton came by and threatened everybody a few minutes ago, so…"

"Yeah, I got it. There's nowhere to go, and if you try to escape, they'll beat you with ropes," Malai said, then muttered, "Doesn't mean I'm not going to try though."

"Just don't be stupid about it," Katie said. "No plan is better than a dumb plan, and a good plan is hard to come by. There's a reason we're all still here."

Malai harrumphed and opened her mouth to retort, but the cook opened the back door, spoke to them in her native tongue, and beckoned them to enter.

Stretching and yawning, the others stood and followed her inside. Katie and Sally started on the eggs while Tucker began prep-work for the rest of the meals. Malai stood around chewing on her nail as the others went about their tasks, and Katie sighed internally. She waved the girl over. "You do this, and I'll help Tucker."

Malai joined Sally at the table. "What am I doing?"

"Cracking eggs," Sally said as she broke another and dropped it into the bowl. "Have you ever cooked before, Malai?"

She shook her head, her black locks gliding across her back.

"Just jump on in, and I'll show you the ropes."

Leaving Malai in Sally's capable hands, Katie gathered the vegetables that were needing to be chopped and joined Tucker at his prep station. Malai picked up an egg shell and daintily tapped it on the side of the bowl.

Katie pursed her lips to stifle a laugh. "A bit spoiled, isn't she?" she whispered to Tucker.

"Lay off her," Tucker mumbled. "She's brave is what she is. First day here and she's not huddled in a corner crying."

Katie raised her brows as she glanced back at Malai. *Second day here. Third day kidnapped.*

Perhaps Tucker had a point, but it was a weak one. Malai, however, caught Katie watching her, and her nostrils flared.

Katie returned her attention to her own work. She hadn't done anything to piss the new girl off yet, so what the hell was that look about?

After finishing off the cucumbers for lunch's salad, Katie fetched the carrots from the walk-in cooler. On her way back, she caught Malai eyeing her again, a look that started at her feet and went slowly up to her head. It would be the second of several unpleasant observations.

Everywhere Katie went, Malai's gaze followed as well as her look of disapproval. After the fifth time, Katie slammed her knife onto the cutting board and demanded, "What?"

"What do you mean?" Malai asked.

"You keep staring at me."

The corner of Malai's mouth raised. "Have I been? Guess I've just never seen a real-life whore before."

"Malai!" Sally chided.

Warmth rushed to Katie's cheeks. The embarrassment from last night, forgotten until now, returned, but with it also came anger. It was a false accusation, but one she could not defend herself from.

Malai stepped around the table. "I mean, that's what you are, isn't it? You bang your master for better food? A better bed?"

"She doesn't have a choice, Malai," Sally argued.

"You don't know what the hell you're talking about," Katie snarled.

"Katie…" Tucker pressed his hand on top of hers. Warning her.

Malai chortled. "I saw how you went off with him last night. Followed him out like he was the piper. You little slut—"

"She does not have a choice!" Sally slammed her fist on the table. "He would kill her if she—"

"Where the hell is your dignity? Your backbones? They sure as hell won't get *me* without a fight!"

"Then fight back," Katie said through gritted teeth. "Fight back with everything you've got, Malai. But don't come in here talking like you've been through what *I* have and tell me what to do about it. You do what you have to survive. And I'll do what I have to."

Katie laid the knife beside the vegetables and stepped past the others to the back door. According to the clock, time for jobs was in five minutes anyway, so she stormed out of the kitchen, swatting her blurry eyes.

She stopped by Louie's first, but he wasn't there yet, so she exited the mansion. Her tears rolled down hot as she marched down the path. Katie fetched a rake from the shed and started moving bits of mulch around to look busy. If she looked serious enough in her work, perhaps no one would poach her, pulling her away from the ocean and the sound of the water lapping against the shore. Her mind swirled too much for her to focus on anything else but the rhythmic fall of the waves.

"Are you alright?"

Katie spun around to face Jared standing on the path, stretching his arms, sweat gliding down his forehead. One earbud stayed in his ear while the other rested on his shoulder. Clearly, he had just been on his run.

"I'm fine." She dug the rake into the mulch. "It has—" She was going to say, "It has nothing to do with you," but that wasn't remotely true. It had everything to do with him. "The new girl's just a jerk is all."

"Anything I can help with?"

Katie laughed shortly. "You mean flog her?"

"Katie—"

"No." She planted the rake on the ground and faced him fully. "No, Jared, there's nothing you can do to fix it. Just get us out of here, okay?"

Jared lingered for a moment longer, and Katie returned to her raking. Finally, he continued his jog up the hill and around the corner, and once he was gone, Katie paused in her work. The sea breeze swept over her, chilling her slightly through her thin shirt.

Why had what Malai said bothered her so much? She and Jared weren't actually sleeping together.

It was something she said about dignity…

Katie brushed her fingers through her matted hair then across the scar running the length of her cheek. When had she lost her dignity? Her pride in who she was? She couldn't remember when it had actually happened. Everything had just turned into a blur.

They were going to destroy Midas, but would it be enough to return even that?

*   *   *

After taking a quick cold shower and eating another protein bar, Jared pulled on his green polo shirt and re-entered the hall of the staff quarters. After double-checking to see that his door closed snuggly behind him, he headed for the docks.

As Jared entered the foyer of the mansion, the sound of giggling reached his ears as Tucker and Malai stood by the front door, chatting. When he stepped onto the tile entryway, they clammed up immediately, their gazes fleeing to the floor. Tucker took Malai's arm and led her out the door.

Jared's stomach soured. He hadn't meant to startle them. Anxiety skittered down his arms, jostling his fingers. He knew he should go to his room, meditate, and pour a cup of tea, but after such a sleepless night, he'd be left fighting the nods more than ever. The bar, however, stood open and empty. Jared helped himself to a shot of whiskey.

Just one to still the nerves.

Upon stepping outside, the sea breeze licked through his hair and he tasted salt—a sensation he was still not used to. Living in the hills of Tennessee most of his life, he was more used to being struck with pollen or warm rain than salt.

Katie had moved on to wherever it was she went during the days. Instead, Tucker and Malai worked with the landscaping team trimming back unruly bushes. Tucker saw Jared approaching and started knocking dirt off his hands, but Jared grabbed the boy under the arm, pulling him from the flowerbed. Tucker stumbled onto the path, and Jared shoved him on ahead of him. Malai watched, slack-jawed, and Tucker gave her a look with his lip upturned.

"What the hell?" Tucker muttered once they were away. "I was coming."

"Appearances," Jared said. "She's new. She needs to get the memo. I let my guard down with her off-island and don't want her to get the wrong idea."

"No reason to take it out on me." He rubbed his arm.

Jared didn't reply. Some things were more important than Tucker's feelings.

As they entered the vehicle bay, Jared glanced at the camera in the corner and closed the door. "The boat we brought in yesterday needs to be cleaned."

"You mean the boat you kidnapped Malai in?" Tucker sneered as he grabbed the cleaning bucket from the workbench.

"It was out of my control, Tucker," Jared said. "I didn't go there to kidnap her. My job was to steal drugs."

Tucker's sneer lingered as he stomped down the dock to the most recent arrival. Jared followed him down the wooden planks and leaned against the post to which the boat was tethered. "You don't believe me?" Jared asked.

Tucker glanced at him before grabbing a container of wipes and running them over the seats. Jared dug out a cigarette, lit it, and stared out over the ocean. *Do I really believe myself at this point?*

"I met with someone shoreside," Jared said. "A friend of mine with enough money to rent a private army. He's getting something set up right now. We've managed to whittle down Midas's men to half. If we can get—"

Tucker rubbed the vinyl vigorously. "I don't give a shit. If you were going to help us, you would have done it by now."

"These things take time."

Tucker removed the next cloth with a rip and took to shining the next seat with as much vigor. He muttered something beneath his breath.

"What was that?" Jared asked.

Tucker slapped the cloth onto the seat and straightened. "You had me flogged."

"I told you, Tucker, I saved your ass from getting shot."

Tucker ripped another wipe free.

"I'm doing what I can here, Tucker. Which isn't much at the moment, but I'm trying—"

"Well, then try harder!" Tucker shouted. "Or just leave us. Take Katie and go. But all these *promises*…Just leave me out of it, okay? I don't want to hear any more promises."

"Tucker, I'm just—"

"Leave me alone!" Tucker exclaimed. "Okay? Why don't you be like the other Watchers and go kick your feet up in your office, smoke, or do whatever the hell it is the others do? I just want to be left alone." Tucker turned back to his bucket, pulled out the glass-cleaner, and sprayed down the windshield until it was dripping.

Jared continued to puff on his cigarette until the ash hung long and fell into the ocean. Then he turned on foot and trudged to his office. He closed the door and immediately the feeling of claustrophobia rippled up his back, but he swallowed it down. Tucker needed his space right now, but he'd come around.

Jared peeked out the office window to see Tucker scrubbing down the front of the windshield. At least, he prayed Tucker would come around. At this point, the kid knew too much. If he spilled his guts and…

In the bottom drawer of the desk, Jared found a bottle of Jack Daniels. He knew he should stop, but temptation won and he poured himself a glass.

The door to his office opened, and Jared dribbled part of the liquor onto his beard as Randall entered. He hid the glass behind a stack of papers.

"Warner, what do you have on your agenda for today?" Randall asked.

"Uh, nothing much," Jared said, wiping the liquor off his face with the back of his hand. "Kid's cleaning the Speedster. Other than that…"

"Good. I have a job off-island for you today. Quick pick up and delivery. Shouldn't take too long." Randall picked up the bottle of Jack Daniels from the desk, frowning at the empty glass sitting beside the stack of papers. "Little early to be drinking, isn't it?"

"My predecessor left the bottle. I was just giving it a test run."

"Yeah, old Bob was quite the fish. Grab the keys, and I'll meet you down by the boat."

Jared stopped before the lockbox where all the keys for the boats were kept and typed in the code while Randall tramped down the dock in his combat boots. As he walked past Tucker, Randall shoved the boy in the back, and Tucker fell into the water. Jared started for Tucker, but the boy bobbed up after a couple of seconds. Without a look back, Randall hopped into the speedster and started programming coordinates into the GPS by the wheel.

Jared grabbed the key and followed after Randall while Tucker fished himself out of the ocean. The boy glared at Randall's back as he clenched and unclenched his fist. With some interest, Jared realized he was doing the same thing. He pressed his palms to his sides and forced them to be as still—or at least not as obvious—as he joined Randall in the boat. "What am I picking up?"

"The boss man, Warner."

The whiskey nearly resurfaced.

"Don't look so pale, Warner!" said Randall. "After our little mission in Thailand, the boss has taken a liking to you as well. In fact, he specifically requested you pick him up so you'd have a bit of time to chat."

Randall smacked Jared on the back and returned down the docks. As he walked past Tucker, Tucker stood straight before him, although he did not meet the big man's eyes. Randall's grinned and shoved Tucker back into the drink before turning to Jared with a wave. With his best impression of a smile, Jared raised his hand in farewell.

As soon as Jared was out of sight, he shoved his fingers down his throat and vomited, hoping to remove the alcohol from his system. It takes around thirty seconds for some of the alcohol to be absorbed into the bloodstream, he knew, but the majority lingers around for twenty to thirty minutes. He wasn't sure how long it had been since he took the first shot, but hopefully it wouldn't impair him too much.

Dammit! Why had he done that?

His hands vibrated against the wheel of the boat. The shaking took over his whole frame, and his teeth chattered. Jared wrapped his arms around himself and doubled over as the tremors racked his body. Thoughts tore through his head, all of them jumbled and nonsensical. Jared closed his eyes and tried to ground. *Feel the chair beneath you. The floor under your feet.* Each time he nearly grasped the feeling, it fled from him like a skittish cat.

Jared fumbled a cigarette out of his pocket and finally managed to light it after several tries. He puffed away on the roll, allowing the ash to crumble onto the floor. Once the roll was down to a nub, he chucked it into the ocean and fished a pack of CBD gum from a hidden pocket.

Jared chewed on the piece with vigor, the tremors aiding in the pulverizing motion. Slowly, ever so slowly, the rush of adrenaline dissipated. His mind latched onto the feeling of the chair beneath him, of his feet on the floor, of the sea breeze and salt rushing over him. Although his concentration waned a few more times, he was able to bring it back. The tremors diminished, the choking sensation around his throat loosened.

Jared fired up the motor once more and pointed the boat in the direction marked by the GPS coordinates. For a long time, he stared out over the ocean concentrating on one thing: the vast blue waves before him, their steady lapping against the sides of his vessel.

Through the mire a tangible thought finally emerged: *What does Midas want with you?*

Randall said he had found favor with Midas. Was it that simple? Jared doubted it. More likely, Midas desired to get a closer look at Jared, to size him up.

To see how best to devour you.

The tremors returned in haste, but Jared gulped and shook his head. Midas may well be suspicious of him, but if he had made the connection between Jared Kelley and Jack Warner, he doubted Midas would willingly get on a boat with him.

Unless you're driving to your own execution.

But that didn't make sense either. Why waste the gas? Two in the back of the head would be just as effective on the island as off the island. Jared was still part of Midas's pack at the moment, not part of the prey. At least he hoped so.

For the next hour, Jared tumbled these thoughts through his head, never landing on a better answer. "What does it matter?" he muttered to himself finally. "Whether or not I'm walking into a trap is a moot point. Either I'll end up dead or I won't. My fate is beyond my control at this point. All I can do is roll with the punches."

After that, time rolled by much faster, and before he was ready, an island emerged into view as if springing up from the depths of the ocean. The island was small, perhaps a mile in diameter. The land curved almost in a semi-circle at one end, and a dock extended into the water.

Jared hesitated at the edge of the bay as his breathing accelerated and his knuckles turned white on the wheel.

Screw it.

He pushed the throttle forwards and sidled up to the dock.

Several trees clustered together along the edges of the island, but the center around the house was a manicured lawn. A clean, sandy beach spread along the length of the bay, a retaining wall holding back the rest of the island. Stone stairs led up to a large, three-story house covered in sandstone. The house had multiple peaks of various sizes and a shale roof. Four massive vertical windows looked out over the bay beneath the tallest of the peaks.

Mechanically, Jared exited the boat onto the dock and tethered it. It seemed no one was home. At least he had yet to be ambushed.

"Warner!" a voice called from the stony path, and Jared cupped a hand over his eyes. Midas strolled down the path toward him. He wore khaki pants, a pale yellow button-down, and flip-flops.

Jared had never seen Midas in anything less than a suit and now he was wearing flip- flops? Designer flip-flops, but still…

Midas smiled broadly and extended his hand. "Glad to see you found your way alright."

Jared mustered a smile and shook the man's hand firmly. "GPS is a great invention. Do you have any bags for me to load or—"

"Oh, we'll leave in a little bit," said Midas. "I invited you early for lunch. Please, please, come on up to the house. Everything should be about ready."

As Jared followed Midas up the walk, he scrambled to wrap his mind around the situation at hand. What in the ever-living hell was going on?

Midas led the way into the home through two massive oak doors. Vaulted ceilings rose nearly two stories, and a staircase commanded a corner to his right. On the left, chocolate-colored leather sofas and chairs formed three sides of a square, facing a stone fireplace. A coffee table made from a massive horizontal cut of a tree trunk sat in the middle of the seats. The exterior bark was still present, but had been sanded and stained a deep walnut color.

A balcony ran along the opposite side of the room with a dining area beneath it and a kitchen just visible behind a peninsula cabinet. Out onto the balcony stepped a thin woman in her forties with close-cropped black hair. Her pink dress came to her knees, and a golden pendant hung from a thick, black cord around her neck. She pressed her hands against the rail of the balcony and smiled down on Jared. "Mr. Warner! Thank you for coming today!"

Midas smiled at the woman as she glided down the stairs. "Warner, this is Jamey, my wife."

Jared's mouth fell ajar, then he clamped it shut. Had he entered an alternate dimension during his boat ride? Or did Midas just introduce him to his wife?

He had a wife? For how long?

Did Addison know about her?

The woman extended a dainty hand to him, and Jared swallowed hard as he gripped it. "It's good to meet you, Mr. Warner," she said. "Rich has told me a lot about you."

"I—uh—it's good to meet you too, ma'am." Jared released the hand and rubbed the back of his head.

Before Jared knew it, Midas—or rather Richard—and Jamey had seated him at the table in the breakfast room. The cook came in shortly thereafter with a plate of tender, juicy ribs that fell off the bone. Unfortunately, Jared could barely taste them as he struggled to keep up his manners and remain in time with the small talk. All the while his gaze kept wandering to the ring around Jamey's finger and the matching one on Midas's. Had he missed it before?

"So," Jared said, finally coming up with a fitting question that was both casual and investigatory, "how did you two meet?"

Midas finished off his Bloody Mary and draped his arm over Jamey's shoulders. "We met in college."

"*I* was in college," Jamey corrected. "You were hanging around picking up girls."

Jared crumpled the cloth napkin in his hand. *I'll bet.*

Midas laughed. "That's true. I unofficially audited a few classes, but I was less of a book person and more of a people person. I was diagnosed with dyslexia when I was a kid, but I think, in a bigger way, living in the world rather than reading about it had a greater appeal. Thankfully, Jamey here is quite the bookworm. It makes up nicely for my lack of interest in the written form."

"So, you're involved in the business as well?" Jared asked.

Jamey giggled. "Oh, honey, without me, Richard would still be blackmailing city councilmen for zoning changes and tax breaks. He certainly wouldn't be living on a private island with princes and heads of state on his speed dial."

"This is true," Midas said, and Jared took another sip of wine to hide his sneer.

"My father was the US ambassador to Spain for most of my childhood," Jamey continued. "So, I grew up surrounded by politicians, donors, fixers, all of those shakers and movers. And I knew how the game worked. So when we met, it was just the perfect match."

Jared chuckled, shaking his head. "You two sound like soulmates."

Midas slid his hand across the table, taking Jamey's into his own. Jared nearly vomited.

"So, what about you, Mr. Warner?" Jamey asked. "Do you have a special someone?"

Jared shrugged and swished the wine in his glass around. "There was a girl back home, but she ended up going with some other guy. Last I heard, she had been knocked up by him, so, no. Not really."

"Oh, I'm sorry to hear that." Jamey's pink lips curved downward. "Well, don't worry. You'll find someone who fits you just right. It might take a while." Her gaze flitted to Midas. "But it'll work out eventually."

"Yeah," Midas said, "our relationship has never been easy. A lot of on again, off again, but, as you probably know, our business ran into a few snags a couple of years back. That more than anything brought us together. We've been married almost a year now."

Jared inclined his head. Great. So now he had to add *this* psychotic relationship to his guilt roster.

"Now, I'm sure you're wondering why we asked you all the way out here," Midas said. "Truth be told, I'm looking to promote you, Warner. How would you like to have Stanton's job?"

Jared nearly choked on the ribs. "I—uh—come again?"

"Randall told me about the job you and he ran in Thailand. Like clockwork, he said. Not to mention how you proved yourself with that fiasco with Lionel. I've even spoken to your old bosses. All of them sing your praises. In fact, it seems like every job you're given flourishes."

"Or turns to gold," Jamey said with a smile hidden behind her glass. Midas eyed her before continuing.

"People respect you, Warner. You're smart, likable, a born leader. And Stanton, well, I'm starting to think he doesn't have what it takes to run his operation."

"Especially after the camera brouhaha," Jamey said.

"It's time for a fresh face. Would you be willing to be that fresh face?"

Jared sat dumbfounded. Another promotion? It wasn't like he was a super spy or anything. If anything, he was just trying to survive and make it day-by-day. Why the hell was he such a good bad guy?

But secondly, his mind raced at the benefits of such a proposition. If he had Stanton's job, there would be no need to plant the virus. All of the information regarding Midas's operations would be at his fingertips. Not only could he take out Midas, he could control the very power he wielded. *He* could be puppetmaster over all these influential parties who allowed his captivity and the captivity of his people to take place. Everyone who turned a blind eye or helped Midas would be his to destroy.

He would get his revenge.

Finally.

"Hell, yes. I'll be your guy."

Midas grinned and clamped a hand over Jared's shoulder. "Good to hear it, kid. You'll do great."

THE MIDAS TOUCH

Jared gazed over his shoulder to see Midas still swiping through his tablet as he leaned back in the seat, socked feet propped up on the rail of the boat. The wind swept across the man's hair revealing a receding hairline typically masked by his usual style. He had changed back into his suit, although the tie hung loosely around his neck and his shoes rested on the floor beside him. The ring he had left on the island.

"That son of a bitch…" Midas muttered.

"What's that, boss?" Jared asked.

Midas glanced up at him. "Oh, it's nothing really. I downloaded the *Times* onto my tablet before we headed out. It seems one of the guys working on my congressional campaign managed to secure his own seat in congress." One side of his mouth raised in a sneer as he sucked on his lip.

Jared looked out to the ocean ahead to hide the smirk rising on his face. *You're welcome, you bastard. You're going to lose more than an election by the time I'm done with you.*

"Don't you just love the ocean?" Midas asked. "There's just something about it. Something so free."

Jared's brow quirked as he stole another glance over his shoulder.

"I spent most of my childhood wishing for such freedom. Nothing like being stuck in a tiny town in the middle of nowhere."

Jared held back a retort. *Take being stuck on a twenty-acre farm behind an electric fence, you son of a bitch.*

"You grew up in Tennessee, right Warner? Did you live in the country or the city?"

"The suburbs mostly," Jared said. "A couple of foster families, lived on a few acres, but most were suburbanites."

"Most of my days were spent in my dad's two-by-four hardware store his grandfather built."

"Sounds pretty normal to me."

Midas shrugged. "It was for the most part. More than anything, it was terribly boring. Talking all day every day to the same people. Having the same conversations over and over again. How's the weather? Same as last week.

"My dad wanted my half-brother and I to run the store together once he was gone. He thought us being together *all* the time would make up for the fact that his mother wasn't my mother. Ian was all about running the store. Hell, he became a CPU to do just that. But the store was a dead-end job going nowhere. First chance I got, I moved to Chattanooga. It wasn't Atlanta, but it was bigger than Tellico."

Was this the same guy that put a gun to his head and pulled the trigger a couple of years back? How did a smalltown boy with a normal, boring childhood get to that point?

But then Jared shook his head. Did it really matter? So, he wasn't quite the psychopath Jared had believed him to be. The guy still murdered hundreds of children. Jared's people. His friends.

But as Jared watched him scroll through his tablet now, he looked weak, pathetic almost. He was so calm, so relaxed in Jared's presence, Jared could draw and fire his weapon before Midas could swipe the page again. As a child, Jared had viewed Midas as a giant with fanged teeth almost. How many times had Jared sat up drenched in sweat after dreaming about him?

But he was just a guy.

And he'll bleed just as easily as any other man…

Maybe he should stop the boat right there, subdue Midas, and make him do just that. Jared had bled enough under this man's hand. Perhaps it was time to get his revenge, once and for all…

"Hey! We're almost there!" Midas dropped his feet to the floor, stirring Jared from his bloody thoughts. "Excellent time, Warner. That might be a record." Midas slipped on his polished shoes and tied the laces.

A record? Doubtful. Flattery as a manipulation tool was the more likely answer for such a compliment, but Jared just muttered, "I aim to please," in reply.

Midas stood and placed a hand on Jared's shoulder, and Jared strained not to shrug it off. "One thing before we get into port. Not many people know about Jamey, so if we could keep that a secret, I'd appreciate it."

"My lips are sealed," Jared said as he decreased the throttle and swung the boat into the dock. Randall met them portside, and Jared tossed him the rope.

"Welcome back, boss." Randall grinned. "I take everything went well?"

Midas gripped the post and pulled himself onto the dock. "Warner's on board. We'll make the change after the party tomorrow."

"Good to hear it!" Randall slapped Jared on the back as Jared joined them on the docks.

"Until then," Midas said, "we'll keep our little arrangement between the three of us."

As they made their way up to the mansion, Jared kept his eye out for Katie, hoping to catch her alone and tell her the news. She might not be happy with her reduced role in this venture, but that was something Jared was sure she'd get over in the long run. He had never hoped for this level of success, and now that it was here, he could hardly believe it.

Katie was cleaning Louie's bar—probably her last task of the afternoon before dinner prep. She cocked her head to the side, probably confused as to why he was walking with Randall and Midas with a stupid grin on his face.

"I ran out of cigarettes," Jared told the Watchers. "I'm going to stop by my room and catch up with y'all later."

Neither Randall or Midas paid him any mind, so he entered the staff quarters, waited five minutes for them to continue on to the dining room and looped back to Louie's bar. Katie frowned at him as he walked over her freshly mopped floor to grab a bottle of scotch from the shelf.

Louie stepped in from the back, eyeing the bottle of scotch, but Jared glared at him, and he slunk off. Jared poured a glass and spoke through still lips as he brought it to his mouth. "I have good news. Can you get on laundry pick-up tonight?"

Katie pressed her mop against an invisible stain. "I can trade with Tucker, sure."

"Good." Jared set the empty glass on the counter. "See you then."

*　　*　　*

Only five baskets of laundry were set outside the doors of the staff quarters that evening. All of the other staff were out collecting the guests for tomorrow's party, and Midas hadn't been there long enough to fill a basket. If Katie stacked them, she could get them all in one go, but she planned to take them one at a time to give Jared a better window. He must have been waiting for her, however, because the door opened the moment she bent over his basket.

He leaned against the doorframe, smoke trailing from his cigarette. For the sake of the camera, Katie kept her head lowered as she stood upright. Jared took her arm and pulled her inside.

"So, what's so important it couldn't wait until tonight?" she asked.

A grin filled Jared's face as he tamped out his cigarette in the ashtray on the table. "I got another promotion."

"Congratulations? I guess?"

"I'm getting Stanton's job."

Katie's mouth fell open. "But—what about Stanton? What's Midas going to do to him?"

Jared shrugged. "Don't know, don't care. The transition is supposed to go down after the party. Randall's going to be supervising and training me before I take on the role fully, but getting the blackmail information won't be a problem after that. You're off the hook."

Katie continued to gawk. Had Jared truly impressed Midas this much?

"Katie, with this level of access, there's something else we need to consider. We will have enough information to destroy Midas easy. But what if we held onto this blackmail material for ourselves? In the same way Midas has used this information to destroy lives, we could force them to…"

Katie sank onto Jared's bed and pressed a hand to her forehead. "Jared, these people who are being blackmailed aren't just going to sit back and let you dictate their lives. They'll come after you."

"Then I'll recruit guys for protection. I'll—"

"And how are you going to pay for them? Through the drug trade? Through money extorted from corrupt politicians?"

"We'll dispense with the really bad stuff. Maybe stick to marijuana or—"

"Jared, I don't want to be in control of some drug empire or to live my life wondering if someone is about to stab me in the back. I just want to go home."

Jared drew out another cigarette and played with it as he leaned against the wardrobe. "Katie, I don't know if there's anything left for me to go home to. Jack Warner is one of the most wanted criminals in the States. There are people who can connect Jared Kelley to Jack Warner back home. Coming here, participating in Malai's kidnapping, I don't think that's just something I'm going to be able to walk away from."

"So, what are you going to do?" Katie asked. "Stay here until you fully turn into Jack Warner?"

"I'm still going to take down Midas. I'm still going to—"

"No. You are going to turn into Midas. Not at first, maybe, but eventually."

"You think I could turn into him?" Jared balked. "The guy murdered hundreds of children!"

"And you nearly shot Tucker! You would have if I hadn't been there."

Jared pounded his fist against the wardrobe, and Katie flinched. "I am not one of them!"

Katie flinched at the increase in volume, but then, shoulders heaving, Katie raised her head, meeting his eye. "Yet."

Jared sneered. "You have laundry to fetch. I suggest you get to it."

Katie drew near to Jared, and his breath caught, expanding his chest. "Yes, Goldie," she said with a curtsey, and Jared's nostrils flared.

Katie left the room and gathered up the laundry. Part of her wished to take back those words, but the other part was proud for saying them. After Tucker, after Malai, someone needed to wake him up to what he could become.

GUNPOWDER
AND LEAD

"Warner!" Stanton smacked Jared in the chest with the back of his hand, causing Jared to jump. "You alright tonight?"

Nelson and Midas, the other occupants of the table, also turned their attention to Jared, and the hair on the back of his neck raised. Ignoring the sensation, Jared stirred the remnants of his wine glass before downing the last bit. "I'm fine. Just tired is all. Didn't sleep well on the mainland."

Or at all last night. Everything around him seemed to pass like a blur, and he found himself doing unnecessary double-takes.

The wine probably wasn't helping. In a moment, he tallied how many drinks he'd had that day and then wished he hadn't. Two shots before the boat trip, a glass of wine at Midas's, a shot at Louie's, and two more glasses of wine at dinner.

The Watchers picked up their conversation once more—mainly jokes and tall tales of jobs they worked and women. Jared leaned back in his chair and pressed his hands to his face. The drabble was generally rough, but he found it intolerable tonight. He'd had a life's worth of their bullshit. Not to mention the additional ruse he was forced to bear: the secret promotion that Stanton knew nothing of.

Jared tried his best to remain indifferent to Stanton's fate, but things were never that easy. Stanton had been Jared's greatest ally since he had arrived on the island, yet he was about to betray him. Watcher or not, the prospect churned his stomach, and Jared poured another glass of wine to silence the sensation.

"Why don't you turn in, Warner?" Stanton asked.

Jared glanced to the kitchen window to see Katie in the back washing dishes. Their eyes met, and she looked away.

Oh, and there was always that. Nothing like fighting with Katie to add stress to his already overloaded system. It had just been an idea, dammit. And not even a fully-fledged one at that. What a low blow she had taken calling him Goldie. Didn't she know he was here for her?

"Warner." Stanton grabbed his arm. "Did you hear me?"

"Yeah, I heard you. I'll go get some rest." Jared set his mostly full wine glass down, pressed his palms against the tabletop, and stood. As he thought about returning to his room, he winced as he remembered the planned call to Alec tonight. Katie wouldn't get off for a couple more hours, so he wouldn't be getting to sleep until midnight or later. Probably later. When he got to his room, he was going to load up on coffee. The last thing he needed was Katie griping about his drinking to add on top of all this.

As Jared placed his hand on the dining room door, it swung back. Randall stood in the doorway, one meaty hand around Malai's arm, and the other around Tucker's. Tucker glanced up at Jared through a red, swollen eye as blood dripped from his nose and busted lip.

"What the hell happened?" Jared asked.

"I was going to ask you the same damn question, Warner." Randall shoved the kids further into the room. Malai stumbled forward, but Tucker collapsed to one knee. Randall kicked him in the stomach.

"Stop!" Malai cried. "Please! Haven't you hurt him enough?"

Randall kicked him again, and blood oozed from Tucker's mouth onto the carpet. Malai rushed at him and Randall, but she froze inches from him with the barrel of his pistol pressed against her forehead. He had retrieved the weapon so fast, Jared hadn't even seen the motion.

Randall shoved her back a few paces. "Not another move, princess."

Midas slammed his cloth napkin onto his plate and raked his chair back across the carpet as he stood. "What the hell is this, Randall?"

"Caught the kid gassing up a boat, trying to escape with his girlfriend here," Randall said.

Tucker's red, swollen eyes flitted up to Jared then away.

Jared's stomach churned against the wine. *You stupid, stupid kid!*

Stanton leaned back his chair on two legs. "Did he try to hotwire it again?"

"Nope." Randall drew a key chain from his pocket and tossed it to Jared. "Look familiar there, Warner?"

Sure enough, it was a boat key. But how had Tucker gotten it? He always made sure the kid wasn't watching whenever he typed in the code.

"I don't know how he got this key. I didn't give it to him."

"Kid said the box was open."

"I—I don't know how that could have happened. I *always* lock the box back. I—" Then Jared remembered what was going on when he got the key for the Speedster that morning. Randall had shoved Tucker into the ocean. Had he forgotten to lock the box back during that moment?

Tucker glanced back up at Jared for a second, then away once more.

"This is the same kid that hotwired the last boat?" Midas asked, and Randall nodded. "Then he's officially become more trouble than he's worth. Take him out and shoot him."

"No!" Malai screamed. "No! You can't! It's not his fault!" Stanton stood and grabbed her around the middle and dragged her toward the kitchen. "No! Stop!" she cried and flailed.

Katie stood in the bar window clutching her pendant necklace as Malai was dragged back.

"Come on, jackass." Randall dragged Tucker to his feet as the boy clutched his stomach. "Let's get this over with."

"Not by yourself, Randall," said Midas. "This is your mess, Warner. You get to clean it up."

Jared's head bobbed up and down in a nod he did not feel. Blood drained from his head and he grew suddenly dizzy. With mechanical steps, he followed Randall out of the dining hall, through the foyer, and down the steps of the mansion. Tucker scrambled with his feet, attempting to get away from the bigger man, but the brute's hold was too much.

"Please," Tucker begged. "Please, don't do this. I won't do it again, I swear. Just flog me. Flog me, please. Please, don't kill me."

Jared stared at the ground, barely perceiving when it changed from asphalt to grass.

"Warner—Warner, please," Tucker said. "Please, don't let him kill me. Please, I'm sorry, don't—"

Randall laughed, his belly heaving. "You're barking up the wrong tree there, kid. Warner's colder than *I* am."

"Please!" A tear streamed down Tucker's cheek.

Don't let them see you cry… The voice in Jared's head rang loud as if the speaker were beside him now. Landon's voice. It was what he had told Jared when they were about to be executed. *We're going to go out as men, do you hear me?*

Dead leaves collected around Jared's feet as the wind ripped through the trees, chilling him to the bone. The pines around the graveyard always looked like tall sentries, feasting off the remains of his friends. His final destination was always this place, but he never thought his own feet would take him.

"Warner," Randall's voice broke the illusion. Warmth returned to Jared's flesh and the pines dissolved into palms. "Have you ever executed anyone before?" Randall shoved Tucker deeper into the copse of trees. Tucker's pleading had turned to whimpers as he stumbled on before his captor.

Jared gulped. "Just the woman I hit before coming here."

"There's a trick to it so you don't end up sprayed with brain matter. I'll show it to you."

Jared bit his lip until it bled and warmth flowed down his chin.

"Augh, this is as good a place as any," Randall muttered and kicked the back of Tucker's leg. Tucker fell to his knees with only Randall's grip around his shirt collar to hold him upright. Randall drew his pistol from the small of his back and racked the slide.

Tucker crumpled to the ground covering his head with his hands. "Please! Please, no! Jack—Jack, please!"

A few more days, you stupid son of a bitch, and then we would have been home free. You couldn't wait a few more days?

Randall grabbed Tucker's hair and pulled him back up. Warm tears streamed down Jared's cheeks.

Why couldn't you just have trusted me? Why couldn't you wait?

Randall pressed the gun against the base of Tucker's skull, and an explosion sounded. The birds above them tore from the coppice of trees, fleeing the sudden sound. Then Randall's body hit the ground.

RED TIDE

Smoke wafted out of the barrel of Jared's pistol, curling and twisting as it dispersed. The birds cried and shouted, and Jared felt as if they were shouting at him, "What have you done? What have you done?"

Jared swayed as he lowered his gun and tucked it back into his holster. Then he glanced at the stars, just visible through the trees. The latitude and longitude were too different from his Tennessee home to determine the time.

"They'll be expecting us to bury you," he told Tucker, his voice still calm despite the tremors coursing through his body. "We have maybe an hour before they know something's up."

Tucker turned to him slowly, shoulders hunched around his ears. Upon seeing Randall lying in a pool of blood, he swallowed hard. "I didn't…I didn't think you were going to help me there."

Jared glanced at his watch without fully discerning it. "Get up, Tucker. We need to move."

Clutching his stomach, Tucker rose to his feet on wobbly knees. He grabbed the bark of the nearest tree with his nails and leaned against it. Then he retched.

Sweat soaked Jared's collar, and his own stomach lurched at each of Tucker's heaves. He fumbled the satellite phone from his pocket and punched in the numbers. Twice, he had to cancel out the wrong digits, his hands shook so wildly. Finally, it rang for Bryan.

"We need extraction now," Jared said as soon as the line connected.

"Are you blown?" Bryan asked.

Jared looked at Randall's body. "Soon enough. Did you hire your army?"

"Uhm…sort of. We can be there in two hours."

"I'll be dead in one. We'll head for the boats, and we can rendezvous for extraction at these coordinates…" Jared grabbed Tucker's arm and scrawled a line of numbers as legibly as his trembling hands would allow down the kid's forearm as he listed the same to Bryan.

"We'll be there," Bryan said, and Jared hung up.

"Do you have your wits?" Jared asked Tucker.

"I—uh—" Tucker scraped the sweat off his forehead with the back of his hand and cleared his throat. "I think so."

"Get to the boats, fuel up the Speedster, and sabotage the others. I'll go get the kids."

"The cameras on the docks…that's how I got caught last time."

"I'll take care of them. And Tucker, if the Watchers are closing in and we're not going to make it, leave us."

"Leave you? But—"

"Do not hesitate. Get the hell out of here, Tucker. Better for one of us to survive than none of us, understand?"

Tucker cleared his throat twice more and nodded.

Jared held the boat keys and satellite phone out to him. "This is it, Tucker. We're going home."

*   *   *

Katie smashed her hands against her ears and squinched her eyes closed tight. Even through the flesh of her palms she heard Malai chanting, "It's my fault, it's my fault, it's my fault. . ." as she rocked in the corner with her legs tight against her chest. Even through the thick walls of the mansion, they had heard the shot.

A single shot. An execution.

"Katie—" One of the little ones tugged on the fringe of her tattered shirt. Wide, brown eyes peered up at her.

Katie took a staggering breath. "Yes, Selena."

"I'm scared." Selena's lip trembled and her eyes were glossed with moisture. Katie picked her up and pressed the child's chest to her own. Her own tears she let fall behind the little girl's back. "It's going to be okay."

With the smallest of sounds, the door opened and Jared entered halfway, his hand gripping the door jamb with pale knuckles. The other workers retreated against the back wall, eyes down. Selena dropped from Katie's grip and buried her face into Sally's belly as Katie stood between them and their captor.

Blood speckled Jared's face and shirt. Had he fired the shot himself? Clamping a hand to her mouth, Katie let out a torturous moan.

Seeming not to notice, Jared peeked into the hallway then back. "We need to go. Now."

But Katie stood frozen in place, unable to process what he had said. Her fingers grew numb. The room grew fuzzy at the edges and Jared swayed in her vision.

"Katie—" He stepped in the room, letting the door click shut behind him. "Did you hear me? We need to go." He shook her gently by the shoulders.

"Blood," Katie whispered. "You're covered in Tucker's blood."

Jared brushed his fingertips over his face and frowned at the red. "Randall's, not Tucker's."

"R-Randall's?"

Jared glanced at the camera in the corner. "We have a small window. I knocked out the guy in the monitor room, but he won't be out forever. Tucker's at the docks getting a boat ready. We need to go now though, or we're dead."

Tucker's alive? With a shake of her head, Katie dispelled the cobwebs and looked back at the others still huddled against the wall away from them. Sally's wide eyes pleaded for an explanation, but feeling had not yet returned to Katie's tongue.

Returning to the door, Jared pressed his thumb into the keypad and the door unlocked. He peered into the hall once more. "Explain it to them."

"Uhm." Katie pressed a hand to her forehead. "Jared, I mean Jack, his name is actually Jared. He's undercover. He's going to help us escape."

Sally peeled Selena from her leg and spoke to Katie in hushed tones, "I don't know what he's been saying to you, but. . ."

"He's not a Watcher," Katie said. "He's one of us. Jared was taken when he was seven years old, but he managed to get out and—"

Sally's eyes grew even wider as her gaze of suspicion intensified.

"Oh for f—" Jared swore and yanked the back of his shirt up to his neck, exposing the mass of tangled, contorted flesh, now silver and raised above the healthy skin. "You don't get those marks from easy living. I'm one of you, Sally. Now, come on. We *have* to go!" With a shrug of the shoulders, the shirt went back down.

The workers stood staring at Jared, disbelief still written on their faces. Jared rolled his eyes and opened the door wide. "Come or don't, but the window is collapsing."

Katie gestured to Sally to follow, but it was Malai who stepped forward. "I knew there was something fishy about you," she said.

Jared sneered at her as she slipped past him. Katie came next then the others. The wounds had been a decent defense, but the others still remained as far from his as possible as they exited as well. When Katie stepped into the hall, he took her arm. "Keep them together. If anyone spots us, let me do the talking. If anyone starts shooting, run for the boats."

Katie gulped and nodded. "Give me a gun."

Jared considered her momentarily then pulled a piece from an ankle holster. "Your dad said he took you to the range. Do you remember how to shoot?"

Katie's hands sagged from the weight as she took the surprisingly warm weapon. Then she gripped the gun with her right hand and braced it with her left like a saucer. "Shoot for center mass. Don't point it at anything you don't intend on killing."

"Sounds like we got the same speech." Jared stepped ahead of the others to the door, drew his pistol, and shoved the door open with his shoulder. Gun raised, he cleared left then right before sprinting across the asphalt and into the brush. Keeping the gun trained on the road in the direction of the beach, he jerked his head, indicating for the others to follow.

"Come on," Katie prodded them, and the kids took off running to the other side. They crouched in the grass behind Jared as he pressed his body against a tree.

"Stay in the brush-line," he said and slid the gun back into the holster. "Katie, keep them parallel to me and as silent as possible." Stepping back into the road, Jared shoved his hands into his pockets and sauntered down the lane.

With the help of Sally and Malai, Katie corralled the young ones in a mass that traveled with him down the path. For the first time, Katie was grateful for the manicured bushes that ran the length of the road. Soon, they reached the end of the hill and the bushes curved away from the warehouse to run parallel to the shore. No break in the bushes was to be found, however, so they crouched at the bend, waiting for further instructions.

Jared stood with his back to them and lit a cigarette. After a couple of puffs, he whispered, "In groups of two, cross the road to the warehouse."

"What about the light?" Katie whispered back. The light above the warehouse would make their crossing obvious to anyone who might be passing by.

"Just a sec." Jared crossed the street and stepped inside the warehouse.

"I knew there was something up about that guy," Malai whispered. "He wasn't into it as much as his friends."

"Hush," Katie replied.

"Katie," Sally whispered next, "how long have you known Jack was undercover?"

"Since he got here." Sally's face tilted in the dim light, and Katie could sense her questioning gaze. "Jared was in my first camp. He's the one that broke everyone out."

"So…you two weren't sleeping together?" Malai asked.

"No. We're just friends. It was a cover."

Sally chortled. "I wish *I* had *just* friends like that."

The streetlight went out as well as the lights in the front half of the building. Moments later, the cherry glow from the end of Jared's cigarette marked his exit from the shop. He was nearly to them when a voice cried out, "Hey, Warner!"

Jared froze, the end of his cigarette blazing red then dulling. Sharply, he turned on heel and dropped the cigarette to the ground. "Nelson, what's up?"

"You got a cigarette?"

Katie bit her lip. *A cigarette? Dammit! Please, God, don't let us get caught because of a cigarette!*

Jared produced a cigarette for his comrade, and Nelson stuck it between his teeth. He leaned in while Jared offered a light, but Jared's thumb faltered several strikes, and when a flame emerged, it danced and shook.

Katie petted Selena's head and squeezed her close. None of the children moved, and half held their breath. *Come on, Jared. Keep it together.*

Nelson held out his hand. "Let me do it."

"Sorry," Jared grumbled as he passed it over.

"Rough night, huh?" Nelson asked as the flame sparked and caught on the base of his cigarette. "Kid had it coming for some time though. You know that, right?"

"Yeah," Jared barked a laugh and jammed his toe into the asphalt. He looked their way then ripped his eyes back to Nelson.

Nelson glanced their way too and his brow furrowed. "You gonna be okay, Warner?"

"Yeah, yeah, of course." Jared let out a puff of smoke and scratched the back of his head. "I'm out here to clear my head. Muddle through this shit."

"Right, right," Nelson said. "I'll let you be. But if ever you need to talk, just remember we're all in this together, alright?"

Jared nodded. "I appreciate it."

Nelson slapped him on the shoulder and turned for the house. Katie let out a pent-up breath, and the others relaxed as well.

Then Nelson's radio crackled to life on his hip. "Anyone seen Randall or Warner?"

Nelson touched the radio on his hip. "You got your radio?"

"Oh, uh—" Jared brushed his empty hip then palmed his forehead. "No, I forgot it at the house."

Nelson answered on the radio, "I'm here at the docks with Warner. What's up, boss?"

"Send him up to my office," Stanton replied. "If anyone sees Randall, tell him to come too."

"Will do, boss." Nelson gestured with his head to the house. "I'll walk up with you."

Jared shuffled his feet. "Su-re. Let me lock up first." As he turned back to the warehouse door, Jared rested his hand on his holster. He extracted his keys out with his other hand, and they jangled as his hands shook.

Katie adjusted her grip on her pistol. What were they supposed to do if Jared went back up to the house? Keep going to the warehouse? Would they leave without him?

The radio cracked to life with Stanton's voice once more. "Randall is down! I repeat, Randall is down! Nelson, detain Warner immediately!"

Nelson raised his weapon, training it on Jared. The keys fell from Jared's hand, landing on the ground with a crash.

"Take your gun out of the holster and set it on the ground!" Nelson shuffled forward. "Nice and slow there, Warner."

"Katie," Sally hissed. "Katie, do something—"

Katie glanced at the others then at the gun in her hand.

Jared raised his other arm up. "It's a misunderstanding, Nelson. I can explain—"

With his shoulder, Nelson shoved Jared face-first into the wall. He pulled Jared's gun out of the holster and tossed it into the sand beside the warehouse. Pressing his gun into Jared's back, he hissed, "Not a move, not a word."

Katie popped up above the bushes and aimed the gun at Nelson. But Nelson was right against Jared! What if she missed? What if the bullet went through?

The sound of running feet came from the road behind, and a shadow sprinted toward them. Katie turned the gun and fired at the shadow.

The shot went wide right, smacking into a tree beside the shadow, and Stanton leaped for cover on the side of the road. Katie fired again for good measure, and Stanton shot back, his bullets sailing past her through the bushes.

"Shit!" Katie shouted. "Our cover is shit!"

Nelson ran for cover on the other side of the warehouse too, leaving Jared behind. Jared grabbed his gun from the sand and fired toward Stanton twice then once in Nelson's direction.

Lenny screamed as a bullet grazed his arm.

"Sally!" Katie cried. "Get them to the warehouse, I'll cover you!"

Katie rushed for cover behind a tree and fired from that position. Damning the branches, Sally tore through the bush-line, sprinting for the warehouse. The kids followed in a mass, taking cover behind Jared. He directed them into the ocean behind him—the same route Katie and Tucker had tried months before.

Katie stood and fired at Nelson, but the gun clicked. Wide-eyed, she stared at the useless, empty gun. She burst through the bush-line and sprinted for safety against the wall of the warehouse.

"Go!" Jared cried as he slammed a fresh magazine home. "Tucker has a boat waiting. Bryan's going to rendezvous. Get out of here!" He fired at Nelson, and a cry came from his target.

"Give me some bullets first," Katie said, and Jared dumped a handful into her palm. She loaded as quickly as she could. "What about you?"

"I'll retreat once you get to the ladder, now go!"

Katie took off for the ladder, her feet kicking up sand. She stumbled as she entered the water, but she splashed her way on. As he promised, Jared retreated once she reached the ladder.

Katie took the rungs two at a time as the sound of gunfire grew nearer. As she neared the top, Stanton rounded the corner. Jared fired at him over his shoulder, but Stanton didn't flinch as the wild shots landed somewhere across the road. Instead, he aimed down the sites and fired.

Jared smashed face-first into the sand, and a wave of water rushed over him.

"No!" Katie cried.

Jared rolled over and sat up, firing again. Only one shot rang out before the slide shot back, the magazine empty.

Katie fired at Stanton. He fired back, dropped his mag and reloaded within a span of a breath. Jared tried to stand but fell back into the water, clutching his leg. Katie dropped from the ladder, crouched low, and fired again. Stanton retreated behind the warehouse corner.

"What are you doing?" Jared cried. "Get the hell out of here!"

"Get your ass up the ladder!" she cried.

Stanton fired, and the bullets whizzed past her. Jared scooted to the ladder and gripped the rungs. Katie glanced at his leg to see blood pooling on his jeans already. He hopped up the rungs on one leg, groaning as he did so. Stanton fired once more, and Katie attempted a return, but her gun clicked once more.

"Hurry, Jared!" she cried.

Jared looked down at her, face pale in the moonlight. Stanton emerged from the corner, and, facing no bullets, rushed from the warehouse corner. Jared's mouth formed a line as his eyes locked onto hers. "Get out of here, Tucker! We're not going to make it."

A purring sound rose just above the waves as Tucker revved the engine and took off toward the horizon. Their way out officially gone.

Stanton paused in his advance as the boat peeled out, his gaze fixed on the fleeing captives. Then he re-gripped his weapon. "Get down, Warner."

Jared looked down at Katie once more. There was much in that glance. Defeat. Pain. But what else was there to do?

Jared hopped back down the ladder on his one leg. Wincing, he landed in the sand beside her, and the waves lapped around their knees. His pant leg was already dark.

"I hope she was worth it, Warner," said Stanton. "Because this bitch just killed you."

Katie found, strangely, that she didn't really care about what happened to her. If escape was no longer an option, then death was fine. But she didn't want Jared to die. Not because of her.

But Jared said, "Dying is easy, Stanton. She caused me to live again."

"Augh, you've got to be kidding me," Stanton sneered. "I'm going to be sick. Get back to the road. Both of you." He waved them on with his gun, and they walked together, hand-in-hand. Midas and Nelson stood waiting for them beneath the dead bulb above the bay door with guns drawn.

"A boat took off," said Stanton. "I don't know who was on it. The boy and probably—"

"All of them," Midas said. "They're all gone."

"Then we need to go after them!"

"They sabotaged the other boats," Nelson replied. Part of his ear was missing, and blood dripped down his neck.

Stanton looked out over the ocean where the boat had disappeared into the night. "What now, boss?"

Midas eyed Katie up and down, and, for the first time in years, she held her chin up, meeting his eyes.

"You haven't won," he snarled. "I own everyone in this part of the world. Your little friends out there are going to be intercepted by my boats and shot. I will still win and with—" he glanced at Nelson's bleeding ear and the blood pooling on Stanton's arm— "minimal casualties."

Jared laughed, and Midas narrowed his eyes. "What?"

"You narcissists are so predictable," Jared said. "You run an operation based on a tiny island near some third-world countries. You're a has-been, Midas. Irrelevant but to a few."

Stanton slugged Jared in the nose. Jared crumpled to the ground, and Katie lunged for Jared to help him, but Nelson grabbed her arm, dragging her back.

"I trusted you!" shouted Midas as he dug his heel into Jared's bullet wound, causing him to squirm. "You son of a bitch! You could have had everything!"

"I don't know," Jared managed with a shaking voice once Midas let up. "Do *you* have everything, Stanton? Because *he* was offering me your job! Isn't that right, Midas?"

Midas's thin lips curled as Stanton turned to him. "You were going to replace me, boss? With this kid?"

"He's lying," Midas said. "It's just a way to—"

"He blames you, Stanton, for the cameras in the rooms." Jared pressed his hand against his leg and red pooled around his fingers. "I must say, I had quite a bit of fun watching you guys go around blaming each other, all while confiding in the guy who planted them in the first place."

Midas ripped his gun from the waistband of his pants. "Who the hell are you? Interpol? CIA?"

Jared smirked. "I'm unaffiliated."

"Who do you work for?" Midas ground his heel into the wound again, and Jared cried out.

"Stop it!" Katie pleaded. "Please!" Nelson smacked her, stifling her protests.

"Get them inside," Midas ordered. "We'll get to the bottom of this."

After dragging him inside the warehouse, Stanton bound Jared to a straight-back chair in the center of the vehicle bay while Nelson stood over Katie with his gun drawn but arms crossed.

"Surely we have some jumper cables around here," Midas muttered, and Stanton wandered off to find them, pulling open drawers, checking in cabinets, all while clutching his bloody arm.

"Don't expect me to tell you where they are," Jared replied as his good foot tapped against the cement floor. Blood formed a pool beneath his wound.

Midas bent over him, meeting his eye. "You've got spirit, kid. It's probably why I liked you so much. But you're a lot denser than I thought you were. Do you think you won't talk? Everyone talks."

"Come on, Midas. We both know you'd be doing this whether I had secrets or not. My keeping them is just my way of telling you to get bent."

"Boss," Stanton said, "what about the girl?"

Midas glanced over his shoulder at Katie, and she lowered her head. He sauntered over to her and pressed his gun against the top of her head. "Tell me who you are, or I blow her brains out."

Jared's eyes locked with Katie's, and she nodded, understanding his intention.

"How do you think she's survived you for this long, Midas?" Jared asked. "Your men torture her for the hell of it. Torture her, kill her, it makes no difference. She knows how to escape you."

Midas laughed. "What the hell are you talking about?"

"Katie," Jared said levelly, "you don't need to stay here for this."

And with permission granted, Katie closed her eyes and felt herself ascending, leaving her body, watching as if from above. Midas shoved Katie in the chest, but she remained in her trance-like state. He slapped her, but she had been smacked around so many times, it barely registered.

"Neat trick," Midas muttered as he re-holstered his weapon. "Too bad you can't do that. Now, where were we?"

As Katie began to float above them, she stopped. A sound came to her, just over the waves of the sea lapping against the dock. A buzzing sound. Was it Tucker's boat returning?

"Well, let's see," Jared said. "You were going to hook me up to a car battery, and I was going to tell you shit."

Katie arrived back in her body and blinked. The sound was louder. More distinct, but still, she could not place it. Judging from the expressions of the others, they had not heard it yet.

"Cut off his shirt. If he's one of Arhrit's men, he'll have tattoos," Midas said.

Stanton flipped open his switchblade and sliced through Jared's shirt. The black-and-red phoenix sprawled across his flank and up the side of his chest. But other lines and scars crept around from his back as well, silver and raised above the skin.

Jared grinned at Midas as recognition dawned in the man's eyes as to the meaning of those scars.

"What the hell?" Stanton gripped Jared's neck and pulled him forward. He yanked on the shirt, exposing the mass of torn flesh across his back.

"I'm not as good at dissociation as Katie," Jared smirked, "but I'm not new to this rodeo either, boys."

The whirring grew louder, and for a second, the moon disappeared.

"So, this little visit is personal, is it?" Midas sneered.

"Give the man a gold star!"

"How disappointing it must be for you to have come all this way to 'destroy me' only to die tonight. For nothing."

"Oh, I destroyed you a long time ago, Midas. I'm just nailing your coffin shut," Jared said. "You know the problem with victimizing children? They grow up."

Midas's brow crunched as he studied Jared, but no sign of further revelation crossed his face. Jared cocked back his head and laughed. "You still don't recognize me? You really are slipping, old man. Why the hell was I ever afraid of you?"

Midas stepped forward, inspecting the phoenix tattoo and the scar rippling above the ink. "No way in hell," he whispered as he read the word 'LIAR' carved in Jared's flesh.

"You really should have loaded that second bullet."

Midas snarled. "You son of a bitch!" He grabbed Jared's thigh and squeezed. Jared howled in pain, masking the sound of the ever-growing whir. Midas pounded his fist against Jared's face in a flurry of punches.

"No," Katie whispered. The shadow on the horizon grew, but Jared had seconds, not minutes.

Nobody paid her any attention as she rose to her feet. Midas pressed into Jared's wound again, and Jared cried out, weaker this time.

"Stop it!" Katie lunged at Midas, but he shoved her back. As she made another go at his hands, Midas shook her free, and she fell at his feet. "Stop it! Stop it, please!"

Midas reached for his gun, but his eyes grew huge to find the holster empty. He turned to Katie where she knelt doubled-over, groveling. Then with a smirk, she raised up and fired his gun, striking him in the center of his chest.

Jared knocked his chair over sideways, striking Stanton's legs. Stanton toppled to the ground with the chair on top of him. Katie fired at Nelson before he could finish his draw, and blood soaked his shirt. Stanton freed himself from Jared's chair, drew his pistol and aimed, but Katie's remaining bullets hit him center-mass, and he fell dead on the ground.

The whirring sound roared as a helicopter rushed over the boat house to the mansion. It hovered over the drive and ten guys in black dropped from ropes to the ground below. They cleared the mansion first.

Jared, still lying on his side, nodded to Katie's still-smoking gun. "I see your dad gave *you* the advanced course."

As Katie righted his chair onto all four legs, Jared grunted. His breaths were heavy, and his face was pale. Using Stanton's blade, Katie cut through his bonds. "I'll look for something to stop the bleeding." An old oil rag was the best she could find, and she pressed it against his wound. "Hold pressure," she ordered, but Jared's hands were nearly limp.

"Katie, I—" he began, his voice weak.

"Get down on the ground!" One of the raiders rushed at Katie, rifle raised, and she backed away, both hands in the air.

"My friend! He's hurt!" she cried.

"I said get down on the ground!"

Katie lay on her stomach, hands stretched out before her, and her arms were secured behind her back. Another raider dragged Jared from the chair, and he crashed to the floor with a feeble moan. His hands were secured as well.

"Katie," Jared whispered, "I love you."

"Hang in there, Jared," she told him. "It's not time for goodbyes. We're almost there. Stay with me."

Into his radio, the raider spoke words Katie did not recognize. She guessed it to be Thai. Who were these guys?

"Please," she said. "He's hurt. Can't you see that? He's been shot."

"Shut up!" the man ordered.

With no one holding pressure to his wound, blood flowed freely from it once more, sliding across the slick concrete of the bay.

"Hold on, Jared," Katie pleaded.

If he heard her, he made no sign of it. Jared stared at an oil spot on the floor for several moments, then his eyes shut.

"Jared!" Katie shouted, and his eyes opened and shut once more. "Jared, no! You stay with me!"

"I said be quiet!" The raider raised the butt of his gun above her head.

"Stop!" another man shouted from the bay entrance. Bryan tossed his helmet to the side and ripped off his balaclava. "She's a friendly. Katie, where's Jared?" She nodded to him, and Bryan swore. "Get a medic!" he ordered to the raider before rolling Jared over.

The raider muttered something in Thai and spoke into his radio once more. Bryan pressed his balaclava to Jared's wound, and it was saturated almost immediately.

"Medic!" Bryan shouted. "Do you have one of those? Or at least a med kit?"

A woman in tactical gear with a caduceus on her lapel joined them and felt for a pulse on Jared's wrist. She quickly moved to the neck. "Friend or foe?"

"Friend. A good friend. And so is she." Bryan cut Katie's restraints and the medic passed them both supplies from her dufflebag.

"Mr. Rosenbaum," said the medic, "get his vitals. Girl, you hold pressure. I'm going to start an IV while they come with a stretcher. If your friend here is going to live, we need to get him off this rock immediately."

As Katie pressed the gauze to Jared's wound, he let out a moan and his eyes flickered open. At first, his gaze was glazed over, but then it latched onto his friend. "Hey, Bryan," he said feebly.

"Hey, yourself." Bryan blinked through tears. "Hang in there, buddy. I don't want to have to explain this one to your sister, do you hear?"

"This one is alive." The raider nudged one of the bodies with his foot. "Do you want to save him too?"

Horror-stricken, Katie turned to see Midas's chest rising and falling with shuddering breaths as he watched them from the corner of his eye. A red blotch grew ever wider on his chest and his face was paler than Jared's. His mouth moved as if trying to speak.

"Friend or foe?" the medic asked, pressing two fingers to Midas's throat.

"Foe," Bryan croaked.

"Then I won't give him morphine," she said and returned back to Jared.

For the next few minutes, Midas continued to watch them, his blood-covered chest rising and falling. Rising and falling. And then it stopped.

Fire leaped from the windows of the mansion as black smoke rose in a tower above the island as they lifted off in the helicopter. Jared lay on the floor in a canvas stretcher beside three hundred pounds of heroin. Two duffle bags propped up his legs and a tube filled with blood dripped into his arm from a bag suspended on a hook above his head. The medic continued to take his vitals every so often, but stated she had otherwise "stabilized him."

But the hand Katie clutched was so cold and still that the medic's words provided little comfort. The expression on Bryan's face as he gnawed on his thumbnail did not assure her either, and as Katie brushed a lock of his brown hair from Jared's face, she pleaded, "Come on Jared! We've come so far. Don't leave me now!"

An explosion came from the mansion below them, and fire poured out of the roof. Smoke and ash lingered outside the helicopter windows for several minutes until they cleared the area.

"Did you get the laptop?" Katie asked Bryan.

He stopped gnawing on his thumb for a moment to shake his head.

"What? Bryan! That was the whole point of the—"

"Not my call, Katie."

"What do you mean, 'not your call.' You hired these people!"

The medic chuckled as she slid her stethoscope into her ears and pumped up the blood pressure cuff around Jared's arm once more.

"They're not mercenaries," Bryan said. "They're Arhrit's men."

Katie's mouth fell open. "Arhrit? The drug dealer? Malai's dad?"

"Yeah, as strange as it sounds, money can't buy everything, Katie. Especially when no one will take it." Bryan leaned against the wall of the helicopter. "My mom's the primary account holder on my credit card, and since she didn't even know I was *in* Thailand…well…let's just say the transaction didn't go through. So, I contacted Arhrit instead."

"But why didn't he get the laptop?"

Bryan shrugged. "He didn't want the giant target on his back. And now that I think about it, I wouldn't want that sort of target on our backs either."

"But all the people who supported Midas, who turned a blind-eye to what he did—"

"The laptop is destroyed. Midas is dead. You're not. All of our people are free, and no one will be rebuilding this organization from the ashes. Take the win, Katie."

But Katie's stomach churned as she watched the tower of black smoke grow smaller and smaller in the distance. Her chance at vengeance, at exposing every last person who allowed this atrocity to take place, was gone. Those cowards who turned a blind-eye while children were starved and murdered to save their miserable selves—they would get a free pass. They would return to their lives and sleep calmly in their beds tonight.

But she wouldn't. Not with the memories that plagued her.

The helicopter hit turbulence, and Jared rose up, grabbing for his leg. Upon seeing Katie and the medic above him, he swung wildly at them.

"Hold him down!" the medic ordered, and Bryan and Katie grabbed his arms.

"Jared, it's okay," Katie said. "It's me." But he twisted and tried to break free of their grasp. He swept his leg into Bryan's knee and roared with pain.

The medic jabbed a needle into his arm through the sleeve, and Jared's eyes grew wide as his pupils dilated. Then he fell back onto the floor, out cold once more.

The medic recapped the needle. "It's just a sedative. Should keep him out for an hour or so." She shoved the stethoscope back into her ears and pumped up the cuff once more.

The helicopter passed over a couple of towns before landing in a jungle clearing. Arhrit's men unloaded Jared's canvas stretcher onto the thick, brambly grass, and Katie and Bryan sat cross-legged beside him while the others buzzed about, unloading and packing the heroin into trucks waiting at the edge of the clearing.

Jared's color had improved after receiving two bags of blood, but the shadow of blood on his leg bandage continued to expand.

"Ma'am," Bryan said to the medic, "tell me the truth. Is he going to make it?"

The woman lit a cigarette and clutched it between her teeth as she set up another bag of fluid. Her headlamp swayed and bobbed as she moved. "He'll probably make it, sure. Don't know about that leg though. Tourniquet needs to come off soon, or he'll lose it."

"I be sure to get him best medical treatment possible," a voice said above them, and Katie peered up in the darkness, unable to make out the face. "You don't remember me, Katie?" The light of a phone illuminated the speaker's face as he grinned from ear to ear.

Still, Katie struggled until the memory finally clicked. "Zhang?"

"Zhang!" Bryan leapt to his feet and enveloped the boy in a hug. "What are you doing here?"

"Your girlfriend messaged me on Facebook!" Zhang said. "I talk to Dad. He pulling strings to get you home."

"Your English!" Katie said. "It's a lot better."

"Private tutor. Better than Bryan."

Bryan looked to the boxes of heroin being loaded up. "And the Chinese ambassador is okay with all the drugs?"

Zhang waved his hand. "This is Dad's real job. Why you think assholes take me? But no matter, you come with me, and Goldie go to a hospital."

"I go where he goes," Katie said, reclaiming Jared's hand.

"Uh, no." Zhang said. "Goldie need hospital. That mean official papers, everything. You get smuggled out. Safer that way. No politics."

"But—" Katie ran her thumb over Jared's hand. If she let it go now, would she ever hold it again?

Zhang knelt beside her. "Katie, I trusted you in *your* country. You trust me in *my* country. Okay?"

"Look, you two," the medic said. "If we're going to save the leg, we need to move."

Bryan wrapped an arm around her shoulders. With a sob, Katie let go of Jared's hand, and two of Arhrit's men picked up the stretcher and loaded him into the back of a panel van.

Come home, Jared. Please.

FORGOTTEN LIFE

Like most kids growing up, Katie had imagined clouds to be made of cotton balls, or at least the fluff that emerged from the seams of her beloved doggy bed companion, and her flight to Grandma's house when she was five years old had only intensified that belief. During that trip, she had wanted to open the door of the airplane and leap into the clouds, sure that they would catch her and let her play with the sundrops. It had been a nice fantasy. A happy fantasy.

She had not had such fantasies in a long time, happy or otherwise.

Now, as Katie looked down upon the clouds, all she could wonder was how much rain could gather there before it tumbled to the earth.

It was a Jared-like thought if she had ever heard of one. Had he always been this way—thinking only of reality and never make-believe? Or had Midas taken that from him too? Because she couldn't imagine a Jared, big or little, that saw images in the clouds or created worlds in his mind. She couldn't imagine him happy. Just as she could not imagine herself happy again either.

The last few days had not helped. Sure, nothing evil had befallen them during that time, but each step of their journey home had been plagued with new faces, new situations, new fears.

Zhang had put her and the others on a slow boat to Hawaii manned by a group of smugglers. According to his promises, there had been no illegal content or activity on the boat (that was going to be on the return trip), but the men had made them nervous, nonetheless.

In truth, however, they could have been saints from Heaven and they still would have made them nervous.

Even though he had other options, Bryan had elected to go with them, reasoning, "I'm the only one with a gun and enough cash to get us out of a jam if we get in trouble."

Katie had appreciated the gesture. In fact, without him, the trip would have been sheer torture. He acted as their leader, speaking with the sailors on their behalf and ensuring everyone had what they needed. During the journey, Katie realized she had not known much about him from their old camp other than the fact that he smoked pot, but he proved to be a smart, capable kid. He was great with the young ones too—his experience as a Hut Leader no doubt helped with that. Also, the Disney movies on his laptop helped time go by much faster than it would have without him.

When the ship crossed into American waters, it was immediately swarmed by Coast Guard vessels. No shots were fired, nor was any violence of any sort taken, but the men in guns rushing in had been another terrifying experience. Bryan had been in contact with the FBI since leaving the mainland, so they were expected. That didn't make it less scary.

Ever since then, they had been in the custody of the United States Government. They had lacked for nothing. The food was excellent, the hotel room was fantastic. The interviews conducted by the FBI, however, were not.

But finally, after everything, it was over. She was going home. And on Bryan's private jet no less.

Leida had met them at the base of the steps, her golden hair glowing in the sun. It was not up in her customary braid, but hanging long in waves down her back. When she saw Katie, her face lit up, and she ran to her arms wide.

The girl was larger than Katie had remembered, but the reason did not compute until Leida's abdomen pressed against Katie's. It was bulbous and firm, and not well hidden beneath Leida's clothes.

"I'm so glad you're okay!" Leida had said as she cupped Katie's face.

"Good to see you too, Leida," Bryan remarked. "Are you glad I'm okay?"

Leida grabbed Bryan's collar and pulled him into a kiss. "I am. More than you know."

Katie turned to Bryan, an unspoken question on her lips.

Leida burst laughing. "Yes, Katie, it's his."

And ever since then, they had been flying thousands of feet above the ground, returning to a home Katie barely believed still existed.

It was all too surreal.

Would anyone recognize her when they arrived? Would they be as stumped by her appearance as she had been stumped by Jared's? Her face was marred, her hair matted. If someone handed her a photograph of herself the day before she was taken, she might not recognize it.

And what of everyone else? Bryan and Leida were expecting a freaking baby. She hadn't seen that one coming! Leida had been getting over Dakota last she'd seen her.

Her friends at school would have graduated high school without her. They were probably all caught up in their own lives, looking toward college or jobs or whatever. What was Katie looking forward to?

"Excuse me, ma'am—" Katie jumped at the voice, not having seen the stewardess approach from behind. How had she managed to sneak up on her? Katie started berating herself for her carelessness before taking a shuddering breath to remind herself of where she was, of how safe she was.

"Sorry." The woman smiled, her red lipstick stretching across her face. "Would you like something to drink? A soda? Water?"

"Do you have any tea?" Katie asked. "Chamomile?"

The smile faltered then recharged as the stewardess glanced at her boss, the young man in the seat across the table from Katie. "I'll see what I can find. And for you, Mr. Rosenbaum? Ms. Kelley?"

"I'm good," Bryan said.

"Tea sounds good to me," Leida, who sat beside Katie, said, patting Katie on the knee. A flash of sunlight reflected on the giant stone around Leida's finger as she returned the hand to her swollen belly. The stewardess nodded and returned to the back to collect their beverages.

"Have you heard any word about Jared?" Katie asked.

"According to Agent Rogers, he beat you guys back to The States by a couple of days," Leida said. "But the FBI won't tell us where he's being kept. Some mix-up about the Jack Warner thing."

So Zhang had kept his promise. That was a relief.

Katie found her gaze being pulled to Leida's belly once more. It was hard not to be drawn to it. "I don't mean to pry, but does Jared know about…"

Leida giggled, and Bryan paled. "No," Leida said. "But that's his own fault. He hasn't exactly been easy to reach lately."

Katie grinned as she leaned back in her seat, shaking her head at Bryan. "He's gonna kill you. . ."

"Maybe I'll ask Cara to pour me something too after all." Bryan rose and strolled to the back. "Something more powerful than chamomile, perhaps."

"Jared will huff and puff, but that's all he'll do. He loves me *and* Bryan. And it's not like Bryan can't afford to get married or anything."

Katie laughed as she took in the couch, the wide-screen TV behind their seats, and the two model-like stewardesses that served them on Bryan's private jet. Bryan being a millionaire had not been something Katie had anticipated. But it was hard to envision any beaten and battered kid being the child of such wealth.

Katie tugged on the edge of her giant shirt, a maternity shirt borrowed from Leida that hung on her shoulders like a sack. At the hotel, she had tried to fix her hair, but it was a pointless venture. She couldn't even bring a comb through her hair.

Her hair…She hated to meet Dad and Alec with hair like that. There was nothing to be done about her scar, but her hair? Why had she let it get that bad?

The stewardess returned with three teas and a disappointed Bryan. "They won't serve me alcohol until I'm twenty-one," he muttered.

Katie giggled. The kid had just come from Myanmar where he busted up a drug cartel and a human trafficking ring, and still, not even his own staff would serve him drinks.

"Katie," Leida said, "I hope you don't mind, but I was wondering if I could look at your hair for a minute."

Instinctively, Katie touched her tangled strands. "Oh, I don't know if there's anything you can do about them, Leida. I'll probably just end up getting it cut off."

"Cut off?" Leida said. "But that would be a shame! I love your hair! I always wanted to ask you if I could braid it, but never got up the nerve."

Leida like *her* hair? Leida, with the perfect golden locks? Katie's face grew warm and she looked away.

"If you're not comfortable, that's okay," Leida said.

"No, it's not that. It's just—do you really think you can do anything with it?"

Leida grinned. "I can try." She slid out from the table and collected a bag sitting a few rows over. "I picked up a few things this morning thinking we might have this conversation. Just sit where you are, and I'll take care of it."

Leida misted Katie's hair with a spray bottle before massaging coconut-scented conditioner into the tangled strands and working it all the way to Katie's scalp. Katie glanced at Bryan who was pretending not to pay attention as he played on his phone. "Leida, I should warn you about the…you know…"

"The lice?" Leida asked, and Bryan glanced up before resuming his scrolling.

Heat rose to her cheeks once more. "I don't want you to get it."

"Won't be the first time." Leida pulled another bottle from her bag containing delousing medication.

Katie pressed her hands to her face to hide the tears collecting in her eyes.

"Oh, what's wrong, Katie?" Leida touched her shoulder, and it bounced up and down.

Katie shook her head. "It's nothing. I'm just—I'm such a mess."

Leida wrapped her arms around her trembling body and pulled her to her chest.

"Leida stop! You'll get it!" Katie tried to pull away.

"Katie, look at me," Leida said. "Look at Bryan. You are one of us. And neither of us are afraid of little bugs." She chuckled. "We're both afraid of a lot of things, but not that. So, please. Let me help you, okay?"

Katie nodded and swiped a tear away with a roll of her shoulder. Leida squeezed her hand and returned to her spot behind her. As she worked to untangle and untwine each of Katie's matted locks, it was as if bits of her mind were being untangled as well. People in her past life may not recognize her or know her any longer, but her people, her old-yet-still-new friends knew not only her name, but who she was and what she had lived. And for the first time in so long, Katie felt safe. And protected.

And loved.

Jared gripped the plastic hospital bed rail and pressed his head into the limp pillows. Grimacing, he closed his eyes as sweat dripped from his brow, down his face, and onto the already soaked sheets.

Focus on your breathing. Focus on the breath coming—and going. In—and out.

He opened his eyes and stared at the tiled ceiling, the melon-sized water stain in the corner, the metal rungs holding up the open curtain by the door. His fingers dug into the mattress as he focused on the water stain, counted his breaths to ten before starting over again. The knife-like pain in his leg gripped all of his thoughts, but slowly, his focus on his breath allowed another sensation in.

Thirst. He was thirsty.

Jared glanced at the water pitcher on the bedside table. Clenching his thigh just above the wound to stabilize his leg, he raised up and reached, but the pitcher was just beyond his grasp. With a groan, he shifted his hips until his good leg ran out of slack from the handcuff locked around his ankle, tethered to the bottom bedrail. His fingers grasped the blue plastic handle of the white tankard, and he dragged it into bed only to find it empty.

Jared dropped it onto the mattress. "Please," he said to the man sitting in the corner, turning pages of a Playboy. "Please, can I have some water?"

The man crossed his legs and turned the next page of his magazine. The metal plate on the upper right chest of his black button-down shirt identified him as police of some sort, but without his contacts, Jared could not discern the writing on it or his shoulder patch.

"Please, officer, sir," Jared tried again. "Just a little water. Please."

The man peered at him over his magazine. "Just a little water, huh?"

"Yes. I haven't asked you for anything. A little water, please."

He smacked the gum in his mouth. "I can get you a little water." Setting the magazine to the side, he stood and scooped up the pitcher.

Jared collapsed back onto his pillow. "Thank you."

The officer stepped into the bathroom, where Jared expected the sink to be, but then he saw the sink mounted on the wall next to the door. A splash sounded, and Jared's stomach sank. The officer returned with a full cup of toilet water and set it on Jared's table with a smile. "There's your water, ass wipe." Then he sat and picked up his magazine once more.

Moisture collected in the corner of Jared's eyes, but he pressed the heel of his hands into them and forced the sensation back.

The door opened and the sound of conversation from the hall filtered into the room. "Who are you?" the cop barked at the newcomer.

"Agent Rogers, FBI."

Jared dropped his hands and gazed up at the man brandishing his badge. *Thank God.*

"About damn time." The officer rolled up his magazine. "Wondered when you Feds were going to show up."

Rogers inclined his head. "How are you doing there, Jared?"

The officer waved his hand dismissively. "He's fine. Better than he should be, if you ask me. Doc says he'll make a full recovery. But that's what these damn perverts are like, you know? They're like cockroaches. Just can't kill them."

Jared pinched the bridge of his nose and peered up at Rogers. *Get rid of this guy, please?*

He had tried arguing with the cops earlier, but there was no point. What had really happened on the island had not been communicated, and he had been stuck with the label ever since.

"I'll take it from here, Officer—?"

"Jackson." He extended his hand.

"Jackson." Rogers nodded. "I'll remember that."

The officer collected his belongings and left, and Jared sighed with relief. But then grimaced again as another shot of pain rushed through his leg.

Rogers took the now free seat and dragged it to his bedside. His face screwed as he leaned back in his chair. "Listen, I know you have this thing about not taking pain meds, but you look like you're in agony. Maybe you should—"

"Have you ever had a bullet in your femur?" Jared asked through gritted teeth.

"Uh—no?"

"I asked for pain meds. The nurse said she'd ask the doctor. That was yesterday."

Rogers rose and moved to Jared's bedside. After searching for some time, he found the call light buried beneath a stack of linens far out of reach. Upon pressing the button, a ding sounded overhead.

"Can I help you?" a voice came from a speaker behind the bed.

Into the device he said, "This is Agent Rogers with the FBI. I need a nurse in here now, please."

"One moment."

A few moments later, the door opened and Jared's shrew of a nurse entered with a smile plastered across her face. "What can I do for you?"

Rogers tossed the call light onto the bed. "He needs pain medicine."

Her smile grew. "Still waiting on the doctor." Then she winked.

Roger's face contorted as his balled fist pounded on the bed rail. Jared winced as he shook the whole frame. "This man is my confidential informant! The information he has supplied us has led to the rescue of more than two hundred children! Go get him pain medication! Now!"

The woman jumped, raised both of her hands, and turned for the door. Rogers swore at the closed door. "I am so sorry. I would have—I don't know—sped or something had I known this was going on."

Jared rubbed his eyes again. "It's fine."

"No, it's not fine! Dammit!"

Jared chuckled then cringed from the effort. The nurse returned with a vial and syringe and took hold of Jared's IV. She wouldn't look at his face, so Jared stared at hers in revenge. "Can I get a new pitcher and some ice water, please?"

"Sure," she whispered as she depressed the plunger on the syringe.

A warm sensation flooded Jared, and his eyes grew wide. Almost immediately, the pain relaxed like the end of a muscle cramp and the ceiling swam with a different sensation. "Thank you," he muttered.

Rogers harrumphed.

The nurse turned away and pulled out a computer mounted to the wall on an elbow hinge. As she typed away, Rogers continued to glare at her back. "Oh, thought you'd like to know," he said. "Your *girlfriend* is on a flight home. Her family's waiting for her at the airport."

Jared sat up dizzily. "How is she?"

Rogers shrugged. "Alive. Which is more than I hear can be said about Midas. Your work?"

"Actually hers. But I can claim it if—"

He held up a hand. "Clear case of self-defense. Nobody will be coming after her. Her *father* sends his thanks, by the way."

Jared glanced at the nurse, whose face had turned crimson as she stared intently at the monitor. "I'll be right back with your water," she whispered and stepped out.

"So, I'm a confidential informant now, huh?" Jared asked, massaging his upper thigh. "When'd that happen?"

"Two years ago." Rogers pulled a file from the briefcase he had brought. "After you sign these backdated forms that is."

Jared laughed. "Agency wanting to take the credit now, huh?"

"Let's just say you've won a little favor with the bureau by returning an agent's daughter. People are feeling a bit—paternal about you right now." He set the paper on the bedside table and scooted it over Jared's lap.

"You too, I take it?"

Rogers sneered. "The nurse is just lucky those pain meds worked as quick as they did, otherwise she had a lot worse coming her way."

Jared nearly signed his alias to the paper instead of his actual signature. He realized he had only signed his own name a handful of times before. First, he signed nothing, with all his work being credited to Addison. His secret messages had been his initials marked by pin prick. Then for over two years, he had been Jack Warner.

"When do I get to go home?" Jared asked as he set the pen down.

"Once the hospital releases you, we have a few stops to make," Rogers said. "Hopefully not much longer. Then you can get on with your life."

It would be strange, learning to be himself again. Finding out who he actually was. Part of him did not believe that he would get that chance, that something else terrible would happen before he lived such a life. Looking back, he certainly had not thought he'd live this long or survive so much. He had learned how to die.

Now he would have to learn how to live.

PEACE?

Katie ran her finger over the peeling varnish of Mom's upright piano. It had been nearly three years since she had touched a piano, and the instrument felt alien beneath her hand today.

When Katie had entered the house for the first time, the same house they had lived in through her childhood, the same house that Mom had died in, a knot had settled in her throat.

Dad's leather recliner sat facing the TV like it always did. The upholstered couch still showed a place mended by Katie when it tore the summer before high school. Even the missing knob on the staircase was still missing.

If Mom came back to life right now, she would recognize Dad, although his hair was a little greyer and further back on his scalp. She would recognize Alec, even with his new limp and cane. But would Mom recognize her?

The limping. Her heart had shattered when she had learned about Alec's loss. He put on a good face about it, but still. Jared could have warned her. He *should* have warned her, dammit. But there had been nothing mentioned.

Right now, Dad was out at the store, and Alec had to run by his college campus that morning—he had dropped out for the past few years but was trying to get back into his classes for the coming semester. It was as good a time as any to play, and if she royally screwed up, no one but her would hear it.

Katie slid onto the leather covered piano bench, careful not to snag her pants on the already-loose buttons. The keys were cool and smooth. She found her place on the scale, took a deep breath, and pressed her fingers into the keys. Music flowed from the instrument, sweet and smooth, and Katie closed her eyes, losing herself in the sound, allowing it to wash over her.

Clare de Lune, her mother's favorite. At the melody shift, Katie smiled as she found her way with ease. Her fingers remembered even if her mind did not fully recall it.

There had been a lot of that lately—acting by instinct rather than thought. She knew how she should be around her family, what to say and when to say it. But, just like this piano that had not been serviced in years, everything had also been slightly out of tune.

The first broken key had shown up the night she came home. The night of her first full-blown panic attack. He had called her Katie Belle, the name he had created but that Midas had used for the past few years. Suddenly, she had been back in the tiny safe house room where he had hurt her.

She had shot him herself. So why did she continue to feel his claws around her throat?

Katie's fingers continued along the keys, rising and falling as appropriate. Then came the ending. A shift, a crescendo, but Katie found herself back at the beginning of the stanza. She opened her eyes, frowning as her fingers continued to play that portion again. The melody led into the crescendo once more. Next was a triplet and—

The wrong note tore through the melody, jarring her nerves, and she gritted her teeth as she started the stanza again. More notes faltered and failed. How did it end? The melody flowed through her mind, but she could not find the right keys.

Katie slammed the cover over the keys. How did it end? Hours and hours she had practiced. For hours and hours she had sealed this piece in her mind. In honor of Mom she had played it, but now the corruption of the melody made it unrecognizable.

Katie caught a glimpse of herself in the mirror fixed to the top of the piano. The scar, still pink, looked back at her. And next to it sat her freshman school picture. In the picture her face was smooth, untarnished. Her eyes were clear and not encircled by gray.

Katie grabbed the picture frame and smashed it into the glass, shattering it. She knocked over the bench as she stood, rushed up the stairs to her room, and buried herself beneath her blankets.

She was out of tears, so she lay there still as stone, staring at the wall. *How does it end? When* will *it end?*

Her cell phone buzzed in her pocket and, upon retrieving it, she stared down at it dumbly. Another friend request on Facebook. Yippee.

She scrolled through her news feed, studying the happy faces of her family and friends from before. Then she scrolled over a somewhat familiar face. But was that truly her? And whose baby was it hanging on her hip?

Compelled by a half-formed desire, Katie clicked on the phone icon next to the name and waited.

"Oh my gosh, Katie!" Michelle's voice came through the line. "You're alive! Are you home?"

"I just got home a little bit ago, yeah." Katie rubbed her hand over her face. Now what?

"Katie, it's so good to hear your voice. How are you doing?"

Katie pulled the covers off her head and looked around the too-familiar room. "Not so great."

"Yeah, coming home is rough. Wanna talk about it?"

Katie crunched her eyes tight as a tear glided down her cheek. "Yeah, Michelle. I think I do…"

"So…You gonna get out or what?"

Jared laughed in his throat at Rogers' question, but continued to hold on to the car door handle. The two-story house with the screened-in front porch stood stalwart across the yard, waiting on his entry.

Two weeks had passed since getting out of the hospital. Once he was discharged, Jared had been swooped up by the FBI and taken to multiple meetings and debriefs with people who were supposedly important but that Jared didn't know. One claimed to be the United States President, and since no one had refuted him, Jared assumed that was true. To him, it didn't matter. He told his story and interacted with these people the same way regardless of who they were.

Tiredly.

Between the loss of blood, the pain medications, and the sheer exhaustion that had swept over him since everything had ended, it was the only way he could interact. Now, the most anticipated and the most stressful meeting of all was before him.

"Your parents love you, Jared," Rogers said. "I know you don't always get along, but—"

Jared shrugged. "We get along fine. And I know that. I love them too. It's just—I don't know…Something about coming home."

"It's never what you expect."

"No," Jared said softly. "It's just—they expect things from me. Things I can't give them."

Rogers ran his thumb over the emergency brake. "I don't think it's things they want *from* you, Jared. I think it's things they want *for* you. Most of all, I think they want you to be safe and happy. Running off and joining a human trafficking ring probably wasn't high on their list of things they wanted for you. But if you're afraid of disappointing them, well, I don't think any parent in their right mind would be *disappointed* in you."

Jared looked to Leida's window where he had crept into the house for what he truly thought was the last time. He had snuck in so he wouldn't have to see their disappointment. But leaving had still been easy. Staying would be harder. His imagination had not taken him back here, to these people. Yet here he was again at their door.

Movement took place behind the screen, then the door popped open a crack. Mom peered out, but only slightly as if not believing what she was seeing. Then she smiled, scraped back a rogue strand of graying hair, and stepped onto the sidewalk.

Rogers jabbed Jared in the arm with his elbow. "Either step out or get dragged out."

Jared allowed a smile and pushed open the car door while Rogers rounded the vehicle and pulled a set of crutches from the back.

"Told ya I'd bring him home, Marie," Rogers said, handing the crutches to Jared. "Although, he's a bit rougher for wear than I'd have liked."

Jared hobbled to his mother one step at a time. His leg was getting better, but still sore. Mom pressed a soft hand to his cheek before pulling Jared into a hug, and he wrapped his crutch around her as well.

"I'm so glad you're home!" she said into his shirt.

"Me too, Mom."

Tugging on his arm she said, "Come inside! And you too, Agent Rogers."

"No, ma'am. I have to go to the office," said Rogers. "But it was good to see you. Take care."

Still clutching his arm, and throwing off his balance, Mom led Jared to the door. "You must be starving," she said. "I just finished dinner."

As Jared stepped inside, Dad enveloped him in his thick arms, kissing him on the top of his head. Jared tensed, but forced himself to breathe through the rounds of affection. Next was Leida hugging him tight. As she did so, however, Jared frowned at the lump pressing against his stomach. He held her at arm's-length and studied her large belly.

Bryan sat on the couch far across the room, his cheeks and neck crimson. His shoulders rose nearly to his ears as he watched Jared closely.

Jared's nostrils flared as he took in the guilty expression. But then he shook his head. "I should be mad," he said. "But I'm just too tired for mad."

"Not to mention I saved your life!" Bryan blurted.

Jared grinned. "Been preparing to use that one, have we?"

Bryan smiled, his straight-white teeth gleaming. "Maybe."

Raising Leida's left hand, Jared took in the massive sparkling stone mounted on her ring finger. "When's the wedding?"

Leida beamed. "In five days, actually."

"Five days!" Jared dropped her hand. "And nobody mentioned this to me?"

Leida pulled back her hand and adjusted the ring on her finger. "You weren't exactly easy to reach. We've been planning the wedding for months, Jared. It's not like we're heading off to Vegas or anything."

"Well, am I invited or anything?"

Bryan stood and shoved his hands into his pockets as he crossed the room. "I was kinda hoping you'd be my best man, if you got back in time."

It was Jared's turn to redden. "Oh, I—uh—sure. I guess."

"Great!" Leida clapped her hands together. "Because I already made an appointment with the tailor tomorrow to get you fitted for your tux. I don't know about the crutches though. Maybe we could get you a cane like Alec? He's one of the groomsmen. Maybe we'll get Dakota one too to balance things out."

"Dakota is in your wedding too?" Jared asked. "He's your ex."

"But he's Bryan's friend too! And he still lives nearby. So, after your tux, we can go check out the venue and go over your role and…"

Jared stopped listening as his sister listed off the itinerary for the next week. Instead, he sank into the couch and rubbed above the mostly healed bullet wound. He tried to listen, but she kept on talking. Soon, Jared was fast asleep.

*　　*　　*

Jared didn't intend to keep tuning Leida out, but her incessant talking had turned into white noise over the course of the car ride. He didn't remember her talking so much. Was it wedding jitters? Or had she taken up a coffee habit? Regardless, she seemed content as long as he interjected an occasional grunt or nod, so Jared continued staring out the front window, daydreaming about his motorcycle. Maybe she could drop him off once they were done at the tailors.

As they passed over the bridge onto the north shore, boats rushed below them on the river. So, the river *was* populated by watercraft. Jared tallied how many months it'd take working for Uncle Nate to buy himself one and sneered. One consulting job would have covered the cost entirely. Now, if he wished to save up for an apartment *and* buy a boat, it would take months if not years.

Leida turned into a strip mall and parked the car next to the front door of the store. She brought around Jared's crutches, still babbling, and led the way through the front door.

Spotlights hung over various feature items, lighting up the brown and gray walls, and the hardwood floors echoed off Leida's heels. There was not much merchandise lying about, but judging from a passing price tag, not much inventory would be required to keep this shop afloat.

Jared scratched the stubble on his chin. "I take it Bryan is paying for this?"

"Well, we know who's *not* paying for it," said Leida. "Since the FBI commandeered your accounts and all."

A young man with the same hairstyle as Bryan approached with a plastered smile but quirked brow. Clearly, he had overheard the comment, but ignored it. "Can I help you with something?" he asked as his eyes ran over Jared's half-brown, half-blonde hair, plain white tee, thrift store jeans, flip-flops, and crutches.

If Arhrit's men hadn't burned up his luggage, he too could have been wearing Armani.

"I'm Leida Kelley. My brother, Jared, is here to get his tux fitted for the Rosenbaum wedding." With her manicured nails, vogue clothing, and handbag, Leida fit right into the joint. Bryan's mom must really like her in order to have permitted such purchases.

"Yes, right this way." The attendant's grin intensified as he escorted them toward the back. He paused at a curtain and had them wait for a moment as he said to someone on the other side, "The fitting for the Rosenbaum wedding is here."

"The dead-beat brother finally decided to show up, huh?" a man replied.

Jared's mouth popped open as Leida giggled.

Dead-beat, huh? What has Leida been telling people?

Pink collected around the ears of the attendant as he pulled back the curtain. The tailor, a slender octogenarian with a tape measure around his neck stood from a low stool. Upon seeing his clients so near, he reddened too, but Jared kept his face flat, revealing nothing. The man would have to wonder.

During the fitting, a flash memory of being inspected by Camp 7's boss came to mind, and Jared involuntarily opened his mouth before clamping it shut. No one else seemed to notice the motion, but perspiration sprouted across his brow nonetheless.

All the while, Leida lounged on a velvet sofa with her legs kicked up over the side and played on her phone. "When are you going to see Katie?"

His sister knew what she was doing, waiting to ask a question like that while he was forced to stand still. Nothing like a captive audience.

Leida dropped her feet to the floor. "You like her, don't you?" Warmth rose over Jared's neck, and she continued, "Have you told her how you feel?"

Jared recalled the drunken confession. "I told her, but it was bad timing."

"Then tell her again! What are you waiting for?"

"I'm sure she's busy trying to get her life put back together and doesn't need me complicating things."

"You know, for a smart guy, you're sort of stupid sometimes. You're one of the few people on the planet who know what she went through."

"Yeah, Leida, I do. Which is why she doesn't need me coming around reminding her of everything."

The tailor kept marking the hem, and Jared repressed his desire to tell him to speed it up and get him out of the damn hot seat.

"You don't think she's having enough memories without you?" Leida asked.

"Right now, she needs to focus on spending time with her family and get back to her normal life. I'm sure the last person she even wants to see right now is me."

"Uh-huh," Leida said. "So, I can just disregard this last text asking when you're coming by to see her then."

"She—she asked that?"

"Yup," said Leida. "Came through just now."

That sounded more like an expectation rather than a wish. Perhaps Jared was wrong. Perhaps she *did* wish to see him. He asked the tailor, "How much longer until we're done here?"

The sun crept across the floor like a slowly approaching tide until it rose above the level of the bed and into Katie's eyes. She watched as dust motes floated across the light, swirling and tumbling. Outside, a bird chittered happily. Katie considered throwing her pillow at the window to scare it away.

The night had come and gone without any sleep from her. Each time she closed her eyes, she could feel Midas's breath on her cheek, Randall's hands on her shoulders. Ghosts, both of them. Had they chosen her to haunt for eternity?

Now morning was here, and she was supposed to get out of bed, eat breakfast with her family, smile and pretend she was doing better. Why wasn't she doing better?

If ever she forgot what had happened for a moment, the terrors would rush back, drowning her in a memory so vivid she left the real world before her. And on days when she had not slept the night before, it was always worse. Before stepping out of bed, she knew it would be a bad day. The therapist had told her this could happen after a traumatic event, but this didn't feel normal.

The door opened silently and Dad peeked in. "Hey honey," he said after seeing that she was awake. "I've made some breakfast."

Katie forced herself up onto her elbow. "Alright, Dad. I'll be down in a little bit."

"Love you, sweetheart. See you in a minute then." He closed the door.

Katie collapsed back down onto the mattress. The chirping bird continued merrily with his song, and this time, she did throw the pillow. He continued on, unphased by the projectile.

The phone on the nightstand buzzed, the screen illuminating the ceiling above it. Katie snatched it up and opened the text from Leida. "Jared's coming to your house."

Katie sat up and tucked her legs beneath her. "When?"

"I don't know," Leida replied. "He was gone when I woke up. He left a note."

She dropped her legs to the floor. Jared was up before the sun most days she had known him. He could be here any—

A motorcycle approached their house and turned into the driveway.

"Shit!" Katie hopped up from the bed and stood turning circles in the middle of her room. Clothes were all over the floor instead of hanging in her closet, the mirror on her dresser showed she'd grown a rooster's tail in the night, and the sweat stains on her nightshirt gave her a clue as to how she smelled.

Katie grabbed the cleanest shirt she could find from the pile and the pair of jeans she had worn for the past three days. She was tempted to rip her brush through her hair, but took time on this project: her hair was thin enough as is.

"Katie?" Alec's voice came from beyond the door. "You have a visitor."

"Coming!" she called as she slapped on some deodorant. Then she paused before her mirror. A line of make-up products sat at the base of it, but she had not yet found a good combination to minimize the scar. Most of the time, it just looked caked on and funny, almost more noticeable than if she did nothing at all.

Jared had seen the scar before. Hell, he'd been the one to stitch it up in the first place. He would notice what she was trying to do. She turned for the door instead.

Standing at the base of the stairs stood the blonde-haired kid from Camp 1. He was a few inches taller and more filled-out than when they had first met, but with his contacts in and the beard gone, he looked like himself once more.

Katie realized she preferred the beard. It made him appear the age he acted. Even still, was he really only twenty?

Alec entered the living room with eggs and sausage smothered with gravy heaped on his plate. Jared's gaze followed the food.

"Nice cane," Alec said. "What is that? A Hurrycane from the drugstore?"

Jared raised up the shiny blue cane with a four-pronged base. "My grandfather lent it to me. It's from when he got his knees replaced." His gaze wandered to Alec's plate of food once more.

"You're checking out my food more than you are my sister. Wanna kiss it?" He pushed it up toward Jared's face, and Jared pushed it away with a smile.

A pang of jealousy tore across Katie's chest as she descended the stairs. She felt as if she should be introducing Alec to Jared, but they already had history she had not taken part in.

"You're not planning on being in Leida's wedding with that thing, are you?" Alec nodded to the cane.

"I—uh—"

"Let me see what I got." Alec turned down the hall beneath the stairs. They had turned Dad's old office into his bedroom on the first floor so he wouldn't have to climb so many steps. Alec walked with a limp, but only slightly. Katie often forgot about the prosthetic until they left the house and he brought his cane along. If it hurt, he didn't complain.

"Hey, Katie," Jared said as she stepped onto the landing. His eyes were soft as they looked into hers. He was one of the few people who didn't keep staring at her scar. He was also one of the few people in her life now who hadn't seen her without one.

"Hey, Jared," Katie replied. Then she slipped her arms beneath his and rested her head on his shoulder. He wrapped his arms around her back, and she snuggled tight against him. The woody smell of his aftershave mixed with his cigarettes and the lavender essential oils he diffused regularly. Each scent rooted her in the embrace, connecting her with the past but also making her feel safe at the same time.

Alec re-entered the living room with a cherry-stained cane. The top was carved, antiquated brass, engraved with his initials. "This is what *my* grandfather gave me."

Jared took the walking aid and studied it. "I think your grandfather likes you more than mine."

"All y'all need are some striped vests and funny hats," Dad said as he entered from the kitchen. "Then you could form a barbershop quartet. Jared, I made you a plate, son. Come on and eat. You too, Katie."

"Thank you, Agent Thompson," Jared said.

Dad winced. "Peter. Go with Peter."

"Too weird. Thompson?"

"That'll do."

"Can I call you Peter?" Alec asked.

"Absolutely not."

Katie smothered Dad's eggs in gravy to hide the dryness and tucked in with the others. Jared ate a little slower, like he always did, but showed no signs of leaving half the food on his plate.

"So, Jared," Dad said. "Tell your father thanks for nothing for getting me that job. I'm getting carpal tunnel from grading all those term papers."

Jared dabbed his chin with his napkin. "Would you prefer to get carpal tunnel writing up the report Rogers is having to make?"

"Ha! I hadn't thought about that. You and Katie sure did make quite a mess, didn't you?"

Katie tried to smile as she attempted to think of something to contribute to the conversation, but her mind was blank. The gravy did not hide the dryness and the eggs stuck to the roof of her mouth.

"Almost as bad as the foul-up *you* created at Camp 1," Jared said. "That is, after ten years of not being able to find me."

Dad leaned back in his seat, a smile playing on his lips. "Now you're getting nasty."

Jared laughed. "Yeah, I suppose it took you a while, but you got it in the end. I'll give you a little credit for saving my life."

"Yeah, and don't forget about that either, kid."

Katie followed the back-and-forth banter with bitterness. Two years ago, Jared was sitting alone sloshing gruel out of his bowl with his trembling fingers. Now he could socialize easier with her family than she could.

He had sat with Midas too, telling jokes to the Watchers. When he called her ugly, they had laughed. Jack Warner would shove her, block her way out of doors just to frighten her. He implied horrible things about her.

He saved her.

Katie jolted as she slipped out of her trance-like state, returning to reality. The table beneath her hand came away with a moist impression. Dad and Alec continued talking, not noticing her absence.

But Jared watched her from the corner of his eye while he took a sip of orange juice. "You okay?" he mouthed behind the glass.

Katie pressed her hands to her face and nodded. She was glad Jared was here, but how could her mind sort between the dichotomy of her experiences with him? In one regard, he was everything that represented safety and security to her. In the other regard, he reminded her of everything that once threatened her. Could what they had work?

Alec rose from the table. "I have to be at work in about thirty minutes. Maybe call next time before dropping by if you want to hang, huh?"

"He's not here to see *you*," Dad teased.

Jared grinned and set the glass back down. Katie tried to match the smile, but her mind was too rattled to cling to anything genuine.

"And I have those papers to grade." Dad set his coffee cup down and stood. "Oh, the drudgery…"

"He's lying. Dad *loves* working from home in his pajamas." Alec grabbed an apple from the basket on the counter and munched on it as he returned to his room. Dad, however, made a show of checking his watch before pouring another cup of coffee and heading to his office upstairs.

A torrent of sweat formed around Katie's neck as she was left alone with Jared.

Jared finished off the food on his plate and limped his dish over to the sink. "Do you want to take a walk?"

"What about your leg?"

"It's got a couple of miles in it before it starts hurting too bad." Jared picked up the brass cane from where it leaned on the table.

They walked in silence for a time, up one street of the neighborhood then down the next. Jared kept looking at her hand, and she wondered if he was going to take it, but he never did. She didn't offer it.

"How are you doing, Katie?" Jared asked. "For real."

Katie shrugged. "Getting back to normal."

Jared stopped and turned to her. "What the hell is normal?"

"You know." She shrugged again and slipped past him. "Seeing my old friends again. Getting my life back together. I'm looking at getting my GED so I can join them in college next year."

The lines on Jared's brow depressed as he matched her speed, even with his cane. "That's good," he said evenly.

"It is good. Are you going back to work for your uncle?"

"As soon as my leg heals."

Silence fell over them once more. As they rounded back to Katie's house, she noted sweat collecting on Jared's brow. "Do you need to rest?"

"No, I'm good." He studied the pavement ahead.

"You're lying."

"I'm well-known for my lies. You're not."

"What's that supposed to mean?"

"How are you doing, Katie? And don't tell me good."

She stopped at their driveway. "Why don't you believe me? Just because you floundered around after coming home doesn't mean I will."

"How many flashbacks did you have while eating breakfast this morning? How much have you been sleeping? And don't tell me a lot because the red around your eyes tells another story."

"You don't know what you're talking about."

"I know *exactly* what I'm talking about. What I don't know is why you're lying about it. Why you're lying to *me* about it. I've been watching you live this hell for months now. You're not fooling me."

Katie sucked on her lip. "What do you want from me, Jack? I mean, Jared?" She corrected the slip quickly, but winced knowing he had heard it.

Jared looked toward his motorcycle, propped up in the driveway. "This was a mistake. I should go. You obviously need to spend time with your family and work this stuff out."

Katie grabbed Jared's sleeve. "Wait! No. I—please don't go yet."

"You don't even know who I am."

"You're Jared," she said. "It was a slip of the tongue. I know who you are. You're my friend."

Jared ran his thumb over the seat of his bike. Were there words available for her to speak so he would understand? All of her thoughts were warped and wrapped together, hopelessly tangled.

"I—I think I love you Jared, but I don't know," she said.

Jared rubbed his toe in the concrete. "You know how I feel about you, but why bring this up now?"

Katie pressed a hand to her forehead and took a couple of steps back. "I don't know. I just...I can't think. My head is spinning and—" She inhaled a ragged breath.

Jared took her hands and led her to the steps. "Just sit down for a moment."

A sob escaped her throat as he sat on the stairs beside her. Jared wrapped his arm around her and she pressed her tearstained face against his chest. "I don't have what you want," she cried.

He brushed a rogue strand of hair back. "And what do you presume I want?"

"I wish—" her words came out in heaves. "I wish we had just done it, that night in your hut. I wish we had, because my first time was—my first time was with *him* and—"

"Oh shit, Katie. I don't—"

"I'm so screwed up, Jared."

His arms shook as he held her tight. "I wish I could fix this for you, Katie. But I'm not sure being together before you were ready would have solved anything. And I'm not some weird puritan that would ever blame you for what happened. I don't expect, need, or want anything from you. Please, believe me in this."

"I believe you." Katie pulled back from his chest so she could meet his eye. "What I mean is, I don't know how it will go between us since—since all I know is—"

"I know you're worried about that, but I'm not. Not really. We've got a lot of shit to work through, and that's just another piece. In the meantime, as long as you want me here, I'm not going to go anywhere."

Katie pressed her head against his chest, and he squeezed her tight.

"Besides," Jared said, "the FBI said I couldn't keep the money I made while undercover, so I'm broke. I had to steal twenty bucks from my mom's purse for gas. Where the hell *could* I go?"

Laughter rippled from Katie's chest, the first true laugh she had released in recent memory.

They sat together on her porch steps watching the occasional car pass by. Not saying much, just being present. Katie leaned her head against Jared's shoulder as the morning warmed. And without intending to, she fell asleep against him.

*　　*　　*

As Jared held tight to Katie, he berated himself for not having better words to say, for not having anything, really, that would make it better. At least he had made her laugh. That was something. He had missed her laughter. While he racked his mind for something else funny to say, he was surprised to look down and see her eyes closed as she rested against his shoulder.

Seriously?

Was she afraid of him or not? Because people didn't sleep against those they were afraid of. Why were girls so freaking complicated?

Jared leaned against the porch column and watched the lazy street as a few cars passed by. After a while, his hip fell asleep, all except the wound, which shot pain down his leg. He extended it as gently as possible so as not to wake Katie and flexed his foot up and down to return blood flow.

He hated being still. Better to do mindless chores than to sit still. As the morning progressed, the heat caused a wave of drowsiness to settle on Jared too, however. That and the rhythmic, hypnotic breathing of Katie. He leaned his head on the porch column and closed his eyes.

A car alarm went off a couple of doors down, and Jared and Katie leaped to their feet, both turning around in circles, locating the source. With a flip of the wrist, Jared's knife was drawn at the ready. But another neighbor stepped out of his house and clicked the button on his key lanyard, silencing the sound.

Jared and Katie looked at each other in their states of heightened readiness and laughed.

"What were you going to do?" Katie asked. "Fight off the car with your pocket knife?"

With a smile, Jared folded the blade and slipped it back into his pocket. "I don't know. Old habits."

Katie's gentle smile held him captive. She was studying him. What did she see?

"I'm glad you came, Jared. Even if I am a mess." She ran a hand over her soft, wavy hair.

Jared grasped the porch column behind him and eased himself back onto the steps. He straightened his leg out and massaged the wound. "I know I don't talk about it, but I do know what you're going through."

She inclined her head then sank into the seat beside him. Katie slid her hand into his, and Jared pressed his palm against hers, his heart drumming inside of him. Electricity zipped up his arm.

"I know," she said. "If anyone knows what it's like to be dominated, it's you."

The electricity ceased and turned sour in his gut.

A flash of Clayton's fist crashing into his face while he lay pinned to the ground raptured him from the porch and back into the trunk, hog-tied and waiting for more. Another flash of Clayton torquing his arm until it ripped out of socket. Then of a door leading to a dark room he didn't enter. Next it was Midas's gun pressed against his head followed by the click.

"Yeah, something like that." Jared slipped his hand from hers and stood once more. "Are you coming to the wedding in a couple of days?"

"Of course," Katie said. "Alec is a groomsman."

Jared measured the time to be almost noon. "Well, I hate to leave, but I promised Leida I'd help with the wedding stuff. Picking up—food and things." Jared winced at his own lie, but as he had never been to a wedding, he didn't really know what things were required. He just hoped eating at a wedding was something people did.

"Oh," Katie said. "Oh, okay."

Jared paused, leaning against the porch column. *Just stay. She didn't mean anything by it.*

But he didn't like how it made him feel: weak, vulnerable, and helpless once more. For years now he had fought to escape from that version of himself and suddenly it was back.

"Well—" Jared shrugged. "I guess I'll see you then." He leaned down and kissed her on the cheek. Katie smiled at him, a gentle yet confused smile. Then Jared took his bike, kicked it to life, and roared back down the street from where he had come.

All the way home he chided himself for leaving like this, but all the way home he didn't turn back. When he arrived at the house around mid-afternoon, Leida and Bryan were in the living room writing out place cards.

"Why are you back so early?" Leida asked.

Jared shrugged in reply as he hobbled to the stairs with Alec's cane.

"You blew it, didn't you?"

"Shut up, Leida."

LIFE WITHOUT GOLD

The music changed for the entry of the bride, and Jared shifted to stand straight as a pencil as she took the first step down the aisle. The wedding coordinator had gotten onto him for slouching yesterday—three hours into the rehearsal as his leg pounded and his headache started crushing his skull from all sides. He could feel her eyes on him now from the back of the room behind Leida's poofy veil.

The woman disliked his late arrival to her wedding plans and did not seem to care that he'd been shot getting his girlfriend out of hell. Her only concern was that she now had to deal with four canes instead of one—Bryan and Dakota had decided to use canes too as a last minute 'theme.' Jared couldn't decide whether it was charming or down-right goofy.

Leida looked stunning, of course, as she walked in-step to the music. The soft lighting caught her hair, causing it to gleam. Her dress trailed the floor while patterns of lace crept up from the bottom to her hips. There was no hiding her belly, yet the dress still seemed to make the abdomen smoother than it actually was. A trick of the eye, perhaps?

Dad walked stiffly, as if wearing a suit of armor or other restrictive clothing. As he looked down on Leida, however, a soft smile spread across his face. Undoubtedly, he had given up hope for this day.

Fate had been kind.

The venue was a ritzy place north of Chattanooga, and the bridal party had been provided rooms on location for last night and the coming night. Jared had seen glimpses of Katie since they had been there, but his presence had been needed so frequently, they hadn't had a chance to speak. Today, when he saw Katie in the third row on the bride's side, his mouth went dry once more.

Her face was smooth, all except the scar that is. It was minimized by make-up, but still visible. She wore a green floral skirt and a sage top that tapered at the waist in a tasteful fashion. Her hair was curled and held up in a bun while a braid ran over the top of her head. Jared was not sure how that worked, but then again, he wasn't sure how girls' hair really worked in the first place. Leida had fired him from braiding her hair at age five, preferring to do it herself.

Not that he blamed her; his work was pretty awful. Now her hair was done up in a compilation of loops and braids all pinned together by a thousand bobby pins. Well, one hundred and seventy-six to be exact, but close enough.

The service was long and hot. Although the pastor was a talented orator, he really could have summed up the most important points. He had been Jared and Leida's pastor when they were little, and could not help but tear up here and there about their whole going missing thing and how it affected everyone and blah blah blah.

During the reception, Jared found a random chair and just sat. Until the wedding coordinator dragged him to the bridal party table, that is, to his assigned seat. He sat grumpily and sipped on the punch his mother brought him. Mom also slipped a pair of Tylenol across the table with the punch, and for that he could have kissed her.

"Think you could smile some?" Bryan asked. "It's your sister's wedding day."

Jared glared at him. "There's nothing in this punch but sugar and flavoring, is there?"

"It's a dry party, yes. Leida and I are both under age. So are you, if you remember correctly."

Not according to my fake ID. That had been another one of the perks of being someone older: fewer questions and fewer rules.

"Is there anyone at this table legally old enough to drink?" Alec asked.

"I am!" Sedonya waved from the other side of Leida. "As of last week."

Jared swirled his drink around the glass cup before downing the rest. Then he spotted Katie sitting with her dad a few tables over. "I'm gonna go mingle," Jared said, finding his cane once more.

"I think mingle implies talking to more than one someone," Leida said as he stood, but Jared ignored her as he slid past Alec and Dakota back into the fray once more.

Most people gave way to the guy leaning on a cane, but a few still had to be gently pushed in order for Jared to get to her table. Once there, he completely forgot anything he was going to say to her, so he went with his usual "Hey, Katie." And after a nod to her father, "Thompson."

Thompson smiled at Jared then looked at his daughter. "I'm gonna get some cake."

Once he left, Jared took the seat next to her. "You look nice in your—dress, skirt thing."

"You look nice in your tux." Katie smiled and sipped on her drink.

"Katie, about the other day—"

"Jared!" a voice said from above, and Jared could have punched them until he realized it was Michelle standing at their table.

"Oh my gosh, Katie?" she cried and wrapped her arms around her. "How are you since we talked?"

Jared's brow came to a point. They had talked? Recently?

Katie returned the embrace, holding on to her for some time. "I'm figuring it out," Katie answered.

Michelle found a seat behind her and dragged it close. "Is the surrealness wearing off yet? It took a while for me."

"It was," Katie laughed. "But today feels a bit weird with Bryan and Leida of all people getting married."

"I know what you mean!" said Michelle. "I was thinking that just the other day!"

"How's your daughter?" Jared asked, and Katie looked between them in question. Jared bit his lip. The question had been genuine, he wasn't trying to start anything and hoped Katie would see that too.

"Good." Michelle pulled out her phone. "Her adoptive family sends me pictures and I see her on the holidays." The picture on the screen was of a beautiful toddler girl with her black hair pulled up in pigtails on either side of her head. "Can you believe she's almost two?"

"Almost two, so—" Katie said, then turned pink. "I'm out of the loop. I'm sorry if I—"

"It's fine," Michelle said. "I'm at peace with it. It took some time, lots of therapy, but what happened happened. And my boyfriend and I are navigating through it." She nodded to a guy at the food table holding two glasses of punch. The guy scowled at Jared, and Jared rubbed the back of his head.

"But anyways, I just wanted to say hi. I'm glad you're back, Katie." Michelle hugged her once more.

"Thanks, Michelle."

Once she was gone, Katie leaned across the table. "She had Ian's baby? Oh, my freaking gosh."

"A very fertile group, our people," Jared muttered. "Katie, I've been meaning to—"

"Did you know?" Leida plopped down into the chair beside Jared. For a very pregnant woman, she sure got around quick. Bryan sat down beside her.

Jared tilted his head to the extreme side to look at her. "What?"

"Have you seen Dakota's plus one?"

Jared glanced across the way to find Dakota and his date snacking on hors d'oeuvres. "Today? Not until now." He took a cup of cashews from a cup on the table and popped some into his mouth.

"You knew, didn't you?" demanded Leida.

But Jared just frowned and looked at Bryan, who was busy inspecting his nail beds. Gonna make me the fall guy, huh? Jared opened his mouth to reveal Bryan's knowledge of this new development then sighed. It was his wedding day, after all. Mercy would be Jared's wedding gift.

"Dakota might have mentioned it," Jared said. "So, I called Paulina and cleared the air. I didn't think to mention it to you, because her beef was mainly with me anyway and it's now been resolved."

"Resolved?" Leida scoffed.

"We were kids, Leida. And we were in hell. I want to move on and live my life for once. If that means being…" He glanced over to where Dakota and she now stood watching them. Perhaps it was their repeated glances that had clued them in on their conversation, or perhaps it was intuition. Either way, they started making their way to them through the thick cloud of guests. "If that means being acquaintances again, then I'm going to let it ride."

Jared would not call Paulina his friend. Some wounds went too deep for that, but after living among true evil for so long, he had no more grudges left to give her.

"Hi, everyone," said Paulina softly as she approached. Her hair was soft and smoother than Jared had ever seen it before, and it was pinned up off the back of her neck in rolls of curls. She looked very nice tonight, but she also clung tight to Dakota's hand. Her smile was close to forced, not in an unhappy way, but in a nervous way as if afraid of what was going to happen next.

"Hi, Paulina," said Jared with the best smile he could manage with his aching leg. "Cashew?"

Her shoulders dropped in relief, and meekly, she accepted a few bits from the cup Jared raised to her. "Thank you, Gol—I mean, Jared. Leida, I must say, you look so beautiful. And your hair is amazing."

Leida folded her bright pink lips inward as her chest expanded and held. For a moment, Jared feared she would turn blue, but then she released the breath through her nose. "Alright, fine," she relented. "Hi, Paulina. Welcome to my wedding."

Jared nodded at Leida approvingly then claimed a few more cashews for himself. Dakota and Paulina took hold of the backs of chairs and started to sit. "Whoa, now, hold up!" cried Jared. "What are you doing?"

"I–uh–" stammered Paulina.

"Not just you, all of you," said Jared, motioning to the others who had come to sit. "Don't y'all have a wedding or something to host?"

"And aren't you the best man?" laughed Leida.

"We talked about this. I'm not giving a speech. My job is done, so if you wouldn't mind, I'd like to take this moment to talk to Katie."

Beside him, Katie giggled, but said nothing more.

"Oh, he's just cranky because he got shot," Leida said.

"That's right, I did get shot. Again. So, please, can we?" Jared motioned for them to move on. "I've been trying to talk to her for two days now."

Once the group had indeed stood and walked away, chuckling and snickering at Jared's demands, Jared looked at Katie, shook his head, and sighed.

"Want to go outside?" she offered.

"Hell, yes," he said and grabbed his cane.

*   *   *

By the time they stepped outside, the sun was half-sunk behind the trees. The wedding venue was on forty acres of land situated on a plateau overlooking a deep valley where the last rays of light shimmered and danced on the tall grasses below. A path ran along the rim of the plateau overlooking the vista, and Katie and Jared walked along this path until the sound of the party faded. They rested there on a bench the venue owners had courteously placed.

She kept looking at him, trying to decipher his face, to understand what was going on inside that mind of his, but the only thing his face gave away now was the pain in his leg as he massaged the wound.

"When is your leg going to get better?" Katie asked.

"Doc said I can use it as much as I can tolerate it, but it'll be sore for a while still. I'm hoping by the end of the month, I can return this to your brother." He lifted the brass handled cane. "Katie, about the other day—I'm sorry I left so abruptly. There's a lot of shit I'm working through too and—"

Katie slid her hand into his, capturing the warmth of his fingers as she intertwined hers into his. He had nice hands. Strong hands, albeit calloused and worn. She liked the way they felt against her small, petite fingers. She had wondered if she was going to hold that hand again and now didn't want to let it go.

"Katie, I want you to know I'm not expecting anything from you," he said, running his thumb over the back of her hand.

"I know," she said, and met his eyes with a smile. Those green eyes that watched her so carefully.

"Then may I—may I kiss you?"

"Yes."

Jared smiled his soft smile. His hand pressed against her cheek, as his fingers slid into her hair. He brought her near and their lips touched.

The taste of cashews and cigarettes took her aback momentarily, but the gentleness of this kiss, the softness of his lips, caused her face to flush with warmth, and her heart pattered. It wasn't their first kiss, but it was their first kiss of freedom. One shared without wondering if it would be their last. And she savored it, the good and the bad of it, for the future was in it too.

Acknowledgements

This was the first line on the previous book's acknowledgement page: "This book has had a long and eventful journey filled with hope and heartbreak, but thanks to a bevy of support from friends and family, it has made it to the finish line!"

Is it possible to double that sentiment? Because I can hardly believe this series still exists, and it would not without all of my friends, family, and readers.

To all those who had a direct hand in making this dream a reality, I offer my love and sincere thanks. To my beta readers and critique partners: Kale Sartor, Kyle Johnson, Alyssa Swann, Concetta Swann, Bertha Hague, Kathleen Thorp, and Elaine Barker. As always, a special thanks to Andrew Rucker Jones who holds all technical questions regarding the series in his hands.

With all my heart, I thank my family, especially my husband for listening patiently to twenty different versions of the same chapter without spontaneously combusting or walking away from my nonsense. Thanks to my mom for putting up with my never-ending questions about children's responses to trauma, and to my sister for cheering me on, even when things got rough. Thanks also to Nana, who has now read more of my books than anyone else!

Did You Enjoy The Midas Series?

Consider Leaving A Review!

The Midas Series is not just an entertaining tale, but a story that demonstrates the real-world psychological effects that child abuse has on those who have suffered from it. As the daughter of a social worker, kids from hard places hold a special place in my heart. My hope that kids or even adults who have suffered trauma will find comfort and strength from seeing their experiences reflected in others. But the impact of this story will only be felt if that know that these books are out there for them. Leaving reviews does not just let others know you liked this work, it incentivizes platforms such as Amazon to advertise it to others. It does not take much time to leave a review, but the help that it brings to the series cannot be understated!

Scan the QR Code below to let others know how much you enjoyed the story!